Eggart stared at .... er.
"Unsere Ehre Hei..................... ....yalty.
"Deutschland Er.... .... —Germany Awake!—had
been the Nazi slogan during the 1920s.

"What does this mean?" Eggart asked Barentz. The
leaflet ranted about some plan for action by SS
supporters.

Barentz took a deep breath. "It is the Werwolf's belief
that the Military Tribunal at Nuremberg must be
brought to an end. He intends to deliver a gift to
Nuremberg."

Eggart puzzled over the meaning of the threat. *"Ein
Gift für Nürnberg?"* he asked. What kind of present
could the Werwolf have in mind?

Then it suddenly dawned on him. He had not
translated the word *Gift* from German to English.
Gift, in German, meant "poison."

THE NUREMBERG GIFT

Robert Conot

BANTAM BOOKS

TORONTO · NEW YORK · LONDON · SYDNEY · AUCKLAND

THE NUREMBERG GIFT
A Bantam Book / June 1986

ISBN 0-553-25712-9

Published simultaneously in the United States and Canada

Bantam Books are published by Bantam Books, Inc. Its trademark,
consisting of the words "Bantam Books" and the portrayal of a
rooster, is Registered in U.S. Patent and Trademark Office and in
other countries. Marca Registrada. Bantam Books, Inc., 666 Fifth
Avenue, New York, New York 10103.

PRINTED IN THE UNITED STATES OF AMERICA

KR   0 9 8 7 6 5 4 3 2 1

For
Chandler Flickinger

Introduction

Shortly before Germany collapsed in 1945, Josef Goebbels, chief of German propaganda and head of the home front, launched a campaign to establish an organization of *Werwolves*, an underground resistance that would continue to struggle against the Allies. Goebbels's propaganda convinced the OSS and SHAEF—the Supreme Headquarters of the Allied Expeditionary Force—that this resistance would be centered on an Alpine Redoubt in southern Germany and Austria; and General Dwight D. Eisenhower based his strategy in the last days of the war on that assumption.

The Alpine Redoubt turned out to be a myth; but members of the SS did, in fact, establish a Werwolf network to perpetuate the organization, stage incidents, and await an opportune moment for a resurgence. It was the task of the CIC—the American Counter Intelligence Corps—to root out the SS Werwolves.

Unfortunately, the severe cutbacks in the American army and the development of the Cold War soon gutted the campaign against the SS. Out of the Werwolf organization emerged Odessa, which facilitated the escapes of Adolf Eichmann, Josef Mengele, and Klaus Barbie, and laid the groundwork for the continuation of the SS mystique and the emergence of successor rightwing organizations. Members of the SS with knowledge deemed important for the combat against the Soviet Union were whitewashed by the OSS and its offspring, the CIA.

A large proportion of the OSS and CIC records dealing with this period have remained classified because of the

American government's sensitivity respecting the legality and morality of bringing former SS members into the United States. But I succeeded some years ago in obtaining a key file dealing with CIC operations against the Werwolf resistance, and subsequently spoke to some of the participants in the action. During the course of my research on the Nuremberg trial, which led to my book, *Justice at Nuremberg*, I obtained information on the alarm that the SS activities set off at that time.

For a number of reasons, the story of the Nuremberg Gift lends itself better to fictionalization than to straight history. But I think the reader will realize from the details and descriptions that the account has a strong basis in fact. I hope that it will be accepted as a tribute to the CIC and to all those who were engaged in tracking down the SS after World War II.

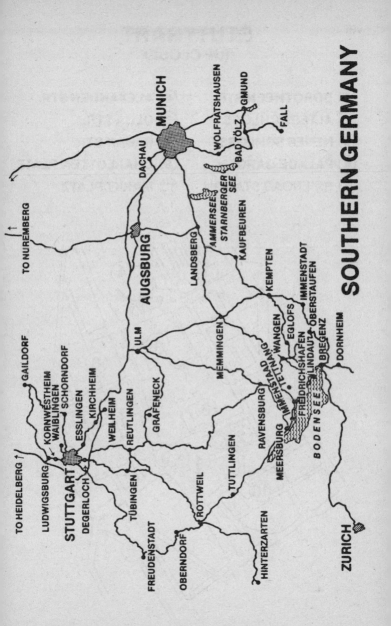

SOUTHERN GERMANY

STUTTGART
(UP CLOSE)

1. DOROTHEEN STR.
2. ALTES SCHLOSS
3. NEUES SCHLOSS
4. PALACE GARDEN
5. RAILROAD STATION
6. ALEXANDER STR.
7. OLGA STR.
8. URBAN STR.
9. CHARLOTTEN PLATZ
10. MARKT PLATZ

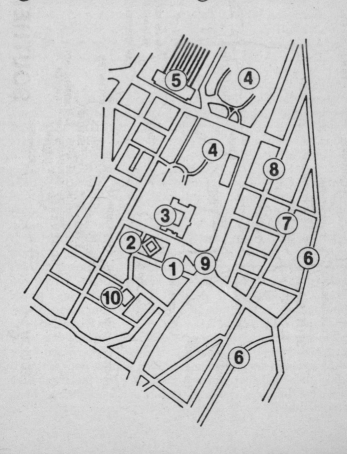

I

Sergeant William Eggart would remember the date, Thursday, March 15, 1945, because it was the eve of his twenty-fourth birthday. There was an excitement in the ranks. It was not only the tension before battle, but a sensation that victory was in the offing. At one o'clock in the morning the Americans set up searchlights on the west bank of the Blies River and lighted the east bank like a football field. Against the garish ghost-white glare, orange-scarlet tracers from 40-millimeter antiaircraft guns and quad .50-caliber machine guns mounted on armored cars crisscrossed geometrically and disappeared like darting insects into the dark of the forest. Muzzle flashes from the cannon of M-4 tanks created a rhythmic lightning. Shells bursting like Fourth of July rockets sent red streaks of shrapnel thudding into the earth.

The Germans put up little resistance, and within thirty-six hours Sergeant Eggart caught sight of the Siegfried Line near Blieskastel. Looking like dragon teeth, three parallel zigzag rows of concrete antitank pyramids formed a gleaming white geometric pattern across the brown countryside of neatly laid out fields and roads interspersed with farmhouses. Behind the dragon teeth was an antitank ditch eight feet wide and twelve feet deep. The pillboxes were interconnected and placed so that they provided supporting fire for each other. Constructed more than seven years earlier, many were hidden beneath grass and brush that had grown over them. The Siegfried Line was five hundred yards in depth and could have been formidable; but the German army was exhausted. The

1

Germans had few tanks, little artillery, virtually no air support, and never enough ammunition.

On Sunday morning, March 18, the American chaplains held services in the field and invoked God's blessing on the troops. At 12:30 P.M. the Forty-fifth Division attacked. Contrails of white phosphorus twisted about the pillboxes. The tanks clanked up like green-brown beetles. Behind them, engineers with satchel charges and bangalore torpedoes crept forward, pushed the explosives under the wire entanglements, and fastened them onto the antitank emplacements. For two hours Eggart watched the attack unfold like a panoramic movie. At a distance of a mile or two it was quite impersonal, as if everything were happening in a sandbox.

It was 2:30 P.M. when the order came to advance. First hundreds, then thousands of men poured through the breech leveled in the line, and fanned out beyond. Here and there Eggart saw men spinning and crumpling as they were hit. But the German infantry, which was supposed to fight from outside the pillboxes to provide support for the machine guns, "buttoned up" inside the fortifications. GI's poured through blind alleys free of fire. Along with other members of his platoon, Eggart dashed right past a pillbox's slits and scrambled to the top of the structure. Panting, the men flattened themselves against the concrete.

Elsewhere, engineers were bringing up beehive charges, fastening them to the tops of the pillboxes, and caving the fortifications in like anthills. One of the men in Eggart's company eased himself to the side of a firing port and shouted, "Come on out, Krauts! We ain't gonna hurt you!"

"Let me take a crack!" said Eggart as he sidled up. His grandparents had emigrated to America from Schleswig, on the Danish border, and he spoke passable German. When he shouted at the defenders, a muffled voice responded from inside. The troops had been told that, if they surrendered, the Americans would shoot them. Eggart tried to reassure them. "With the authority of the Supreme Commander, General Dwight D. Eisenhower," Eggart projected command into his voice, "I guarantee you an honorable surrender."

After a couple of minutes, a white undershirt at the end of a rifle appeared through the firing slit. The Germans, hands over their heads, filed out. It was the first pillbox captured intact. Two stories deep, it contained living quarters beneath the firing bunker. The ceilings were only six feet high, and Eggart had to stoop slightly to keep from scraping his head. As he was interviewing the prisoners, American officers began arriving—a couple of lieutenants and a captain, then a major, then two more captains. It was amazing how word spread over the battlefield, and the officers came to gaze like tourists. They were standing around, talking among themselves and questioning Eggart, when the telephone rang.

The conversation ended as if interrupted by the voice of God. Eggart looked at the officers, then quickly moved to pick up the receiver. He identified himself as Sergeant Breitschneid, who had been in command of the pillbox.

An SS Hauptsturmführer (captain), demanding a situation report, was on the line. Eggart told him that the pillbox was under heavy fire, that the Americans were attacking with tanks and artillery, and that infantry was moving up. He added that ammunition in the pillbox was almost exhausted, and reinforcements were needed.

Eggart's accent made the officer suspicious. He requested Eggart's unit and serial number. Eggart supplied them, then explained that he was a "Volksdeutsche Freiwilliger aus Dänmark," an ethnic German volunteer from Denmark. That allayed the SS man's suspicions. He ordered the pillbox held until the last round of ammunition had been expended.

"What then?" Eggart asked.

The men were to withdraw along the road to Landstuhl and Kaiserslautern, where the units were to regroup and form a new defensive line along the Rhine.

Eggart relayed the gist of the conversation to the group of American officers. The major, a cherubic-looking man of about thirty, exclaimed, "Hot damn, sergeant! Let's run that material up to Air Intelligence and see if they can fly with it!"

Between forty and fifty pillboxes were being captured and blown up each day. In two days huge gaps were ripped in the German defenses. By March 21, all semblance of a front had disappeared. Hundreds of American tanks, trucks, weapons carriers, and jeeps sped down the road to Kaiserslautern, Ludwigshafen, and the Rhine. Fighters and tactical bombers roared low overhead. Twenty miles beyond the Siegfried Line, on the road between Landstuhl and Kaiserslautern, Eggart came accross the end result of his telephone conversation with the SS captain. A squadron of American night fighters had caught a column of Germans retreating along the road. Desperately short of gasoline, the Germans had been using horses, cattle, and dogs to draw guns, trucks, and wagons. For miles, there were burned and overturned vehicles, some of their hulks still smoldering. Hundreds of carcasses and corpses were strewn along the road—like a creation out of Greek mythology, a human head with one arm and the upper part of its torso rested atop the bloated remains of a mule. The stench was terrible, and the Americans picking their way through the carnage bound handkerchiefs over their faces.

The next day Eggart reached the Rhine at Ludwigshafen. At 2:30 A.M. on Monday, March 26, the Forty-fifth Division launched its attack across the river.

Clouds streamed like sheets of ice over the moon. The Rhine flowed swift and dark between the banks. Then the silence was shattered by the roar of the fifty-horsepower motors propelling the boats and the sound of amphibious tanks lumbering like crocodiles into the water. Artillery flashes turned the horizon into a shadow play.

Several men in Eggart's boat were smashed to the gills from *beschlagnahmt* liquor. One man from a Cincinnati German district called Over the Rhine kept slurring, "Now tell me, where the hell are we?"

The answer was, "You're over the Rhine."

"Cut out the shit!" he ejaculated, then repeated, "Now tell me, where the hell are we?"

Like an Abbott and Costello routine, the exchange continued all the way across the river. Piling out of the boat on the east bank, the men moved off at a sprint. Though the sound of small-arms fire rattled through the darkness, it was mostly "precautionary" fire by Americans.

At daybreak, Eggart was moving through the Jaegersburger Wald south of Darmstadt. The men were advancing two abreast along a narrow cart road through the woods, and there was a steady, almost hypnotic rhythm to the softly bobbing heads and jouncing canteens. Ahead, Eggart saw a slight widening of the trees; beyond, a narrow paved road intersected the cartway. Like his companions, he was lulled by the weariness of dawn. He did not know what caught his eye through the branches some fourty or fifty yards down the road; but without even a conscious thought he darted through the trees toward the shadow of a movement, a half dozen men on his heels.

Segmented by the tree trunks, a small black Steyr sedan, seemingly abandoned, was parked by the side of the road. One of the men had gotten a few steps ahead of Eggart. As he burst into the road, Eggart had a warning shout catch halfway in his throat. From the woods beyond, an innocuous pop-pop-pop halted the GI in his tracks; with an astonished look on his face, he turned his head as if someone had called to him, and then pitched forward, dead.

The next few minutes became a surrealistic swirl. The carbine in Eggart's hands flicked tongues of fire. Chips of wood flew from the trees as if splintered off by invisible hatchets. Grenades exploded with the thud of drums. Ricocheting shards of metal streaked incandescent here and there like berzerk grasshoppers. Zigzagging forward, Eggart had an impression of a black-uniformed body disintegrating before his eyes; a disembodied hand flew at him, fingers outstretched as if to gouge his face. He ducked, drove past, and emerged into a small clearing. A German was kneeling on the ground, his hands behind his head. With the carbine extended like a short spear, Eggart plunged toward him. The gun's muzzle crashed into the German's face. He toppled sideways.

The catch of Eggart's weapon was set on automatic, and he had an overwhelming urge to pull the trigger and watch the head disintegrate. Then the German looked up, and all Eggart saw were the eyes: dark, expressionless, awaiting— even expecting—death. Slowly Eggart's finger uncrooked from the trigger. His heart was pounding and he started shaking.

Four Germans had composed the enemy group. Three, dressed in the black uniforms of Himmler's SD, were dead. The GI's dragged them like slaughtered animals to the road. The fourth, wearing the uniform of the Waffen SS, was holding his hand to his shattered cheek. Eggart was herding him toward the car when one of the men said:

"Sergeant!"

"What?" Eggart tried to keep his voice steady.

"Look at your pants leg." He pointed to Eggart's left thigh.

Eggart glanced down. His hand went to the spot. A dark, wet stain was pulsing slowly outward.

II

Eggart had been hit in the buttock, an embarrassing but not serious wound that entitled him to a two-week stay in the general hospital at Dijon. The ward nurse looked as if she had barely survived the First World War, and the buck-toothed chaplain gave talks twice a week to inspire the men to recovery.

Gray-eyed, with straw-colored hair, Eggart had been born on a ranch near Santa Maria, halfway between San Francisco and Los Angeles. His grandfather, who had been a farmer in Schleswig, had settled in California in 1888 and had specialized in raising Holstein cattle. Everyone had had to work hard, and by the time William was twelve he had had two to three hours of chores to do daily. Agile and quick, he played football, and on the small school's basketball team was a starting forward. After graduating in 1938, he entered California Polytechnic Institute at San Luis Obispo; but, still uncertain about what he wanted to do, he dropped out to go to work as a newspaper reporter in Santa Maria and Santa Barbara. Finally, he enrolled as a psychology major at the University of California. In June 1943, at the end of his junior year, he was drafted.

After basic training at Fort Riley, Kansas, he was assigned, because of his knowledge of German, to the Army Specialized Training Program at the University of Nebraska. *"In diese Klasse wird überhaupt kein English gesprochen,"* the professor said on the first day, and from then on the men were allowed to speak only German during duty hours. Anyone who failed to keep up was washed out and shipped to the infantry. Then, in March 1944, as the

7

buildup for the Normandy invasion reached full stride, the army decided it was more important to fight Germans than to talk to them. During the wholesale reassignments, Eggart was given the choice of going to the infantry or of volunteering for the airborne. He volunteered for the airborne.

He did well on the controlled jumps from the tower at Fort Bragg. But on his second jump from a C-46 he landed with his left leg in a rut. Before he could unsnap his chute, the wind dragged him, and his ankle was broken. That had washed him out of the airborne and brought on his appearance as a member of an infantry unit.

During the second week he was in the Dijon hospital, Eggart was visited by Lieutenant Steven O'Neal, whom he had gotten to know when he was studying German in Nebraska. O'Neal was a member of the 307th CIC (Counter Intelligence Corps) Detachment attached to Seventh Army Headquarters. Historically, the army intelligence service, G-2—of which the CIC was a component—had been looked down on by the generals and shorted in the allocation of funds, but finally, thirteen days before D day, a British major general, Kenneth Strong, had been appointed to reorganize the American G-2 section. The CIC, however, was desperately short of personnel: the Seventh Army detachment had only 49 officers and men.

Now, O'Neal told Eggart, there was great concern about the development of a German underground resistance organization. In the fall of 1944, Hitler had given Himmler permission to begin construction of a National Redoubt in the Alps of Württemberg, Bavaria, and Austria. This *Alpine Festung* was reputedly designed to accommodate a guerrilla army, consisting of a quarter million men, that could hold out for months—perhaps years. Throughout the early months of 1945, the concept of the redoubt gained credence among Allied intelligence, and rumors abounded. Thousands of tons of supplies were reported being stashed in mines and tunnels, and entire airplane factories were supposedly being constructed underground.

On March 25, a few days before Eggart was wounded,

Seventh Army G-2 had published a report indicating that the Germans were concentrating many of their remaining elite units in the mountains. Every night the Königswusterhausen radio transmitter, the most powerful in Germany, broadcast instructions from Goebbels for Werwolf actions and the formation of resistance groups. The German people were to take to the woods and the mountains and live like *werwolves*—human wolves. They were to wreak vengeance on anyone who cooperated with the conquering armies.

"We're up to our balls in trouble. And when I say balls, I mean eyeballs!" O'Neal told Eggart, and invited him to transfer to the CIC.

"Good God!" Eggart was startled. "What do I know about intelligence?"

"Nothing. So that makes you even with the rest of us," O'Neal retorted. "We're all studying Steve Canyon and hoping to meet up with the Dragon Lady." He pointed out that Eggart's command of German and his background in journalism and psychology made him a logical choice for an investigator.

Eggart, of course, jumped at the opportunity. Even before he was released from the hospital, O'Neal started processing a security clearance on him and feeding him material. Eggart read *SHAEF Directive Number 7*, which contained instructions for the CIC in occupied territories. He studied the G-2 report on the *Alpine Festung*, and the *Basic Handbook of KL's*, a complex and remarkably accurate compilation of German concentration camps and their SS personnel. He went over the issues of the *Weekly Intelligence Summary* for the past several months. After being briefed, he was checked out on a snub-nosed .38-caliber Smith and Wesson "Police Special," the standard CIC weapon.

The second week in April, the CIC detachment moved across the Rhine to Darmstadt and established its headquarters in a villa on the Friedrichsplatz. Ten days later, Eggart was still feeling his way, when O'Neal said to him, "We've got a bunch of lower-echelon SS locked up in a wing of the jail. You'd better check them over. See if they'll tell you anything. Hold anyone who looks important. Then let's get the rest out to a POW camp."

Eggart had questioned three-fourths of the prisoners when, on Friday, April 27, Johannes Barentz was brought to him. Barentz was squat and muscular, not more than five feet five inches tall. His black hair had been shaved high on the temples and the back of his neck in the German SS fashion, and now, as it was growing out, it looked like a beret sitting on top of his head. He marched in stiffly ahead of the guard, and reflexively came to attention before Eggart.

Then, Eggart saw him flinch and jerk back as if struck by an invisible blow. As Barentz turned his head, Eggart caught sight of the left side of his face. His cheek was discolored and swollen. Eggart sucked in his breath—the scene in the woods four weeks before flashed before him: the German kneeling; the carbine barrel smashing into his face; the instant decision between killing him and taking him prisoner.

"*Setze sich!*" Eggart motioned Barentz to the chair.

There was an awkward tension, yet a bond encompassed the two men, as in a re-encounter between an executioner and a prisoner reprieved at the instant of death. But, when he spoke, Eggart made his voice dispassionate, as if he had never seen Barentz before. He asked Barentz the routine questions, and Barentz replied that he had been born in 1922 in Kirchheim-unter-Teck, a town on the road between Stuttgart and Ulm. His father had died when he was a boy, and he had been raised by his mother, who worked as a domestic. At the age of fourteen he had enrolled in the Hitler Jugend, and in 1940 he had volunteered for and been accepted in the Waffen SS.

"It was the greatest moment of my life," Barentz told Eggart. "My mother was very poor. I left school at fifteen and could never have hoped to achieve a higher education. But when I joined the SS, I became one of the elite of the Reich. I was one of the select chosen to build a new order." He made the statement simply and straightforwardly, and with complete conviction.

Nothing during the past few days had shaken Eggart

more than the realization that the SS, which was regarded
with hatred and horror by the people of the Allied nations,
continued to hold an elitist mystique for the Germans.
Even in defeat, many of them spoke of the SS not with
shame but with pride.

Barentz had been assigned to the SS Wiking Division,
half of whose strength was made up of volunteers from
Belgium, Holland, Denmark, and Norway. (Here was
another shock for Eggart! Tens of thousands of men from
Allied nations had fought on the German side.) In June
1941, the Wiking Division had been part of General Von
Rundstedt's Army Group South that had launched the
invasion of the Ukraine. The advance had taken Barentz all
the way to the Caucasus, and he had spent more than
eighteen months in Russia. Early in 1943 the top of his skull
had been shattered by a Russian Katyusha rocket.

"I was sent to an SS hospital in Slovakia," he told
Eggart, "and a silver plate was put into my head. It was not
until I had been there several weeks that I realized all the
doctors were Jewish."

Barentz halted, and it was obvious that it was difficult
for him to continue.

"There had been few Jews in the town where I grew
up," he said. "I suppose there were some in school, but
they were not among my friends—I was poor and they had
money—and when I was twelve or thirteen they were all
transferred to some other school. From the time I joined
the Hitler Jugend I heard only that the Jews were evil, that
they were parasites in the body of the German people and
were the cause of all our troubles. After we arrived in
Russia we all had to read a booklet called *Die Untermensch*,
[*The Subhumans*]. It warned us that we must show no pity
to the Jews, that they were beasts in human form.

"The Jews were supposed to be the masters of
Bolshevism, but we—I—knew there was something wrong.
In the summer of 1941 when we first reached the Ukraine
we were welcomed with friendship offerings of bread and
salt—in the Jewish villages, too! We were startled! We were
confused! I did not know what to think. In the villages they
did not know about Hitler and his program against the

Jews. They looked on us as liberators. An old man told me that he had served as a scout for the German forces that had come to the Ukraine in 1918. Before they came, he said, the Chekha—the Czarist secret police—had organized pogroms against the Jews, but the Germans had stopped all that and treated the Jews well. But after the Germans left came the OGPU, who liquidated the Jewish 'ruling class.' But this time, praise the Lord, the old man told me, the Germans will stay, and the persecutions will come to an end."

"What did you tell him?" Eggart said.

"What could I say? These Jews were not Bolshevists. They were not rich bankers. They were poor hard-working people like my mother. But we had fighting to do. From time to time we heard stories. Jews were being held hostage. In Kiev a lot of them had been shot because buildings had been booby-trapped and scores of our men killed. But we were too busy fighting to ask questions. Anyway, a soldier does not ask questions." Barentz halted. "Can I have a cigarette?"

Eggart put a pack in front of him on the table.

"So then we retreated. Much of the land was like a desert. In some of the villages only a few people were left. There were no carpenters. Why are there no carpenters? I asked. All the carpenters had been Jewish. There were no shoemakers. Why are there no shoemakers? I asked. All the shoemakers had been Jewish. There were no tailors. Why are there no tailors? I asked. All the tailors had been Jewish. There were no doctors. Why are there no doctors? I asked. All the doctors had been Jewish. And now when the children got sick in the village there was no one to treat them, and the people were making medicines out of mud and herbs as they had in the Middle Ages."

Barentz's eyes shifted uneasily. He looked over his shoulder as if to see who else might be listening.

"And then I asked, 'But what happened to all of the Jews?' I am talking to this peasant with a lumpy face who looks like he is growing peas and potatoes beneath his skin. And he gets this sly smile as if I am making a joke. 'They were not happy here,' he said, 'and the German police came and offered to take them to a better land. So they went.'

"'All of them?' I asked.

"'Not all of them,' he said. 'Some ran away. And who knows what became of them? Some resisted. So they were sent off to the best land of all. Paradise.'

"I could not ask him any more questions. No—" Barentz corrected himself, "I dared not ask him any more questions. Soon after that I was wounded. Then there was the hospital. The doctors who saved my life and the lives of my comrades were Jews. They were not the *Untermensch* I had been told about. The Jews in the Ukraine had not been *Untermensch*. I could no longer believe what Goebbels said. But I did not know what else to believe. I was confused. And yes, I was upset. But this was war. And I had to do my duty."

After his release from the hospital, Barentz had been assigned as a Scharführer (sergeant) to the cadre at the SS Junkerschule (officers' training school) at Posen-Treskau. Because of his wound, he was supposed to be limited to light duty. But during the Russian summer offensive of 1944 the German need for manpower had been so critical that he was transferred to an SS antipartisan unit in southern Poland. In December, he suffered a leg wound, and was shipped to the SS clinic at Hohenlychen, north of Berlin.

"I was due to be released early in February," Barentz said, "but I still could not walk well." Even now he limped noticeably. "Some days I had terrible headaches. I was not fit for combat. But the Russians were approaching Berlin. We kept hearing that every man would be needed. I wondered if I would be sent back to the front.

"Then something happened. I was ordered to report to a Hauptsturmführer, who had my papers. He talked to me, and told me I had an outstanding record. Perhaps, he said, I was a man who could serve Germany in its most critical hour. A few days later I received orders to report to a Standartenführer (colonel). He was the highest officer I had ever had to speak to, and I was very nervous. I did not know what he wanted of me. He asked me about my early life, about my mother, about my faith in the Führer and in the SS. These were difficult times, he said, but Germany had gone through difficult times before. It was a time that required strong men and a will of iron. And you, Scharführer Barentz, he said, are a man who has proved that he does not flinch before the gates of hell themselves."

Barentz paused.

"What happened then?" Eggart interposed.

"Another few days passed. I was called back to the Standartenführer's office. To my surprise, another officer was there. He had his back to me, and when he turned my knees almost buckled. He was a Gruppenführer (major general). I stood ramrod stiff, but he came to me, shook me by the hand, inquired about my wound, and had me sit down.

"He spoke freely. I was shaken by what he said. He told me that the Reich SS and Polizeiführer Heinrich Himmler was hospitalized at Hohenlychen with the grippe, and that he had been in conversation with Himmler all morning. The tactical situation was hopeless. The Luftwaffe was finished; there was no more fuel for the planes. The Wehrmacht could still fight, but there was a great shortage of material and ammunition. 'In other words,' he said, 'it is only a matter of time before we must retreat. But where can we retreat to? Germany does not have vast territories like Russia. There is only one place where we can make a stand. In the Alps!

"'But to make a stand in the Alps we must have a support organization throughout the country—whether Germany is occupied by Russians and Americans or not. Every German must be turned into a Werwolf. The SS must continue to lead the struggle, as it has in the past.'"

At the word *Werwolf*, Eggart bolted upright. "Are you saying that you are familiar with the Werwolf organization?"

"Yes." Barentz nodded. "I was assigned as courier to link the Werwolf stations in Baden and in Württemberg."

Eggart had a strange sensation, as if he were listening to a dead man speak. Barentz displayed no resentment toward him and talked without hesitation, seemingly keeping nothing back, as if he were being debriefed by his own superior officer. At Hohenlychen, Barentz said, he had

had to memorize the names, ranks, and addresses of 150 SS men and women from a list provided by Gruppenführer Hans Prützmann, who had been assigned by Himmler to head the Werwolf organization.

For two hours, while Eggart wrote, Barentz related name after name of key members.

Eggart was excited and elated. Everyone in the CIC was talking and speculating about the Werwolves, and the brass all the way up to SHAEF was worried about them. Not only had he stumbled across the first concrete evidence of the organization, but Barentz was enabling him to compile a Who's Who for half of southern Germany.

Finally Barentz uttered the last name. Eggart sat back and looked at the list in front of him. He was perplexed. Barentz had spoken of the idealism that had caused him to join the SS, and though he had clearly been disillusioned, he still seemed to have at least a residue of pride in belonging. Why then was he betraying a mission of such immense importance?

When Eggart asked the question, Barentz breathed deeply. "Can you have my personal belongings brought to me?"

Eggart ordered the guard to bring the envelope containing the contents of Barentz's pockets when he had been captured. Barentz took out a plain, slightly tarnished pocket watch, and handed it to Eggart. "Open the back," Barentz said.

Eggart pressed the small knob that released the catch on the back plate.

"Read it," Barentz continued.

On the inside was an inscription in German: "For my darling Nathan, on his fourteenth birthday."

"I was given the watch for outstanding service," Barentz said. "Thousands of SS men received watches, fountain pens, cameras, and such things. We were told that they were contraband taken from the enemy. But the Russians did not have watches and fountain pens—everyone knew that."

Barentz's face was drained white, and his eyes seemed to project from their sockets. "No. We knew what *enemy* this contraband came from. The Jews." He was breathing hard, and his voice trembled. *"Unsere Ehre heisst Treue,* 'Our honor is our loyalty.' That was our oath, and that was all we were supposed to believe. Obedience and loyalty were everything. Obedience and loyalty were our honor. Germany had become so bankrupt it could not make watches for its soldiers. Honor was taking a watch from a Jewish boy who had been killed or sent to a concentration camp. We, those of us who thought we were serving Germany with honor, were dishonored. From the day I received the watch, I began to hate what I was doing. I began to hate myself."

There was a stillness in the room. The normal background noises in the building, noises that Eggart hadn't noticed before, seemed like rumblings from the netherworld.

"I'll get some coffee," Eggart said.

The coffee helped Barentz regain his composure. On March 19, he continued, he had received orders from Gruppenführer Prützmann to travel from Hohenlychen to Stuttgart and report to Friedrich Mussgay, head of the Gestapo there. On the way he was to make stops in Darmstadt and Heidelberg to transmit messages to the heads of the SD—the SS Security Service—in those cities. When Barentz arrived in Darmstadt, the Americans had reached the west bank of the Rhine, and he had made up his mind that he would do nothing further to aid the Nazi regime, but would let himself be captured. After he left Darmstadt with three Gestapo officials, he had put sugar into the gas tank to disable the car.

Eggart shook his head. He had come within a split second of killing a man who had changed his allegiance. So much for whether a uniform made enemy or friend.

"I am prepared," Barentz told Eggart, "to help in any way I can to bring this madness to an end."

A thought flashed into Eggart's mind. If Barentz had been alienated from the Nazi cause, might it be possible to push him a step further? "Would you be willing to work for American intelligence?" he asked.

Barentz considered a moment. "Yes," he replied.

* * *

Eggart was sky-high when he burst into Steve O'Neal's office and related the results of the interrogation of Barentz.

"Yes," asked O'Neal, "but how reliable is he?" O'Neal's skepticism was deflating.

Eggart declared that he believed everything Barentz had said. What would Barentz have to gain by fabricating such a story? "And look at this list!" Eggart said, punching it for emphasis.

"It is a hell of a list!" O'Neal agreed. After a moment, he continued. "Type up a report. But you'd better get your ass moving. We're pulling out for Augsburg on Sunday."

"What about Barentz?"

"We'll take him with us."

III

It was a motley caravan that started on the journey from Darmstadt to Augsburg. Because of the gasoline shortage, there were virtually no private German cars in operation. But thousands were stored in garages, and these were *beschlagnahmt* by the troops. O'Neal and Eggart discovered a seven-passenger Horch sedan sitting on blocks. Others in the CIC detachment appropriated Opel and Mercedes sedans. The convoy that proceeded down the autobahn contained only two jeeps and one three-quarter-ton weapons carrier—the remainder of the vehicles were German cars.

The advance of the Allies was so rapid and the resistance so scattered that in many towns essential services continued uninterrupted. The conquering American troops were startled to see mailmen on their rounds and streetcars running. French and American units sped along in sight of and sometimes tripping over each other, the French on the right flank and the Americans on the left. On April 23, the French captured Stuttgart on the right bank of the Neckar River, while the Americans occupied the suburbs of Bad Cannstadt and Unterturkheim on the left. Eisenhower ordered the French out of Stuttgart, and on April 26 the 100th American Division moved in. But De Gaulle saw the order as an American attempt to deprive the French of their rightful glory in the final victory, and refused to move the French troops out. For four days the GI's confronted the Third Algerian Division. Then the Americans backed down and left.

Death and chaos tracked each other across the land. In

many of the towns through which Eggart's convoy passed the Gestapo had reigned until the previous day. In every sizeable city, trees and lampposts were festooned with bodies. Crows and ravens tearing at the bloated faces and decaying flesh flapped off noisily as the vehicles approached—the GI's chased the birds with volleys of shots. Hung around the corpses' necks were placards reading: *Those who fear death in honor die in dishonor.* Germans who had knowledge of crimes committed by the security police were hunted down by the Gestapo, bundled into cars, and in gangster fashion bumped off and dumped along deserted roads.

Eggart reached Augsburg during the late afternoon of Sunday, April 29. The CIC moved into a villa that had been the Gauleiter's headquarters. Calls came into the office from outlying districts asking where the Americans were; and the startled callers were told, "They're right here, buddy!"

For the next week, the Gauleiter's villa had the atmosphere of the Grand Hotel on moving day. Rumor was superseded by rumor hour after hour. A wild variety of suspects were brought in. On Tuesday, news came that Hitler was dead, and that Himmler and Göring were struggling over the carcass of the Third Reich.

Dachau was only an hour's drive to the east, and reports of conditions there were of mind-surpassing horror. On Thursday, Lieutenant O'Neal was assigned to head a detail going to the camp, and Eggart assumed he would be going along. That evening, however, a report reached Colonel Campbell, the detachment commander, that Himmler was on his way to his villa on the Tegernsee. Eggart was one of a dozen men picked to accompany Campbell to the SS leader's home in Gmund.

Early the next morning Campbell and the other men started off in three cars. Shortly before they reached Munich, they turned south toward the Starnberger See. As they were passing the northern point of the lake, their attention was attracted by a minuet of vultures. Halting the cars, they trudged toward a meadow fifty yards off the road. In its center a heap of bodies lay like a stack of fallen

dominoes. Other bodies radiated outward in every direction—men and women cut down as they had tried to flee.

A week before, the SS had rounded up 6,700 of the
30,000 prisoners at Dachau and marched them south in an
effort to evacuate the camp. Hundreds of people, many of
them scarcely alive when they left the camp, had died from
fatigue and exposure. Whoever had fallen behind had been
shot.

The Americans spent only a few minutes amid the
shrunken and bloated bodies, a scene beyond comprehen-
sion. Yet it proved only a beginning. Thousands of corpses
lay like markers along the route: Wolfratshausen, Beuer-
berg, Königsdorf, Bad Tölz—the trail led directly to
Himmler's house at Gmund. Everyone in the neighborhood
was rounded up for questioning. But the Reichsführer SS,
the people maintained, had not lived there for years.

While Colonel Campbell conducted the questioning in
an effort to determine the whereabouts of Himmler, Eggart
and four other men were detailed to survey the town and
interrogate anyone who might provide information. They
had just finished speaking to the proprietor of a *Gaststätte*—restaurant—when they were approached by an
elderly woman. Speaking in a low voice which they had
difficulty understanding, she said she had been told that
several men who had escaped from Dachau were hiding in
a cloister near Sachsenkam, some 10 kilometers from
Gmund.

After obtaining Colonel Campbell's approval, Eggart
and two other agents headed for Sachsenkam. They had
great trouble rousing a priest, and even more difficulty
convincing him to let them enter the cloister. He seemed
unable to grasp that there was a difference between Nazi
and American authority.

In a small room near the chapel they found five
prisoners who had slipped away from the death march. The
next day Eggart took them back to Augsburg. Two days
later he began questioning the first, Albrecht Willach, in a
small, jumbled room of the Gauleiter's villa.

Albrecht Willach had worked in Dachau's administration. He was gray-haired and tight-lipped. His skin was

blotched and creased, and his hands trembled slightly; still, it was obvious that he had received the better treatment that was accorded those inmates whom the Nazis considered important. As Eggart spoke in German, Willach interrupted.

"Would it be easier if we used English?" His accent was American.

"You've lived in the United States?" Eggart was startled.

"I spent thirteen years in America," Willach replied. He explained that he had been trained as a chemist and had gone to America in 1925, when he was twenty-seven. He had worked first for the Standard Oil Company of New Jersey, and then for Du Pont. In the winter of 1938–39, his wife's mother had become very ill, and he had decided to bring his family back to Germany for a visit. His three children were completely Americanized—the youngest had been born in New Jersey—and in the summer of 1937 he had taken out his first naturalization papers.

"That means you could have become a citizen in 1939," Eggart interpolated.

"Yes. So I was not worried. It never occurred to me that I could have any difficulty."

"But you did have problems. Why?"

"Like many other Germans, my younger brother had joined the Nazi party during the Depression. He had a university education, and he was recruited by the SS. He joined the SD, the intelligence service, and advanced rapidly. By 1939 he was a Standartenführer. He told me that I must not go back to America, that I would hurt his career if I did, and that it was the duty of every German to work for the Fatherland. When we wanted to return to the United States in May, I was denied an exit visa. My brother took me to see Reinhard Heydrich, the chief of the SD, and Heydrich told me that it was essential that I remain in Germany. My skills were invaluable, he said. I had great knowledge of the American petrochemical industry, and it was my patriotic duty to apply that knowledge in behalf of Germany. I would be given a directorship at I. G. Farben, a large grant for relocating, and so forth."

"What happened?"

"I refused. I went to the U.S. consulate in Munich, hoping that somehow I would be able to take my oath of American citizenship in Germany. Then the war broke out. On November 9, 1939, I was in Munich when an attempt was made to kill Hitler by blowing up the Bürgerbräu Keller."

Willach halted, seemingly collecting his words like scraps of paper.

"Go on," Eggart urged.

"The next day I was in the American consulate. There was some discussion about the assassination attempt, and I said it was too bad the bastard hadn't been killed.

"The following day as I was walking down the street, two men grabbed me and threw me into a car. The next thing I knew I was being interrogated at Gestapo headquarters. Obviously the Gestapo had had spies, or microphones planted at the consulate. At first they accused me of complicity in the plot. They said that the device was so sophisticated that only someone who was a chemical or explosives expert could have made it. I told them I knew nothing about explosives, and after a few days they dropped the matter. I found out much later that they decided the British were behind it."

"And then?"

"I was sent to Dachau."

"What about your brother?"

"I never heard from my brother." His voice trembled. "I never heard from anyone. I was not allowed to write letters. I was not allowed to receive letters. I do not know what happened to my wife, to my children. They probably think I am dead, and—God knows!" He buried his face in his hands.

Eggart waited until Willach recovered. "You worked in the camp administration. You were considered an *important* prisoner?"

"Yes. I was lucky in that, I suppose. It was the only way one could survive six years. I met Elser, the carpenter who built and planted the bomb. A crazy man. Brilliant and crazy! He made a lyre and sat all the time playing it and singing like Ophelia."

"What did you do in the camp?"

"I speak French and Italian in addition to English, so I served as an interpreter."

Albrecht Willach's mention of the fact that he had a brother who was an SS Standartenführer stimulated Eggart's memory. Excusing himself momentarily, Eggart left the room and retrieved the list of Werwolf names related by Barentz. Among the 150 names was a Standartenführer Otto Willach.

"Is your brother's name Otto?" Eggart asked when he came back into the room.

"Yes," Willach replied. "But how did you know?"

IV

A short time later, Eggart, laying claim to an unoccupied typewriter, sat down to compose a report to Colonel Campbell. As he looked at the keys, he realized that the typewriter was German—an SS model that included among its letters the double lightning ⚡ symbol. What the hell! It was appropriate!

In his report Eggart wrote that the nucleus for a Werwolf organization definitely existed. Johannes Barentz had been given his instructions by Gruppenführer Hans Prützmann. Barentz could lead the CIC to Prützmann, and Prützmann might know Himmler's whereabouts.

It was midnight when Eggart finished the report and slipped it into Colonel Campbell's box. At eleven o'clock the next morning he received orders to report to Campbell's office.

Campbell puffed on his pipe. "You think you can find Himmler?" he asked.

"I don't know, colonel. I think there's a good chance we might be able to locate him through the Werwolves. Otto Willach was influential enough to get his brother Albrecht an interview with Heydrich. Prützmann himself is a Gruppenführer and must have a lot of clout. Other than that—God knows!"

"You picked the key words, Eggart—God knows!" Campbell blew a smoke ring that twirled around the stem of his pipe. "But maybe even God doesn't know. Intelligence is putting two and two together to get six. For the last few months I've been kicking myself in the ass because I couldn't figure out what the Nazis were doing. Now I'm finding out the reason I couldn't is they didn't know themselves. Let's see what Kaltenbrunner can tell us."

"Kaltenbrunner?" Eggart asked, surprised. Kaltenbrunner had become head of the SD, the intelligence arm of the SS, after Heydrich was assassinated, and he ranked second in the SS only to Himmler.

"We nabbed him at Alt Aussee," said Campbell. "Sterling example of the superman. Loaded with cigarettes, schnapps, chocolate, submachine guns, and enough counterfeit money to balance the U.S. budget."

Kaltenbrunner towered over the two MPs who brought him into the room. Eggart estimated he was nearly six and a half feet tall. A scar slashed white across his left cheek from his nostril, and above his lip the lighter texture of the skin showed where he had shaved off his moustache in an effort to change his appearance. He should have been an imposing man, but his arms hung loosely, he walked disjointedly, and his head seemed to wobble. Like Adolf Hitler, Kaltenbrunner was a small-town Austrian.

"So, Herr Kaltenbrunner," Campbell said. "Where is Heinrich Himmler?"

"The Reichsführer SS is no longer my concern," Kaltenbrunner replied. "He betrayed Germany, and the Führer dismissed him."

"He is not in the Alps?"

"I do not know. He went to Admiral Doenitz's headquarters, and the admiral asked for an armistice. That is all I know."

"Armistice, Kaltenbrunner? It was unconditional surrender."

"Germany may be defeated. But she does not surrender."

"You surrendered, Kaltenbrunner."

"I did not surrender." Kaltenbrunner's voice was hoarse, his eyes had a desperate, cornered look, his hands were shaking, and he was sweating. "I offered the United States of America the support of the SS and the Wehrmacht in the continuing struggle against the Bolshevik barbarians."

"You do have bad mornings, Kaltenbrunner," Campbell said, pulling a bottle and a glass from the desk. "Some cognac—will that help?"

"Yes. That will help."

Kaltenbrunner reached for the glass even as Campbell was uncorking the bottle. Campbell filled the glass three-fourths full, and Kaltenbrunner drank half of it in two long gulps. His cheeks colored. Within moments he seemed steadier and more erect. Still, his fingers, stained from tobacco, twisted nervously, and he seemed to be trying to keep his hands out of sight.

"Captain Eggart wants to ask you some questions," Campbell continued.

It took Eggart a few seconds to realize that he was *Captain* Eggart. He recovered with a start.

"Are you familiar with Gruppenführer Hans Prütz-mann?" Eggart asked Kaltenbrunner.

"Prützmann? Prützmann was Höhere SS and Polizei-führer in the Ukraine from 1941 until 1944."

"Last autumn, did Himmler assign him the task of organizing the Werwolves to continue resistance in Germany?"

"That is a possibility; yes. The Reichsführer SS had many ideas." Kaltenbrunner drained the cognac from the glass and looked hopefully toward Colonel Campbell.

"What has been done to implement the organization of the Werwolves?"

"Every German will be a Werwolf in the fight against the Bolsheviks." Kaltenbrunner's face was flushed. "That is our duty as the leaders of Western culture. We offer our iron will in comradeship to America and England. We are prepared to make sacrifices. Yes. If we must be Werwolves, we will be Werwolves."

"So Gruppenführer Prützmann heads the Werwolves. Or is it Himmler himself?"

"I know nothing."

"You know nothing about the organization?"

"I know nothing about the organization."

"Do you know Standartenführer Otto Willach?"

"Willach? Standartenführer? Otto Willach?" The name seemed to be vaguely familiar to Kaltenbrunner. "Yes.

Willach. The Heydrich-Thomas clique. A protégé of
Brigadeführer Dr. Thomas. A womanizer. Not to be
trusted."

"Do you know where he is now?"

"I do not know."

Kaltenbrunner was unable, or unwilling, to provide
more information. The interrogation came to an end.

After Kaltenbrunner had been taken from the room,
Colonel Campbell said, "Göring's screaming for his pills,
and Kaltenbrunner's an alcoholic and half a lunatic to boot.
He's dying for a cigarette, but he won't smoke in my
presence. Himmler hated smokers, and he's afraid Heinrich
is hiding in a drawer of the desk. That's the kind of people
who were running the Third Reich."

There was a slight pause. "By the way," said Eggart,
"thank you for the promotion."

"Think nothing of it. Kaltenbrunner won't talk to
anyone below the rank of captain—it's beneath his dignity!"
Campbell puffed on his pipe. "You handled yourself well.
We ought to have at least three or four people on this thing.
Problem is, I'm spread so thin I just can't spare anybody.
Do you think you can work on it by yourself till we get a fix
on what it's about?"

"I'll do my best," said Eggart.

"What approach are you going to take?"

"I've got Barentz and his list of contacts. He has his
instructions from Prützmann. I'll operate him just as if he'd
come straight from Berlin. And then, maybe I can get a tie
on Otto Willach through his brother, Albrecht."

"Separate them."

"Sir?"

"If you're working two agents on a case, don't let either
one of them know the other's working for you."

"Right."

"What do you need?" Campbell asked.

"Authorization. A car. Food. Whatever supportive
materials are necessary for Barentz and myself."

"Good. Of course, you can rely on all our counterintelligence detachments for support if you need it. But the
more self-sufficient you are, the fewer people will know

what you're up to. And the fewer who know, the better. I'll expect reports from you weekly."

Although Eggart's promotion to captain had been fleeting, he recognized that being regarded as an officer endowed him with an authority he did not possess as a sergeant. Since, as an agent, he was authorized to assume any rank or disguise that would enable him to complete his assignment, he took Colonel Campbell's precedent to heart and in the future often passed himself off as a captain.

When Eggart picked Barentz up from the detention cell, Barentz seemed like a starving, whipped dog. Eggart drove to a quiet spot on the brook that rushed past the Mozart cottage, and halted the Horch. A chunk of dark bread, a piece of cheese, a can of beans, and half a K-ration chocolate bar had been left scattered about the car by CIC agents, and Eggart gave them to Barentz. Barentz ate slowly and hungrily. For nearly two hours Eggart questioned Barentz again about the Werwolf organization, and had him recite once more the names and addresses he had been required to memorize. Barentz did not make a single mistake. Eggart asked Barentz about Otto Willach, but the name did not signify anything special to him.

At the end of their conversation, Barentz said he would need a bicycle to make his contacts. He still walked with a limp, and could not afford to be seen with Eggart.

Starting the car, Eggart drove to a German army depot that had been converted into a motor pool, and told the sergeant there that he needed an automobile big enough to carry a bike.

"There's a Mercedes tourer," the sergeant replied. "Take a look at it. The top's shot, and I've got no one to fix it. If it rains, you'll get soaked, but otherwise, it's in fair shape."

Eggart inspected it. The vehicle was about ten years old, an impressive twenty feet long, made out of steel thick enough for an armored car. Spare tires were set on the running boards and cut into the front fenders on both sides. The wood frame that carried the top was down, and when Eggart pulled it up a foot or two he saw that the canvas was in tatters. The heavy leather of the seats was worn but uncut. When Eggart turned the key and pressed the starter, the flywheel groaned two or three times before the engine came to life with a full-throated roar, amplified by a corroded muffler.

"That battery's wiped out," Eggart said.

"I'll replace it," the sergeant agreed.

"What about a bike?"

"Shit! I'm not in the bike business. You'll have to liberate one yourself."

The railroads had been bombed to pieces, the Germans had no gasoline, the Allied armies were appropriating all the cars they could find, and the horses were being eaten; so bicycles were the only transportation left to the Germans. Bicycles were harder to find than cars, and the price of one was two hundred dollars.

While the sergeant went to get a new battery, Eggart was approached by a shabbily dressed man who had been working on a nearby truck. His course was erratic. He shuffled sideways, took two or three steps, then shuffled sideways again. He was a small man, and he finally halted almost directly under Eggart's armpit.

"*Sie wille Fahrrad?*" he asked in Slavic-accented German.

"Yes," Eggart replied in German.

"I—foreign worker," he continued in German, pointing to himself and indicating that he had been a slave laborer. "I know where you can get bicycle."

"Yes?"

The man looked back at Eggart without speaking, as if he had been struck dumb. Eggart glanced down and saw his arm half extended, the palm of his hand upturned.

"Oh, sure!" said Eggart, taking a cigarette from the pack in his pocket and placing it in the waiting hand.

"Ten." said the man.

"Five."

They compromised at eight. The Slav provided Eggart with an address. "Tell them you are from Raskowsky," he said.

* * *

Driving down Fuggerstrasse, Eggart overtook a funeral procession. A pastor in a cassock was leading a dozen middle-aged and elderly men and women who were wearing black armbands. Two of the men pulled a handcart that was loaded with the coffin. Eggart felt a twinge of guilt as he maneuvered around them. Then he realized that things had not changed as much for them as they had for him. A month or two before, the procession would have been going along in much the same way, but the Mercedes would have been loaded with officials of the Reich.

The address the Slav had given Eggart was behind the Augsburg Dom, or cathedral. Eggart twisted the Mercedes through the narrow streets and brought it to a halt in front of an ancient house with a sagging wooden door. Eggart knocked, waited, knocked again, waited, knocked harder, and waited. Finally the door opened a crack. From the dark interior a husky voice asked, "What is it?"

"I am looking for a bicycle," Eggart said.

"No bicycles," the voice replied, and the door started to shut.

Eggart barely had time to shout, "Raskowsky!"

The door reopened. "Ah, Raskowsky. Come with me, please."

The voice belonged to a woman in a long black dress, and she led Eggart and Barentz through a dark hallway and out a rear door. They passed through a courtyard into an alley. They went along the alley, and from there into a small interior garden where a door was set in a gray wall. The woman knocked sharply and a man answered.

"From Raskowsky," the woman said, and left.

The man opened the door and let Eggart and Barentz into a chamber with stone walls and a stone floor. He was working on a bicycle. A half dozen other bikes were propped against the walls. Enough handlebars, wheels, and frames were scattered around to put together three or four more. Aside from the bicycles, the room contained only a five-foot crucifix, suspended from the wall.

"Thirty packs," said the man, setting the price.

The bicycles were a motley assortment in poor to average condition. Barentz looked them over. One had three speeds, but the spokes of the front wheel were bent and both tires were bad. Eggart indicated to the man that they would take it.

"That bike is forty packs," he said.

"With a new front wheel and the best tires you have."

"Fifty-five packs."

Eggart did not argue. On the German market the man was getting $400 for the bike, but at PX prices it was $2.75. Eggart and Barentz waited while he worked quickly and expertly to change the wheel and the tires. A large cross swung loosely from a chain around his neck. When he was finished, he took the bike and led them back to the street.

Barentz tested the bike and was delighted. He loaded it into the Mercedes. Eggart started the engine.

"Religious bastard, wasn't he?" Eggart commented to Barentz.

"He is a Jesuit," Barentz replied. "Times are hard for everyone."

V

On the following day, Eggart started for Stuttgart. Albrecht Willach occupied the right-hand front seat. Barentz was in back with the bike. Heeding Colonel Campbell's admonition, Eggart did not introduce Barentz and Willach to each other. If Eggart were able to recruit Otto Willach, he did not want Barentz to know that he was acquainted with Willach's brother.

The drive on the autobahn from Augsburg to Kirch-heim-unter-Teck, a few miles south of Stuttgart, took less than two hours. The only traffic consisted of American jeeps and trucks, and Americans and Frenchmen in German cars. Eggart had no difficulty passing through the checkpoint that marked the beginning of the French zone, and turned off the autobahn at Weilheim. A mile from the autobahn was a copse of trees, and Eggart parked there at the crossing of a dirt road. Barentz was to cycle to his mother's home in Kirchheim and begin making his contacts with the Werwolves, several of whom lived in nearby towns. Eggart would return to pick him up at 10:00 A.M. on Monday.

Eggart waited while Barentz strapped a parcel containing food to the bike's handlebars. Then Barentz started off. His figure grew smaller with surprising rapidity. It occurred to Eggart that this might be the last he would see of Barentz.

A half hour later, Eggart and Willach approached Stuttgart. A light breeze animated the trees in the woods along the sides of the road. Wildflowers bloomed amid the grass. The road wound upward to the top of a ridge, and they entered the suburb of Degerloch. Some of the houses were in need of paint, but the streets were neat and clean. Along the entire drive there had been so little evidence of the war that Eggart felt as if he were a tourist. In Degerloch the French had established one of their headquarters, and a number of armed men were milling around military vehicles parked in the streets.

From Degerloch, the Weinsteige—named after the steep vineyard path it had once been—serpentined down to the city. Stuttgart lay in a bowl surrounded by wooded hills. Everywhere vineyards had been terraced, and houses were etched into the mountainsides. The road angled to the right, and as it did the entire bowl was opened to view. From one end to the other the center of the ellipse was a field of ruins, as if a giant had battered the city with a mallet. Only here and there a tower—whole, or split like a tree struck by lightning—aspired above the rubble.

"*Mein Gott!*" Albrecht Willach exclaimed.

Eggart whipped the Mercedes downhill around the curves in second gear. It was only ten minutes to Alexanderstrasse, which intersected the Weinsteige along the hillside. To his relief, Willach saw that only an occasional building had been hit here. Apparently, the bombing had been limited largely to the heart of the city.

Alexanderstrasse was lined with genteel brick and stone apartment houses. Eggart halted the Mercedes in front of number 124. He and Albrecht Willach alighted. One of the nameplates at the side of the front door carried the inscription *Otto Willach*.

Otto Willach lived on the third story. As Albrecht and Eggart climbed, Albrecht breathed heavily and twice had to halt. When they reached the third story, Eggart hung back on the steps leading to the landing a half floor below.

Willach pressed the doorbell. A woman of about twenty came to the door.

"I want to speak to Frau Louise Willach, please," Albrecht said, barely able to get the words out of his mouth.

From the interior a woman's voice asked, "What is it, Norma?"

"I don't know, Tante Maria." The girl turned her head to call out. "An old man. He wants to speak to *Mutti*."

Faintly Eggart heard Maria Willach's voice say, "Louise! A stranger at the door for you!"

Louise Willach, a handsome gray-haired woman in her early forties, appeared in the doorway. She was about five feet five inches in height, and at one time Albrecht had been three or four inches taller. But after nearly six years in a concentration camp, he was frail and stooped, and looked shorter than she.

"Yes? What is it?" she asked.

Albrecht Willach tried to speak; but he breathed so heavily he uttered only gasps.

"Are you sick?" Louise Willach asked, moving closer to him, as if to help. She stared at him. "Albrecht?" She seemed to be trying to pierce his eyes, as if she could not determine the answer to her question from his face, but only from his thoughts. "Albrecht!" she screamed, and collapsed in the doorway.

So Albrecht Willach returned home, an old man at forty-seven, unrecognized by his daughter and almost unrecognized by his wife. His two daughters, his fifteen-year-old American-born son, and his sister-in-law joined in the emotional turmoil in the doorway. Eggart waited on the landing until the scene had played itself out and they had moved into the apartment. Since Otto Willach apparently was not at home, Eggart decided not to intrude, but come back the next day.

Continuing his drive down the hillside, Eggart saw how the damage increased street by street as he neared the floor of the bowl. Incendiary bombs had gutted almost every building: the Gothic-styled Rathaus, with its clock tower still standing; the gabled houses on the adjacent Marktplatz; the churches; the large Market Hall; the thick-walled Württemberger Staatstheater, and the smaller Cameo Theater, which had collapsed inward; the water-works, on whose tower the winged and helmeted figure of Mercury still stood poised; the block-long Grecian-columned Königsbau, which had housed a complex of shops; the multitracked railroad station, whose girders had melted and intertwined themselves with cars and locomotives; the Altes Schloss and the Neues Schloss, on the top of whose walls sculpted figures perched starkly against the sky. Only the *Gedenkstein*, depicting two women adoring the crucified Christ for saving their children from the plague, had miraculously survived in front of the burned-out Leonhardskirche.

In the streets, the charred hulks of cars and trucks lay half buried beneath mounds of bricks and stones. Girders twisted in abstract sculptures. Three stories high a toilet hung suspended in midair by its plumbing.

A few people had burrowed into the ruins and were living there like cavemen. On the remains of doorways former residents had posted notices where they could be found. Other inscriptions indicated who had been killed: *"Herr und Frau Gebhardt—tot"*; *"Hedl Bacher und Gertrude Uhl—tot"*; *"Berta und Karl—tot."* More than 4,500 residents of the city had died in the air raids.

Eggart reached Dorothean Strasse and found the partially destroyed Hotel Silber, the former police and Gestapo headquarters, where a small detachment of the CIC was now encamped for liaison with the French.

Eggart introduced himself to Peter Reimer, a CIC lieutenant who had dark, rippling hair, a sharply chiseled nose and chin, and unobtrusive good looks.

"Welcome to the Yank outpost with the French Foreign Legion!" Reimer cracked. The French troops in Stuttgart consisted mostly of Algerians and Moroccans, and, since the confrontation between the United States and France over who should occupy the city, relations between the Allies had been delicate. Although the United States troops had withdrawn across the Neckar River, Lieutenant Reimer had remained as part of a continuing American "presence."

It was a few minutes before 1:00 P.M., and Peter Reimer was on his way out to eat. Inviting Eggart along, he strapped a .45 to his waist and picked up a carbine. Eggart wore his .38 in a shoulder holster beneath his jacket, but was surprised at such heavy armament.

"This fucking town is like the Wild West!" Reimer explained. "West of the Neckar the law is a gun, and the more guns you show the less trouble you're likely to have."

An elderly white-mustachioed Alsatian and his buxom wife were the proprietors of a Gaststätte a half mile away on the slope of the mountain. All public places had been closed to Germans, but the French had in effect turned the Gaststätte into an officers' club. Since the proprietor was Alsatian, the French considered him a national of France, even though he had opted for German residence when France had occupied Alsace after World War I. A dozen French officers were seated when Eggart and Reimer arrived, and conversation bubbled about the room.

Peter Reimer spoke good German and passable French. He was from Philadelphia, where his father was a tobacco merchant, and he had arrived on the other side of the Neckar from Stuttgart with the 100th American division on Sunday, April 22. "We came into Stuttgart from the north and the east, and the French came from the south and the west," Reimer said. "Nobody knew what the fuck was going on. The Bürgermeister surrendered the city to the French at a Gasthof in Degerloch in the afternoon. But nobody surrendered to us. All the bridges across the Neckar except for a couple of footbridges had been blown up. Some of our platoons got across those. Headquarters was scared shitless they and the French were going to start shooting at each other. So I was sent over with a liaison team to tell the French we were advancing in friendship. By that time it was dark. We didn't know where the French had set up headquarters. Try running around in the pitch black in a city full of bomb craters, expecting to get blasted any minute! Finally I had the bright idea to call the Stuttgart telephone exchange. Right away they connected me to the Third Division headquarters at the Gasthof zum Ritter in Degerloch."

The meal took an hour to prepare. Eggart and Reimer spent the time talking, breaking off pieces of the freshly baked bread, and drinking a bottle of tart wine from the Neckar Valley.

"God, it was awful!" Reimer said. "The Gestapo had

strung up several people who'd tried to get away at the last minute, and the bodies were still hanging in the railroad station. Then the Moroccans came in and screwed everything with two legs and a hole between. They got into this girls' home. Had themselves an orgy with thirty broads!"

The rampage had continued for three days. Twenty thousand slave laborers had freed themselves from the camps around the city and taken the weapons from their guards. For months and years they had suffered on starvation diets and seen their compatriots tortured and hanged if they so much as looked at a German woman. Suddenly their distinctive armbands had been transformed from stigmas to emblems of conquerors. Hundreds of the workers had rioted through the streets. They sacked stores and sat down amid the rubble to eat bread and cheese and *wurst*—for many, the first decent meal since the Nazis had hauled them away from their homelands. They drank wine. They set fire to places that they knew were owned by Nazis or still displayed the swastika. A group carted a bed out of a furniture store and met another group dragging two German girls. The bed was set down in the midst of the debris, and the men gang-raped the girls.

"There's nothing so rare as a virgin in Stuttgart," Reimer rhapsodized.

"What have you been doing?" Eggart asked.

"Don't get personal! As a matter of fact, the French weren't paying much attention to what was going on, so I busied myself rounding up the bigwigs. Also, General Devers wanted to get a line on the Werwolves—ah! That interests you," Reimer said as Eggart betrayed himself by interrupting the draining of his fourth glass of wine.

"Tell me more," Eggart agreed. "I *am* interested."

"On Tuesday I got my hands on the Bürgermeister, Karl Strölin. Supposedly, he was mixed up in the July 20 plot against *der Führer*. I'd heard he was the contact man between Field Marshal Rommel and von Stauffenberg—the colonel who planted the bomb in Hitler's bunker. Both of them were local boys. Apparently, Strölin played both sides of the fence. Anyway, he was the survivor type. I figured he'd be a good man to slip into the Werwolves. So I gave him the chance to work for us."

"What happened?"

"He hemmed and hawed. Of course, he'd like to cooperate, but he knew nothing about the Werwolves. They would not trust him because of his past anti-Nazi activities. Then again, even though he opposed Hitler, he could not be a traitor and informer. And so on. So I put him in a bare room in the Reichsbahn Hotel and let him sit there for a day with a big colored guy guarding him. You know Goebbels had been telling the Germans that if the Africans got hold of them they'd salt and pepper them and stick them in a pot of boiling water. And the Moroccans were making holy terrors of themselves in the streets. The Bürgermeister was really sweating. He figured he'd be fricasseed before he got out of there."

"He changed his mind? He agreed?" Eggart asked.

"No." Reimer sighed. "I sent him on to the internment camp at Kitzingen."

It was nearly four o'clock when they left the Gaststätte. Reimer drove Eggart back up along the Weinsteige to the Villa Weissenburg, the headquarters of the French military government. There he introduced Eggart to Captain Mercadier, the commander of the French detachment. After some hesitation, Mercadier agreed to show Eggart the list of Werwolf suspects compiled by Dr. Klett and Staatsanwalt Gaus of Stuttgart. Eggart recognized a few of the names—Gestapo Chief Friedrich Mussgay, Gauleiter Wilhelm Murr, SD Detachment Leader Julius Wilbertz—but overall the list had little relationship to the one prepared by Barentz. Eggart conversed with Mercadier in German, and Mercadier himself questioned the list's trustworthiness.

"The names come from the people who opposed Hitler—in spirit, naturally," Mercadier said. "It's a roster of the local Nazis. Some important, some lesser known. Whether they are members of the Werwolves, who can say?"

Mercadier excused himself, explaining he had much to do to prepare for the next day.

As Eggart left the villa, he asked Reimer what was so important about the following day.

"You don't know? De Gaulle will be here. Stuttgart's going to have the biggest military parade in its history. French retaliation for the German march down the Champs Elysees. I'm sure the French would prefer to hold it in Berlin. But Stuttgart's the biggest city they've got."

The next morning Eggart telephoned Albrecht Willach and agreed to meet him on Alexanderstrasse after the parade. Because of General de Gaulle's presence, the French were on edge. Eggart and Reimer were stopped twice for security checks, and Eggart was glad to have the French-speaking Reimer along. Along two streets Reimer pointed to Werwolf signs that had been chalked on the walls: W with ⚡ or 卐 adjacent. When Eggart picked up Albrecht Willach, Willach apologized profusely for having forgotten about Eggart the previous day.

His family, Albrecht said, had thought him dead. "Otto told them I was involved in the plot against Hitler in 1939. He said he had done everything he could for me, but that I was unrepentant and refused to work for the welfare of the Fatherland. The letters they sent to Dachau were returned, stamped 'unknown.' Then Otto ordered them to stop writing. He said that I was a great embarrassment to him; that to keep stirring the matter up only made it worse. So what could they think?"

Otto had allowed Albrecht's family to occupy two rooms in the apartment. "And for that I must be grateful," Albrecht continued. "They would have had nothing. Nothing! But now I do not know what I shall do. I must get back to America!"

Eggart promised to see if he could help. In the meantime, he thought, Albrecht could probably get a job with the American forces. Gradually Eggart steered the conversation back to Otto Willach.

"Otto has been home very little since the war started," said Albrecht. "Maria told me that he worked in the Reich Central Security Office headquarters in Berlin, and that he was also in France. Apparently he is in some trouble with the French. Maria thinks it must be a mistake. But he is afraid to come home as long as the French occupy Stuttgart."

"Maria is Otto's wife?"

"Yes."

"She's heard from him?"

"Yes. I think he is—well, I think he is not too far away."

"You don't know where?"

"I don't know. But I will try to find out."

VI

On Monday morning, Eggart arrived an hour early at the crossroads near Weilheim where he had let Barentz off. Normally, he smoked little, but now he went through half a dozen cigarettes in an hour. If Barentz did not show up, he would have to go after him into Kirchheim. If Barentz proved untrustworthy, probably the entire operation would be aborted.

It was 9:55 when Eggart saw the speck approaching in the distance. Taking out the powerful German field artillery binoculars he had *beschlagnahmt*, Eggart brought the bike rider into focus. In less than a minute he recognized Barentz. At almost precisely 10:00 Barentz pulled up alongside the car. His face was red, and he was sweating from the exertion.

"I was afraid I would be late," he gasped. His watch had been taken the day before by a Moroccan who had stopped him at a checkpoint. "It was not my watch anyway. Poor watch. Who knows where it will end?"

Barentz was as elated about finding Eggart at the appointed spot as Eggart was that Barentz had returned. In four days Barentz had covered over seventy miles on the bike. From Kirchheim he had made a loop southeast to Owen and Feldstetten, west to Urach, Reutlingen, and Tübingen, and then back to Kirchheim via Neckarenzlingen and Nürtingen. In each town he had gone to an address on the Werwolf list. Several of the contacts had not been there. But he had been given other names, so that the list had, in fact, expanded.

Barentz reported that all the top Nazi officials, includ-

ing Gauleiter Murr, Gestapo Chief Mussgay, and Obersturmbannführer (Lieutenant Colonel) Tümmler, commander of the security police in Württemberg, had left
Stuttgart in a large convoy at midnight on April 20.
Clothes, furniture, dishes, silverware, and booty accumulated from occupied lands and Jewish families had been
loaded onto trucks. The SS plan was to head for the
Vorarlberg and there establish themselves in the National
Redoubt. The convoy, however, had gotten no farther than
Kirchheim when it was bombed. Many people were hit. On
the night of April 22, after a continuous march of forty-eight
hours, the column was on the road between Weingarten
and Ravensburg when the SS learned that the French army
was ahead and had already cut the road to the Vorarlberg.

Everyone had scattered. The Austrian town of
Bregenz, on the Bodensee near the Swiss border, was an
SD intelligence center, and also a headquarters for the
preparation of the National Redoubt. High-ranking SS and
SD officers from all over Germany had congregated there
and at Friedrichshafen.

"Conveniently close to Switzerland?" Eggart asked.
"Yes."

When it was evident that all German resistance was
collapsing, these SS, SD, Gestapo, Kripo (Criminal Police),
and high-ranking Nazi party officials had gathered secretly
at an estate near the small town of Eglofs, halfway between
Bregenz and Kempten. The meetings had gone on continuously during the last week of April. On April 28 an emissary
had arrived from Gruppenführer Prützmann and Reich
Security headquarters in Berlin.

The messenger from Berlin had told the people at
Eglofs that all plans made for the Werwolves were to be
implemented. Himmler was expected to be on his way
shortly to take personal command.

"Fascinating!" Eggart said to Barentz. "What about
Hitler's demotion of Himmler for trying to negotiate with
the Allies?"

"That threw them into confusion. On May 1, however,
they heard that Hitler was dead in his bunker in Berlin.
That resolved the conflict. They were afraid to stay any

longer in Eglofs because they did not want to attract the attention of the French. They decided to disperse and to form the Werwolf network under the code name Ibex."

"Why Ibex?"

"The ibex is a surefooted mountain goat—very hard to track down."

Barentz's report was impressive. Eggart was struck, as he would be again and again, by Barentz's amazing facility for recall. For a few minutes Eggart thought about what to do next. He had obtained a letter from Captain Mercadier explaining that he was an American agent. It authorized the French military government and especially the French Security Agency to provide him with assistance.

"Okay," Eggart told Barentz. "Let's see what we can find at Eglofs."

The drive to the Bodensee took half a day. Eggart traveled self-contained: he strapped five 5-gallon cans of gasoline to the Mercedes and filled the car with food, cigarettes, and chocolate that he could swap for anything else he needed. There was little traffic. The only vehicles he saw were occasional trucks, many of them converted to burn charcoal instead of gasoline. A few groups of Germans, some pushing handcarts or surrounding horse-drawn wagons loaded with their belongings, were on the road. In every town people were trying to catch rides: women, children, soldiers with missing arms and legs, young girls smiling, and old, gap-toothed men. Eggart closed his eyes to the misery; and the Germans seemed resigned to it.

"Mussgay is telling everyone," Barentz said, "that he is uneasy about operating in the French sector. But he is confident there will be no difficulty with the Americans, because American intelligence agents are so bad."

Shortly after four o'clock Eggart dropped Barentz off at Isny, a few miles from Eglofs. They made plans to meet at noon on Wednesday at the Wangen-Lindau crossroads.

Eggart drove on to Ravensburg, a town of narrow, one-way streets, surrounded by a well-preserved city wall. A slender tower like the minaret of a mosque hovered over the old part of the city. Eggart searched out the headquar-

ters of the French Security Agency on Tettnanger Strasse.
The next morning he presented his credentials to a captain.

Eggart knew only a few words of French. The captain
understood English, but did not speak it. So they conversed mostly in German. Eggart said he was interested in
information on a Standartenführer Otto Willach of the SD,
who had served in France. Was there a file on him?

"I will call Lieutenant Roche, who is in charge of our
documents," Captain Rettemond said.

A slim figure not more than five feet four inches tall
with a pageboy hairdo entered the room. While the captain
explained to the lieutenant what Eggart wanted, Eggart
kept looking in some astonishment at the officer, who
appeared to be a fifteen- or sixteen-year-old boy.

"Please follow me, captain," the lieutenant said to
Eggart in lilting, British-accented English. Not until Eggart was walking directly behind the lieutenant did it strike
him—the lieutenant was a young woman!

"What is you interest in Standartenführer Willach?"
she asked.

Eggart explained that he was investigating the Werwolves, and that he had received information suggesting
that Willach might be a member of the organization.

Lieutenant Roche took Eggart into a room filled with
stacks of footlockers. Two clerks were working at tables.
Lieutenant Roche apologized to Eggart. The office was just
being set up, she said, and it would be a long and difficult
task to collect and organize the records. The name Willach
was familiar to her, however; she believed she would be
able to provide Eggart with information.

After two or three minutes, a clerk produced a manila
folder and an envelope from a footlocker. "Let us go where
we can talk," the lieutenant said and led him into a
bedroom of the villa. An ornate bed was in the center of the
room, and they sat down on it. "We are not yet, how shall I
say, completely businesslike?" Lieutenant Roche remarked. "But we sleep here, too. So it is convenient."

She slipped a photo out of the envelope. "Do you know
what he looks like? Here is his picture."

Eggart took it from her. He was surprised that Willach

appeared so young. Willach would be a year or two over forty now, and the picture had probably been taken at least five years before. In the black SD uniform with the oak leaves of a colonel on his lapels he was good-looking in a superficial way.

"Willach was in Amt IV of the SD," Lieutenant Roche continued. "He was on the staff of Brigadeführer Dr. Thomas in Paris. Thomas was the head of Security Police and SD for France and Belgium, the personal representative of Reinhard Heydrich. Thomas was not very efficient— he left efficiency to subordinates. He himself was in a solid position. His daughter was Heydrich's mistress."

Lieutenant Roche was quoting directly from the reports, and apparently summarizing other material— Eggart could not be certain. She spoke unhurriedly and distinctly, without any emotion, and seemed perfectly assured of herself.

"Willach also considered himself to have a way with women. He exploited them. Perhaps that is why Heydrich liked him. One of his jobs was to provide girls for Heydrich when Heydrich came to France. In Rouen, Willach established a brothel, evidently on Heydrich's orders. Microphones were hidden in the rooms. The girls had to practise all the arts the French are renowned for—perhaps falsely. French industrialists, foreign diplomats, German generals—all were entertained in the brothel, and every word was recorded." Lieutenant Roche returned some of the material to the envelope and directed herself to the folder.

"Willach worked under Brigadeführer Thomas to enlist French operatives for the SD and the Gestapo from Fascist and anti-semitic organizations. Later, Willach headed the SD detachment in charge of the economic exploitation of Champagne, French Comte, and Burgundy. He operated not only overtly, but also established a network of agents. Habitual criminals were recruited from prisons and set up as extortionists and racketeers for the benefit of the SD. Willach let Jewish families buy protection, and as long as they had a sou to their name they were not deported. After that—good-bye! Good-looking Jewish girls were given the

option of saving themselves by going into the SS brothel
Willach established in Dijon. Finally, when everything was
in desperately short supply in France, the SS began
operating a black market in France. Naturally, Willach and
other high-ranking officers seized the opportunity to line
their own pockets."

"Was Willach involved in any atrocities?"

"Who can say what went on inside the walls of the
Security Police? But whether a man belonged to the SD,
the Gestapo, or the Kripo, he was part of the gang. Even if
his hands were personally clean, he knew what was going
on. The SD and the Gestapo were delighted to take
criminals off the hands of the Kripo and put them to use.
Robbery, murder, perversion—what they had done in the
past did not matter, so long as they gave faithful service to
the Nazis. I am sure you know, captain, that part of the
modus operandi of the SD, not only in occupied lands but
in Germany itself, was to enlist people who had blemishes
on their records, because these people were the easiest to
control. One misstep, and off to a concentration camp!
Atrocities? I do not think Willach is the kind of man to wash
his hands in blood. But would you not call it an atrocity to
force girls into SS brothels where they had to engage in
perversions the Marquis de Sade would have taken pleasure in?"

Eggart was awed by her. Yesterday, Barentz had
relayed Mussgay's words about the inadequacy of American
agents more or less jokingly. But what the hell—it was true!
The French had been face-to-face with the Germans for five
years. The Americans were Johnny-come-latelies. Eggart
knew little of the organization of the SS—of the intricate
structure that was now evolving into the Werwolves.

Captain Rettemond invited Eggart to join the officers
of the Security Agency at dinner that evening at the
Buchhornerhof, the hotel that had been transformed into
an officers' club in Friedrichshafen. The hotel was a
gemütlich, unpretentious four-story building facing the
strand. Eggart was struck by the difference in the mode of
the American and French occupations. The Americans
were businesslike, shocked, morally indignant. They re-

garded the occupation as the logical continuation of the war, and most of them simply wanted to get on with it, do what had to be done, and go home. The French, in contrast, were moving in like relatives for a long stay. After the humiliation they had suffered and the deprivations of the German occupation, they behaved somewhat like Ceasar's legions; they were imperious, but not as vindictive as they might have been. They wanted to relish the victory. The French military combined élan with joie de vivre. They seemed to have appropriated the best wines and the best cooks.

After dinner Eggart went walking on the strand with Lieutenant Roche. A soft, warm breeze lapped the waters of the Bodensee against the scimitar-curved seawall. The lake was Germany's largest and had its most temperate climate. Eggart and Lieutenant Roche leaned on the railing. A single swan floated by like a snowball in the darkness, its head and long neck tucked into its body. In the far distance the stars faded into the outline of the Alps. Eggart and the lieutenant sat down and leaned against the trunk of a willow. The branches bowing to the ground hung over them like a veil. As the delicate leaves moved almost imperceptibly to and fro in the breeze, they rippled the twin, onion-domed towers of the church in the distance.

"Damn!" Lieutenant Roche said.

"What's the matter?"

"I get seduced by the scenery. I start to associate the politics with the land. It's dangerous. I might forget what bastards they really are."

She did not invite comment, and they did not speak very much. Finally, she asked him where he was from in America.

California, he told her. The Bodensee reminded him a little of San Francisco Bay, where he had gone sailing.

"You can sail a boat?" Her interest perked up.

"Yes."

"If I can get a boat—you will take me sailing?"

"Sure," he agreed.

*   *   *

As planned, Eggart picked up Johannes Barentz at noon the next day at the Wangen-Lindau crossroads. Eggart had obtained a bottle of wine, some cheese, and a loaf of bread at the Buchhornerhof, and they lunched on a grassy knoll.

At the inn in Eglofs, Barentz had contacted two men who had been participants in the Werwolf meeting a month before. An Obersturmbannführer who was referred to only as Siegfried had dominated the meeting, and Barentz had told the men he wanted to meet Siegfried.

The SS men had said they would have to check with Siegfried. Last night Barentz had been taken on a circuitous path to a manor house. He had been led through a side door into a corridor and then to a room lighted by a kerosine lantern. Siegfried was sitting in the shadows behind a table so that Barentz had been unable to discern his features. Siegfried had questioned Barentz closely about his assignment from Gruppenführer Prützmann, had asked him to describe Prützmann, and had obviously tested him. Aparently he was satisfied. Siegfried showed Barentz a page and a half of pass-phrases for message centers in southern Germany. Barentz had memorized them. Later, Siegfried ordered Barentz to take a message to Hauptscharführer Hinsheid, who worked as a waiter in the Hotel Buchhornerhof in Friedrichshafen. Hinsheid was to prepare a coded map of the machine guns, magnesium flares, and explosives that had been taken from the tank works and the Dornier airplane factory in Friedrichshafen and secreted at various places near the Bodensee.

"Hinsheid works at the Buchhornerhof?" Eggart asked, scratching his head.

"Yes."

Eggart laughed. *"Das ist sehr interessant."*

Barentz looked at him, puzzled, but Eggart said, "Go on."

Siegfried had told Barentz that he was cooperating with Gestapo Chief Mussgay, but at the same time he asserted that he had primary responsibility for Ibex. Ibex's first task was to place operatives in the French and American administrations. These would provide Ibex with access to information and supplies, and give its agents greater freedom to travel. Passports, *Kennkarten*, work papers, and other documents would be stolen and duplicated.

"Siegfried intends to carry on his operation from Eglofs?" asked Eggart.

"No," Barentz replied.

Siegfried had indicated that he was awaiting the arrival of an important person from Berlin who would give final approval of the plans Siegfried was preparing. At the Eglofs meeting, the participants had been furnished with false identity papers by the SS. Several members of Ibex were now in the process of using the documents to obtain passes and identity papers from the French occupation authorities. If they had no difficulties, Siegfried planned to shift the Ibex command post to Stuttgart. His training had been in architectural engineering, and he was confident he would be able to find a job in reconstruction work.

"Do you have any indication who that important person from Berlin might be?" Eggart asked.

"Only that the person would have the highest authority. My understanding is that it would be Gruppenführer Prützmann. Or even the Reichsführer SS himself."

When Eggart arrived back in Augsburg and reported to Campbell, the colonel greeted him good-naturedly: "I was beginning to wonder what had happened to you."

Summarizing his activities, Eggart concluded, "Barentz indicated that the important person Siegfried is expecting might be Himmler."

"If it is Himmler," said Campbell, packing tobacco from a pouch into his pipe, "Siegfried will have a long wait."

"Sir?" Eggart looked at him.

"The British arrested him at a checkpoint up north on Wednesday. He bit into a cyanide capsule. He's dead."

"Oh!" Eggart could not help feeling some disappointment.

"However, I am sure there are other big fish to catch." Campbell indicated he was pleased with Eggart's report.

"And since you're free-lancing all over the French zone, I think we'd better tell the French about your activities. It wouldn't do to have them find out that we're running an intelligence operation in their bailiwick, and have them get their hinds up about it. Besides, if you should happen to have to shoot somebody, they'd better know who you are."

"Yes, sir. But what about your admonition that the fewer the people who know about the operation, the better? If we cut the French in—"

"Sometimes one has to take a chance. Of course, all your operatives will be code named. Those names will not go beyond this office. Now, you have this SS man—?"

"Johannes Barentz, sir." Eggart had a picture before his eyes of Barentz eating cheese. Barentz loved cheese the way some people consume candy. "We could call him Käse."

"Käse?"

"Yes, sir. Bait for the rats. Or Grosse Käse. Big cheese for big rats."

"Good. I like that," Campbell said. "Grosse Käse."

The American zone was being divided between the Third Army and the Seventh Army, Campbell told Eggart. The Third Army would occupy Bavaria, the Seventh Army Hesse and Württemberg. The Seventh Army would be headquartered in Heidelberg. The CIC detachment was moving there next week.

VII

On Monday, Eggart packed up his two barracks bags and dropped them into the Mercedes. He gave Barentz a big package of soap, chocolate, and canned goods for his mother and left him at Weilheim, from which point Barentz was to cycle into Stuttgart via Kirchheim. Eggart went directly on to Stuttgart, where he met Albrecht Willach.

The family had received a communication from Otto, Albrecht said. He was in Waiblingen, in the American zone, ten miles east of Stuttgart. He wanted Maria, his wife, to bring him some things. Albrecht gave Eggart the address.

Eggart went to Peter Reimer for help. Reimer obtained the services of two MPs, who followed the Mercedes in a jeep. In order not to cause alarm, they parked the vehicles outside Waiblingen and walked a few hundred yards toward the town. Waiblingen was built on a hilltop and had been surrounded by a moat, part of which was now a brook. On the far side of the bridge that crossed the brook was a hundred-foot tower that had once been part of the city wall. On the wall, houses had been built facing both outward toward the brook and inward toward the town. Between the two rows of houses was a narrow covered passageway, in some places less than six feet high. From this dark passageway doors opened right and left. The number on one of the doors was the address Albrecht Willach had given Eggart.

"*Was ist?*" a voice asked in response to Eggart's knock.

"*Grüss von Hermann. In der dreissigjahr Krieg, es gibt nicht noch Fried,*" Eggart repeated one of the code

phrases Barentz had picked up. He had no idea whether
the declaration that the Thirty Years' War continued was
applicable to Willach, or what the response would be.

"*Ja, gut. Wir haben keine Fried ohne Sieg,*" came the
response. (Yes, good. We have no peace without victory.)

The key turned in the lock. The door opened cautiously. With the two MPs waiting in the corridor, Eggart
and Reimer put their shoulders to the door and burst into
the room. Their charge carried with them the man behind
the door. Caroming against a commode with a built-in
washbasin, they sent a porcelain pitcher of water crashing
to the floor. The pistol the occupant held in his hand flew
against a lamp and decapitated it. Eggart and Reimer
pinned the man against the commode, and a moment later
had his hands handcuffed behind his back.

Stepping back, Eggart had his first good look at Otto
Willach. He little resembled the good-looking, self-assured
SS officer Eggart had seen in the picture shown him by
Madeleine Roche. He was a paunchy five and a half feet
tall. He was wearing baggy pants, and his gray sweater
accentuated the gray streaks in his thinning blond hair.
Beneath heavy lids, his eyes shifted rapidly. His teeth were
tobacco stained, and his breath had a faint odor of decay. He
denied that he was Otto Willach. But a search of the room
quickly turned up his Nazi party membership book and his
Kennkarte.

With the MPs following in the jeep, Eggart and
Reimer took Willach to the CIC villa in Ludwigsburg,
fifteen miles north of Stuttgart. Ludwigsburg had been the
ancestral seat of the Württemberg princes and a magnificent palace was set like a tiara in vast wooded and
landscaped grounds. A short distance from it, on the
opposite side of the street, was the state's large three-story
prison. With the French apparently immovable in Stuttgart, the Americans had established themselves in Ludwigsburg and appropriated the prison. As the number of
German suspects apprehended grew rapidly, other internment camps had been set up nearby at Ossweil and Kornwestheim.

Willach had no idea of the extensive information

Eggart had collected on him. Eggart, beginning his interrogation at three o'clock in the afternoon, was content to let Willach lie and entangle himself. Willach said that he had been an unimportant functionary in the economic administration. He had joined the Nazi party only because it was obligatory. Evidently, he expostulated, someone in Waiblingen had informed the American authorities that a Standartenführer was living there. Truly, however, the rank was all out of proportion to the responsibility he had had.

Eggart had already learned that, in the SS, the opposite was true. During the 1930s, when Himmler had handed out high ranks to recruit intellectuals and university graduates, the organization had become top-heavy. During the war, therefore, promotions had been hard to come by. Many officers had had more authority and performed more important functions than their rank indicated.

It was 4:30 P.M. when Eggart asked Otto Willach to narrate his family history.

Willach, complying, concluded by saying, "And all through the war I have been providing also for the family of a deceased brother. A brother, I might say, who spent many years in America in the service of important firms."

"A brother who spent many years in Dachau. And you let him rot there!"

Willach blanched. "I did not know—!"

"You didn't know I knew."

"Yes. It was a great tragedy. My brother let himself be involved in a plot against Hitler. As you well understand, there could have been no more serious offense in the Third Reich. I did all I could. But as I have told you, I was only a small functionary. I had no influence."

"All your brother wanted to do was to return to America," said Eggart, "but Himmler would not let him, and you secured an appointment for him with Reinhard Heydrich. Heydrich offered him high rank and position in the SD. He refused. He went to the American consulate in Munich, and when the bomb exploded in the Bürgerbräu Keller, he indicated regret that Hitler had not been killed. He was overheard by an informer and imprisoned in Dachau."

"Der Teufel!" Willach's eyes bulged.

"Although you worked in Reich Security headquarters and had access to Heydrich, you were quite willing to let your brother die in Dachau."

"Gott im Himmel! You know everything—but you understand nothing. Do you not think I was under suspicion too? My brother was thought to be the maker of the bomb intended to blow up the Führer! It was only as a personal favor to me that Heydrich did not order him tortured. My brother was offered the opportunity to redeem himself by working for the Reich, but he refused!"

"Quite a difference between you two, isn't there? You never refused anything."

"You think it was easy for me? I had great promise of being promoted to general officer rank. Instead, I was suspended. Investigated. All because of Albrecht. Finally I went to Heydrich. I said, 'My brother is a fool, a traitor; he fell under the influence of the Americans. But I am not his keeper; I am not his older brother. I am his *younger* brother. Surely I cannot be held responsible. What can I do?' Heydrich said that every man must prove himself over and over again. He himself, he said, flew combat missions against Poland as an ordinary pilot, and he suggested that I enlist in the Wehrmacht. I became a Panzergrenadier. A common private. When my lieutenant was killed in the attack on France, I led the men in an assault on a battery of 75s. I was wounded. I was decorated. I was reinstated."

"And of course, to avoid suspicion, you disassociated yourself completely from your brother."

"That is not so. I told you. Heydrich gave orders to offer him a chance for redemption. But Heydrich was assassinated. Once he was dead, there was no one—no one I could turn to." He paused, and Eggart could see that thoughts were flashing through his mind. "But how did you—where did you get this information?" he asked.

"From your brother," said Eggart.

"Albrecht! Alive? A miracle! You see, despite what you say, my efforts were not in vain."

"I thought you were an insignificant functionary without influence."

"Yes. In official duties. It was only my—my acquaintance with Herr Heydrich that permitted me, you understand, to speak freely."

"Then, I presume, when you set up a brothel in Rouen at Heydrich's behest—that was unofficial?"

"Albrecht did not know about that. No, of course not."

"The French have an extensive file on you, Willach. That doesn't come as a surprise, does it? That's why you don't dare go into Stuttgart."

"Captain," Willach said, "war creates terrible misunderstandings. I served my country. I have no apology for that. But I was never a Nazi. I have a university education. There was a terrible depression. I needed a job. The National Socialists were the only ones who offered decent jobs. They put the German people back to work. That was good. But the propaganda—that was quite crazy. And Himmler! Frankly, he was a little off!"

"But you worked for him, nevertheless."

"Suppose General Eisenhower was not entirely right in his head. You would still serve in the American army, would you not, captain? What could you do? It is your duty."

"So you served. But without enthusiasm. Without belief. And you were of no great importance."

"That is absolutely correct."

Hour after hour Eggart continued the interrogation. Darkness fell. Eight o'clock passed. Nine o'clock. Willach reminded Eggart of a sidewinder, wriggling this way, then that. No matter what Eggart brought up that Willach had been involved in, Willach insisted it had all been an accident of war. All could be explained. Yet gradually Eggart wore him down. Willach's answers came more slowly, less glibly, with less assurance. He stumbled over words. His answers were contradictory. Sometimes he made Freudian slips.

When Eggart asked him about the black market operation, Willach admitted that he had been involved, but asserted that he had conducted the operation for the benefit of the French because he believed the occupation was too harsh. He had taken great risks, he insisted. If Himmler had found out, he would have been shot.

"The brothel into which you forced Jewish girls—that was a philanthropic operation, too?"

"I showed them a way out. You must understand. We—you and I, captain—we are Christians. We have a different morality. But French Jewesses—prostitution is nothing new for them. It was just like any other occupation."

"What a fucking shithead!" Eggart spat out in English as Willach looked at him uncomprehendingly. He continued in German: "I think I'll turn you over to the French. I suspect they'll chop your head off. Without malice, of course. But as you say, these are hard times."

It was nearly eleven o'clock. Eggart had carried on the interrogation for eight hours without letting Willach have anything to drink or eat. Willach's face had the strung-out appearance of an old mop.

"You would not do that," Willach responded to Eggart. His voice croaked, and momentarily disappeared altogether. "The Americans are known for their humanitarianism. My family! My poor brother!"

"Your poor brother survived Dachau without you. You've been telling me you did nothing wrong. So what do you have to fear?"

Willach ran his tongue around his lips. "It would not be to your interest."

"What could American interests possibly have to do with it?"

"I have important information. Information of vital concern to the occupation authorities. I will disclose it—in return for—considerations."

"You are in no position to bargain, Willach. You tell me. Then we'll talk about considerations."

"I must think about it."

"Go ahead. Take all the time you want."

"I am hungry."

"After we have finished. Then perhaps there will be *schincken brötchen* and coffee."

"There is an organization," Willach said. "A Werwolf organization of the SS . . ." He began to speak in general terms about the Werwolves. Much of what Willach said

Eggart already knew. Finally Willach asked, "Now, you will not turn me over to the French?"

"I don't see why not. If you've told me everything you know, what good are you to us?"

"*Gott!*" Willach's chest heaved. "You are worse than the Gestapo—though of course I know that only from general conversation." He fell silent for a moment. "I could be useful. Very useful. I do not approve of terrorist methods."

"Yes?"

"I see you do not believe me when I tell you that I did not subscribe to Nazi philosophy. Very well. I have proved myself before. I am willing to prove myself again. I wish only the good of Germany—and America. After all, my brother is almost an American, is he not? I know many people. I have access to much information. You will find my services quite invaluable."

The next day Eggart drove to Heidelberg to report to Colonel Campbell. The new CIC headquarters was across the river from the old city, in what had been an optical research institute. Summarizing the results of his interrogation of Willach, Eggart told Campbell, "He's a son of a bitch. But he knows many of the top people in the SS. In that respect he's more valuable than Barentz. And he has only one interest: looking out for the skin of Otto Willach."

"Double agents are not noted for their integrity," Campbell said. "One takes what one can get."

"We do have the advantage. If we think he's betraying us, we can always turn him over to the French. Better yet, we can let the word slip that he's working for us, and his friends will slit his throat."

"All right. Use him," Campbell agreed.

"What about the French?"

"We won't tell them we have him. That way we won't have to say no to them. You'll need a code name for him."

Eggart thought a moment. "He's such a fucking heel! Let's call him Achilles."

VIII

The next day Eggart returned to Ludwigsburg and informed Otto Willach that he would be working for the CIC. As a cover, Willach was being given a job with the American Food Administration. He would check on and requisition food supplies. For transportation he would be provided with an Opel P-4, since Eggart had difficulty enough driving Barentz from place to place, and Barentz and Willach were not to know of each other's roles. To protect Willach from the French and allay the suspicions of the other Ibex members about how he was able to obtain a job with the Americans, Willach was given false identification papers under the name of Otto Bergauer. He was to keep his room in Waiblingen, but not reveal its existence to anyone. It would provide a secure place for Eggart to meet him.

"In return," Eggart warned Willach, "you will do exactly as I instruct you. Any slips on your part, and we'll turn you over to the French—or worse. I don't want bullshit! I want results!"

Willach assured Eggart that he understood; that he was grateful; that he was prepared to prove he was a man of different caliber than he had been made out to be.

At dusk, Eggart drove from Ludwigsburg to Kirchheim to leave a message for Barentz. As the location for a drop, Barentz had given him the town's old church, an immense fifeenth-century stone structure with massive walls and a tower built as much for defense as homage to God. Barentz had told Eggart that he had put a scratch mark on a stone in the angle formed where the tower was joined to the body of the church, and Eggart had no difficulty finding it. He was screened from the street by a huge tree, and in the twilight blended into the buff gray of the church. The stone could not be removed entirely, but pivoted just enough for Eggart to slip a note into the crack. The note instructed Barentz to meet him at the usual place near Weilheim at ten o'clock on Saturday morning.

Eggart spent the next two days in Stuttgart, and had a top put on the Mercedes at the Daimler-Benz plant in Untertürkheim, across the river from the city. On Saturday morning, Barentz was waiting when Eggart arrived at the crossroads.

Barentz reported that he had made nine contacts in Stuttgart and its suburbs. Everyone in the Werwolf organization, Barentz said, was very nervous, and had looked to him for reassurance because he had seen Siegfried. They seemed disorganized, and would do nothing until they heard from someone in authority.

Fearful that Siegfried might slip away from the manor near Eglofs before Barentz had solidified contact with him, Eggart asked Barentz if he would be willing to return to Eglofs. Barentz answered in the affirmative.

The drive took less than four hours. In order to give Barentz ample time, Eggart told him he would not pick him up until Tuesday. Eggart drove on to Ravensburg, but was disappointed to learn that Madeleine Roche was in Stuttgart.

On Tuesday, Barentz had important news. He had spent two days at the manor with Siegfried. Siegfried had been pleased by Barentz's report of his contacts with other members of Ibex, and had been much less secretive. They had walked in the woods together and spoken about the plan for the organization. Seigfried revealed that he had received the message he had been waiting for from Berlin. From what Siegfried intimated, Barentz thought the commander of Ibex himself had come, or had sent someone in whom he had absolute trust.

"But we still don't know who the Ibex chief is," Eggart said.

"No."

"What about Siegfried's identity?" asked Eggart. "Do you have any idea who he might be?"

"I don't know," Barentz replied. "He says he was a captain in the Wehrmacht, and was wounded and discharged in the summer of 1944. But that is obviously not true."

Barentz went on to say that Siegfried had revealed that he intended to leave Eglofs the following week and go to the military government Reisebüro in Kempten, twenty miles away, to obtain a pass to travel in the American zone. Barentz had asked Siegfried how he was supposed to contact him in the future. Siegfried had replied that if the military government made no difficulties about his papers, he would go to Munich, and on his return come to Stuttgart, where he had been a partner in a machine shop.

"He didn't say why he was going to Munich?"

"He mentioned that his family lived in Bavaria."

"Yes. But what about Ibex? Will he meet someone in Bavaria to obtain instructions? Or has he already obtained instructions and is going there to organize?"

"I don't know. He did say he was pleased he had received approval to reactivate Fehm."

"What is Fehm?"

"A terrorist organization that specialized in assassinations of Germans cooperating with the Allies after World War I."

On the way back to Heidelberg, Eggart thought about how he should deal with Siegfried. If Siegfried were going to Kempten, Otto Willach could be planted at the Reisebüro office to make contact with him.

Eggart stayed up most of the night writing his report, and brought it to Colonel Campbell in the morning. Campbell gave his approval to the plan, then asked, "Do you think Siegfried has received instructions?"

"Apparently. That's why he's moving now."

"Well," Campbell said, "they can't be from Prützmann."

"Why not, sir?"

"Prützmann is dead. I received word on Monday. Actually, he committed suicide at Lüneburg two days before Himmler."

Eggart was surprised. "Then who did Siegfried hear from?"

"That's what you have to find out."

At the Villa Weissenburg, which was the French headquarters in Stuttgart, Eggart met Henri Pittard, the French Security Agency liaison officer with Seventh Army G-2. After Eggart explained the Ibex network and its interzonal nature, Pittard replied that he had received Colonel Campbell's communication, and that the Security Agency would be glad to cooperate.

"By the way, captain," Pittard said, "I believe a friend of yours is here."

It was Madeleine Roche, who accepted Eggart's invitation to lunch. She explained that she was searching for several war criminals in Stuttgart. "Standartenführer Otto Willach—the man you inquired about," she said, looking searchingly at Eggart. "He has a brother who was at Dachau. Albrecht Willach said you brought him back to Stuttgart."

"That's true," Eggart nodded.

"The family claims they don't know where Otto Willach is. Did you obtain any more information?"

"No." Eggart felt uncomfortable. He did not like to lie. But he was now learning that in intelligence work lying is one of the tools of the trade.

He was grateful when the proprietor appeared with wine and freshly baked bread. Madeleine provided an expert appraisal of the wine—she had grown up in Saint-Étienne, in the Rhone Valley, where her father operated an inn. The family owned a small vineyard, which was subdivided and shared with a half dozen uncles and cousins. She had been studying in Paris in 1940 when the

French army collapsed, and had barely escaped from the city ahead of the Germans.

"I don't think any of us realized what terrible things were to come," she said matter-of-factly; but Eggart could see a deep sadness beneath her calm, efficient, sometimes pensive exterior.

After eating, they walked in the woods. They came up behind a middle-aged woman and a boy who were gathering wood and stacking it in a wheelbarrow. Taking wood from the forests was against the law, so when the boy saw Eggart and Madeliene, he grabbed the handles of the wheelbarrow and set off at a run. The woman, her skirt flying, snorted after him.

Eggart and Madeleine laughed as they watched them disappear; then suddenly her laughter died. "You see," she said, "that's how it was in France. One was afraid all the time. Sometimes the German reaction would be like ours— they would laugh at our fright. But we never knew. We had to expect the worst. That was how we survived."

She was really quite pretty. The back of his hand brushed against hers, and his fingers tingled. He looked down at her intently, and had a great urge to kiss her. Her eyes were blue-black, the corner of her mouth had an odd wrinkle, and she had a light brown kidney-shaped mole on her left temple. Momentarily, he saw her in sharp focus; then she took a couple of steps down the path.

"Come on," she said, and her image blurred. "I must get back. I have work to do."

IX

Monday morning Eggart gave Otto Willach his instructions. Willach, accompanied by two CIC agents, drove the Opel to the agency's large villa in Kempten. Eggart, in the Mercedes, detoured to Kirchheim to pick up Barentz.

In Kempten the CIC had appropriated a café across the street from the Reisebüro. Eggart took Barentz into the café through a side door. From behind the shutters they watched the applicants for passes enter the Büro. Willach, who could not be allowed to meet Barentz, was kept at the villa to await the time when Siegfried was spotted.

The Kempten Reisebüro, manned by German civilians, received about forty applications for passes daily. Monday morning went by; then Tuesday. Eggart and the CIC agent who was to photograph Siegfried watched the people go in and out and gather in small groups in the street to await the processing of their papers. They were a shabby-looking lot. Men had few civilian clothes and continued to wear the uniforms of whatever organization they had belonged to. Women were dressed in hand-knitted sweaters and baggy skirts.

When Siegfried did not appear by Wednesday, everyone became edgy. Eggart and the photographer spent the day playing chess in the café. Another game was under way on Thursday morning when, shortly after nine o'clock, Barentz exclaimed, "There he is!"

The man Barentz indicated dismounted from a bicycle. Using a chain and lock, he attached the bike to a grating, then strode toward the door of the Reisebüro. He was about forty years old, quite bald, with an elongated face.

About five feet ten inches tall, he was thin but sinewy. The photographer, hurrying to focus the camera, knocked the chessmen off the board. But before he could click the shutter, Siegfried's back disappeared into the Büro.

When he came out ten minutes later, Siegfried remained near the door. Looking up and down the street, he satisfied himself that nothing was out of the ordinary. The photographer, using a telephoto lens, snapped several pictures of him.

Eggart and the agent-photographer slipped out the side door of the café and went around to the back door of the house in which the Reisebüro was located. Posing as a military government officer checking pass procedures, Eggart collected all the identity papers of the morning's applicants and took the papers to a private room at the rear of the building, where the photographer was waiting. They sifted through the papers, until Eggart found the service discharge Siegfried had presented. Dated 21 August 1944 in Stuttgart, it was made out in the name of Ludwig Siegfried, and carried his picture. The photographer placed it in the window and snapped shots from several angles.

Leaving the papers with the photographer, Eggart returned to the café, spirited Barentz out, and drove him to the CIC villa in Kempten. Depositing Barentz at the rear entrance, Eggart picked up Willach and took him out the front. Willach drove the Opel to within two blocks of the Reisebüro, and they walked the rest of the way to the café. Eggart pointed out Siegfried to Willach, and asked him if Siegfried looked familiar. Willach answered that he did not. Eggart instructed Willach to go to the Reisebüro, file a pass application, then mingle with the other applicants who were waiting to have their passes approved by the military government. He was to work his way up to Siegfried and after a few minutes of conversation mention that he was going to see a sister in Regensburg. He was to offer to take anyone going in that direction, so that the MPs at checkpoints would not fill his car with displaced persons.

Eggart went back to the rear entrance of the Reisebüro, returned the papers to the processors, and during the following hour sat in the café as the scenario unfolded. He had to admire Willach. Siegfried was standing aside, holding himself aloof. But within twenty minutes of presenting his application and emerging from the Büro door, Willach maneuvered three other persons so that they formed a small group that more and more encompassed Siegfried. Although Eggart could not hear the conversation, he was able to follow its development. After a half hour, Willach had Siegfried standing to one side, and Siegfried was obviously interested in Willach's offer. Siegfried pointed to his bicycle, and Willach gestured that it could be tied to the back of the car. Siegfried was pleased. He took Willach by the elbow and engaged him in private and serious conversation. Willach nodded in agreement. Two hours later, when the applications had been approved by the military government, Willach and Siegfried were fast companions.

Four days later, Eggart watched the Opel pull up to the Mozarthaus in Augsburg, where he had arranged to rendezvous with Willach. Concealed on the opposite side of the brook, Eggart waited a few minutes to make sure that Willach was not being followed. Then he whistled. Startled, Willach glanced up. Eggart motioned for him to cross the bridge to the opposite bank.

With Willach seated by his side, Eggart headed the Mercedes for the open country. Willach reported that he had taken Siegfried to Munich. On the way he had stopped at various places to check on food supplies and report to American Food Administration officials. In Munich he had taken Siegfried to several addresses, where Siegfried had attempted to contact friends and locate his wife and sister. After a search of twenty-four hours, Siegfried had found his sister, and from her learned that his wife had returned to the village of Katharinenzell, some distance from Moosburg, to live with relatives. Siegfried had been very cautious; nevertheless, Willach had discovered that Siegfried's real name was not Ludwig Siegfried, but Siegfried Niehbar.

"Does he know you found out?" Eggart asked.

"Yes."

"What was his reaction?"

"He said he had to be very careful. He asked me if I thought the Americans had good target lists. I answered that I thought they were rather poor. He then remarked that he knew he was on the Russian target list."

When Willach had expressed surprise that a Wehrmacht captain should be on the Russian list, Niehbar had replied that he had been involved in antipartisan warfare. Willach, in an effort to elicit further information, had revealed that he had worked in the SD in France. In an obvious testing of Willach, Niehbar had asked him if he knew Obersturmbannführer Rapp. Willach replied that Rapp had headed Operation Zeppelin, the plan to drop Russian volunteers behind the Soviet lines as German agents. Niehbar said he had heard that it was a very successful operation. To the contrary, Willach had continued, the operation had never gotten off the ground because the Luftwaffe had been unable to provide the planes to carry it out.

Niehbar seemed to have been impressed by Willach's knowledge. Willach drove Niehbar to Moosburg and offered to continue on to Katharinenzell so that Niehbar could see his wife. Niehbar, however, had declined, giving as an explanation that the road was too bad. Unstrapping the bicycle from the back of the car, he had pedaled off. Willach was supposed to pick him up again tomorrow in Moosburg.

Eggart was satisfied with the information. He drove Willach back to his car at the Mozarthaus and told him he would contact him in his room in Waiblingen between Saturday noon and Monday morning.

X

Sunday morning Eggart took Madeleine to the first public concert given by the Stuttgart orchestra since the end of the war. Afterwards, they went to the Alsatian restaurant for supper. They had trout smothered in almonds and a bottle of dry Mosbacher wine. Eggart noted that, despite General Eisenhower's antifraternization edict, many of the French officers who filled the room had fräuleins for companions. American GIs were calling it the "nonfertilization order," and it was so breached in practice that another order had gone out making it mandatory for soldiers to carry prophylactic kits at all times.

"This place has certainly been plugged in to the occupation," Eggart remarked.

"I beg your pardon?" She did not understand him.

"Obviously, the proprietors are having no difficulty obtaining supplies. I suspect they are well connected to the black market."

"I suspect you are right." She smiled. He could not recall seeing her smile before. She had the youthful freshness of a happy child's drawing. "How is your work going?" she continued.

"Okay," he answered, and went on to explain that he was still getting organized.

She nodded and looked somberly at him. "You must be careful," she said.

"I am careful."

"No. That is not what I mean. Your reports now go to the French Security Agency also, do they not?"

"Yes. How did you know?"

"I saw one. If I can see, so can others. There are some people in the Security Agency who perhaps do not have the dedication you have. There are many officers among the French occupation authorities who worked for Vichy. They change sides whenever it is convenient. There are men who have been compromised and who have contacts among the Germans."

"For Christ's sake!" Eggart exclaimed. "Are you saying that my reports are being leaked?"

"I am telling you—be very careful what you write. And how you write it!"

After supper they walked along the lake in the Schlossgarten. A few wildflowers penetrated the grass, the survivors of once carefully cultivated gardens. Leaves sprouted here and there from shattered trees. Gaping holes pierced the cameo theater, whose walls had collapsed inward, leaving beams and girders twisting toward the sky like intertwined necks of giraffes.

"It reminds me of Beethoven," she said.

"Why?" His knowledge of classical music was limited.

The Ruins of Athens.

They both felt the strange sense of magnificence the destruction inspired. A few wispy clouds were being blown across the sky. As Eggart looked upward at the sculptured figures on the gutted walls of the Neues Schloss, the figures, not the clouds, seemed to be moving, performing a ballet against the stars. The same illusion had captured her eyes. Impulsively he bent down and lightly kissed her on the lips.

She seemed not to have expected it. She neither withdrew nor responded. For half a minute she looked at him, her eyes very wide. Then, lightly, she kissed him back.

An hour later, as he drove to Waiblingen to see Otto Willach, he wondered if he was falling in love. She was a strange girl, self-assured yet sometimes seeming very vulnerable.

Willach grumbled that it was 10:30 P.M., then grumpily began his report. He had met Siegfried Niehbar in

Moosburg as planned. They had returned to Munich. Niehbar had an address he wanted to go to in the city, but he had not let Willach accompany him. He had returned in three hours, hinting that the people he wanted to see had gone into hiding in the mountains. Willach had to report to the Food Administration in Garmisch-Partenkirchen, and Niehbar asked him to drive via Bad Tölz, where the SS Junkerschule had been situated, and where General Patton had set up his headquarters. In Bad Tölz, Niehbar had told Willach to wait at the bridge across the Isar River, and then had disappeared up one of the narrow streets. Willach did not believe he had gone very far, for he had not taken his bicycle and had returned in less than forty-five minutes. Later Niehbar asserted that there were enough SS men in the mountains to form three divisions—about thirty thousand men.

Thursday and Friday they had driven to Augsburg and Schwäbisch Gmünd. Niehbar had asked Willach if he could continue to accompany him as a mechanic. Willach had replied that he did not know; Niehbar would have to be checked by the American Military Government. Niehbar remarked that if Willach, an SD man, could be cleared, he saw no reason why he should not be, too. "Of course, if you were a *Besatzung's Knecht*—occupation stooge—that might be different."

Willach felt that the remark had been intended to test his reaction, so he had laughed heartily. Niehbar had joined in the laughter. In order to establish greater confidence, Willach had revealed his real name to Niehbar and the fact that he was on the French target list.

In the ensuing conversation, Niehbar had admitted that he had been in the SD also. He said he had grown up in Landshut and had attended the Technical High School of the University of Munich, where he had studied precision mechanics. In 1923, at the age of sixteen, he had joined the *Jungsturm*, the precursor of the Hitler Youth. A professor whom he greatly admired was a friend of Nazi leader Gregor Strasser, and in 1928 Niehbar had joined the SA. After losing his job in 1931 because of the depression, he had become an even firmer adherent of National Socialism.

In 1933, shortly after Hitler's appointment as chancellor, Niehbar had been personally inducted into the Munich SD unit by Bezirksleiter F. X. Helldobler. "I shall never forget the ceremony," Niehbar had said, and started reciting the SD oath. "I swear loyalty to my Führer, Adolf Hitler, to the SS, and to all my superiors." He had halted, then continued. "Of course, all of us who have sworn the oath will have it on our lips even as we go to our graves."

"He was looking at me intently," Willach told Eggart. "It was another test. He wanted me to finish the oath."

"Did you?"

"Yes."

"What is the rest?"

Willach stiffened: "I promise above all that I shall not divulge to anyone who is not a direct superior to me in the SD whatever I may see or hear in the sphere of my duty or position in the SD, and to observe secrecy not only so long as I am a member of the SD, but also after my separation. If I betray these oaths, knowingly, unknowingly, or through carelessness, I give my superiors the right to punish me in any form."

"No matter what you heard or saw, you swore not to reveal it?"

"That is correct."

"Sort of like an eternal pact with the devil."

"I suppose you could regard it as such."

"What was Niehbar's reaction after you recited the oath?"

"I think he accepted me as a comrade. He began to speak quite freely."

"What else did he tell you?"

"He said he had attended the SD school at Bergenbrück, near Bernau. By 1938 he was an Untersturmführer. In January of that year he was sent to Vienna to organize the intelligence operations prior to the overthrow of Chancellor Schuschnigg and the Anschluss with Germany. During 1939 and 1940 he was stationed in Stuttgart, Freiburg, Konstanz, and Bregenz, working in intelligence in the territories adjacent to France and Switzerland. After the fall of France he went back to Vienna. In the autumn of

1942 he went as a Hauptsturmführer to the staff of Brigadeführer Katzmann, the SS and Polizeiführer for Galicia, whose headquarters was in Lemberg (Lvov). In 1943 he was promoted to Sturmbannführer (major) and was made Befehlshaber der Sicherheitspolizei and SD in Tarnopol. In January 1945, during the retreat, he was hit by shrapnel in Hungary and sent to the SS infirmary in Lindau. By March he had recovered sufficiently to go to Berlin, where he saw Himmler, who assigned him the task of helping to organze an intelligence operation, *Unternehmen Bundschuh*, behind enemy lines. When Niehbar returned to Stuttgart, the SS and SD were evacuating the city, so he continued on to the Bodensee, and during the last week in April met with approximately three hundred other SS and Gestapo men at Eglofs to discuss how to continue resistance."

Willach had made a good report. As Eggart had expected, his information was on a higher level and more complete than Barentz's. It corroborated what Barentz had said. The word *Befehlshaber* puzzled Eggart. It had been one of two terms—the other was *Kommandeur*—the SD and SS had used to designate the commander of a place or region. Eggart questioned Willach about it.

"You must understand," Willach said, "that Himmler had his personal chain of command. In every region the Reichsführer SS had his own representative, the Höhere SS and Polizeiführer, and he in turn was the superior of the Befehlshaber. In this manner, orders and reports could travel directly from and to Himmler outside the regular channels."

Eggart nodded. "All right," he said. "You will tell Niehbar that he can ride with you as a mechanic, and I will see that no one takes too careful a look at his papers. You will report every place he goes. But in the future, I expect you to be more aggressive in getting the names of the people he talks to and the addresses he visits."

XI

On July 8, the French, under pressure from General Eisenhower, evacuated Stuttgart. They took with them whatever they could move—machines from factories, beds from hospitals, teaching aids and desks from schools, cattle and chickens from farms. The Germans treated the American troops like liberators. Everywhere people were saying that now things would be normalized. The French and Germans had been enemies for a hundred years, but millions of Germans had settled in America, and America, like Germany, was a Nordic country.

"They want to sweep Hitler and the Nazi era under the rug," Peter Reimer told Eggart, "and they fully expect us to pick up the corners and help them do it."

Whenever Eggart spent the night in Stuttgart he stayed with Reimer, and they became good friends. Eggart, with his German ancestry, could feel comfortable moving among the people. But for Reimer, whose grandfather had been a Bohemian Jewish cigar maker, it was intensely disturbing.

"How does a decent, respectable, culture-loving citizenry get turned into the greatest mass murder machine in history?" Reimer asked. "They were all trundled to church every Sunday and taught to be good little boys. They loved their mothers and honored their fathers. Nobody's more damn moral than the Germans. Then I look at them and wonder—how many notches do they have on their consciences, how many Jewish scalps secreted away? Contemplate that! A whole fucking nation of Jekylls and Hydes!"

* * *

The trickle of returning Jews went almost unnoticed. Of the thousand sent to the Riga ghetto in 1941, forty-two had survived. But that the other 958 had been exterminated—Stuttgarters found that quite irrational! Even firm anti-Nazis would try not to smile. Germans were not murderers. Wasn't it more logical that the 958 had found more congenial homes in the East and chosen not to return?

So the battered buses arrived: one from Ravensbrück and Sachsenhausen; a second from Dora and Buchenwald; a third from Neuengamme; a fourth from Bergen-Belsen; a fifth from Theresienstadt; a sixth from Flossenbürg.

When the bus from Ravensbrück and northern Germany limped in, Reimer persuaded Eggart to come with him to meet it. Thousands of the former concentration camp inmates were still too sick or too weak to travel. Only the stronger could make the journey, yet, even so, many were barely able to descend the steps of the bus. They had spent days on the bus, which halted only for occasional rest stops. They were exhausted. Three and four years before they had been ordered to report to a *Sammellager*, "gathering camp," on the Killesberg in the city, and been told they would be resettled in the East. They had left Stuttgart when it was yet untouched by air raids, and they had embarked on an odyssey through hell. They returned bewildered, broken, still half in shock, to a field of ruins that reflected their own shattered lives. Most had left as families. They returned singly—an old man, a teen-aged boy, a woman young in years but with the lines of horror on her face.

Only a handful of people had come to meet the bus. By the end of the war not more than a score of Jews had been left in the city, all of them the beneficiaries of some special status—they were either highly decorated veterans of World War I, held foreign citizenship, or were married to Christians. An official from the United Nations Relief and Rehabilitation Administration (UNRRA) asked the returnees if they had anywhere to stay. Most gave their old addresses. But some of these places had been destroyed in the bombings, and the rest had been occupied by Nazis.

No firm policy had been established on evicting the Nazis in favor of the Jews. Everyone who had no place to go, the UNRRA official announced, would be taken to a refugee camp until permanent arrangements could be made. A girl shrieked, then dashed back inside the bus. She was sobbing hysterically. An UNRRA official climbed in to talk to her; but after a few minutes he exited again alone.

"What's the matter?" Reimer asked him.

He sighed. "She will not come out. She refuses to go to a camp. I tried to explain to her that it is not a detention camp. But she is hysterical."

"I'll speak to her," Reimer said.

Liselotte Feuerstein was flung across a seat. Reimer told her he was an American official in the military government, that he himself was Jewish, and that he wanted to help her. Slowly her tears subsided. Finally she looked up at him. She was a teen-ager, with black hair, and violet eyes swimming beneath the surface of tears. Despite her emaciated bony figure, she was quite beautiful.

"If you go to the camp," Reimer said, "I promise I will come to see you. I will bring you clothes and food. I will not let you stay there long."

"No!" Her answer left no doubt of her determination.

"But where can you go? Do you know anyone in Stuttgart?" he asked.

She shook her head in the affirmative.

"Who is it?"

She had difficulty catching her breath. "My mother!" The words came out as if they were cracked in pieces.

"Your mother? She's living in Stuttgart?" Reimer was taken aback.

The girl nodded.

"She isn't here to meet you?"

She shook her head in the negative.

"But as soon as you find her you can live with her?" The tears flowed even harder. "I cannot."

The girl was near exhaustion. Reimer was afraid she would collapse. "I have a room," Reimer said. "You can stay there tonight. Do you want to come with me?"

"Yes." Her face lighted up. "Please, yes."

As they drove up the hillside to the requisitioned CIC villa, Eggart chided Reimer in English. Although the nonfraternization rules had broken down completely, to bring a girl into CIC quarters, even if she was a concentration camp victim, was courting trouble.

"Shit!"Reimer responded. His room was below street level on the hillside overlooking the city, and connected with the upper floors by a stairway. It had a separate garden entrance. No one need know the girl was there. Tomorrow they could solve the mystery of the mother.

Liselotte was asleep the moment she lay down on the bed. Reimer covered her with a blanket. "Anyway," he said, "I'm almost old enough to be her father"—a patent exaggeration, since he was twenty-six.

Lisolette did not awaken until eleven o'clock the next morning. When her eyes opened, she bolted upright. She had no idea where she was, and looked wildly and fearfully from one corner of the room to another. Reimer spoke calmly to her and reminded her of her arrival on the bus the previous night.

"I'm sorry," she finally said. "I can't remember anything. I remember only that I ran back to the bus."

Reimer had consulted a WAC the previous night and obtained lingerie and two dresses that he gave to Liselotte. He showed her to the bathroom, turned on the water in the tub for her, and then went upstairs to the kitchen to fetch breakfast. When she emerged from the bathroom the table was set with soft-boiled eggs, cheese, fruit, bread, marmalade, and milk. She gasped. She had not, she said, seen such a feast in years.

She spoke articulately but slowly. Periodically she lay down to take naps. Eggart and Reimer spent the rest of the day piecing her story together.

Her father, a Jew, had been a Stuttgart attorney. In 1927, at the age of thirty-eight, he had married his secretary, a Christian, fifteen years younger than he. Liselotte had been born in 1929 and her brother Edmund fifteen months later. It had not been a happy marriage, and the added stress accompanying the onset of the Nazi era had brought about the divorce of David Feuerstein and his wife Ilena in 1934. A short time later Ilena had married a Nazi party member, Franz Hochheimer.

Liselotte and Edmund had remained with their father. During the *Kristallnacht* pogrom in November 1938, they had been driven from their home. A few days later David Feuerstein had been arrested and sent to Buchenwald. Since Ilena had refused to take Liselotte and Edmund into her home, they had been placed in an orphanage.

Two years later, following the death of David Feuerstein at Buchenwald, the director of the orphanage had informed Liselotte and Edmund that they would be reclassified as "Jewish" from *Mischlingen*, "mixed parentage," unless their mother acknowledged them and took them into her home or agreed to pay for their upkeep. As *Mischlingen* they were considered sub-Aryan, but not outside the protection of German law. As Jews, they would be subject completely to the control of the Gestapo. Liselotte and Edmund had gone to see their mother and begged her to take them in.

"What happened?" Reimer asked.

"She gave us two marks and some chocolates, told us to behave ourselves, and said we would be all right."

In November 1942, Liselotte and Edmund had been transported to Theresienstadt. Liselotte had been moved from camp to camp—Reimer and Eggart did not inquire into the details—and had finally ended at Mauthausen. She had lost contact with Edmund. Probably, he was dead.

Liselotte grew tired quickly, and by six o'clock she was asleep.

"Let's go have a talk with Frau Hochheimer," Reimer said to Eggart.

They found Liselotte's mother in an apartment house in the city's Ostheim district. As soon as she realized they were American Military Government officials, she became nervous and upset. Her husband was at work, she said.

"Where does he work?" Reimer asked.

She had assumed the gentlemen knew that, she

responded. He was an electrician at the Technische Werke der Statt Stuttgart, the municipal public utility.

Ilena Hochheimer was a buxom woman. She had two cherubic daughters, aged five and eight, by her second husband. Reimer told her they had not come to see her husband, but to talk to her about her children.

"My children?" Puzzled, she looked at the two girls.

"Your children by your first husband. Liselotte and Edmund."

"Oh!" She was suddenly downcast. She asked them to be seated.

"Did you know that Liselotte returned to Stuttgart yesterday from Mauthausen concentration camp?" Reimer asked.

"Concentration camp? Liselotte?" She emitted a small laugh. "You are joking. What would Liselotte have done to be sent to a concentration camp?"

"She did not have to do anything, Frau Hochheimer," Reimer continued. "It was enough that she was Jewish. All Jews were sent to concentration camps."

"No. That is not true," she disputed. "How can you be certain? Criminals and enemies of the state—they were the ones put in concentration camps."

"Wasn't your first husband sent to Buchenwald? What was his crime?"

"*Ach*," she said. "He was always talking politics, you know. He was a member of the Social Democratic Party."

"I am not here to argue with you, Frau Hochheimer," Reimer was seething, but spoke in a measured, controlled voice. "Your daughter weighs perhaps eighty pounds. Your son is probably dead. If you want to argue with that—go ahead!"

"But what could I do?" She wrung her hands as if she were knitting with hot needles. "What do you want of me now?" She cast a glance toward her children as if half expecting that Reimer and Eggart had come to take them and place them in an American concentration camp.

"Why did you reject your children?" Reimer demanded. "Why did you not take them in when they came and pleaded with you? You could have saved them."

She shook her head. A tear rolled down one ample cheek. "You do not understand. Franz would not let me."

"Your husband?"

"Yes."

"Why not?"

"Oh—it was so terrible. He told me he would forgive me for marrying David. He said I had been young and impressionable, and it was only natural that a Jew would take advantage of me. That could no longer happen under National Socialism, so what was past was past, but he would hear nothing of Liselotte and Edmund. At the very mention of their names he flew into a fury. He declared he would not tolerate the *Judenkinder*!"

"So rather than oppose your husband, you abandoned your children. You let them be shipped off to concentration camps!"

"But I told you—if I had known! But I did not know. No one knew. I asked Franz, and he said—*Ach!*—perhaps they would be sent to a place like a *Kraft durch Freude*, 'Strength through Joy,' camp. And of course, that was a privilege for German boys and girls. It might be hard, but it was good for the physique."

"And you believed him! What do you think would have happened if you had disobeyed him and brought Liselotte and Edmund to live with you here?"

"But that would have been quite impossible. A wife has promised to obey her husband."

They looked at her without saying anything.

She shifted uneasily. "Besides . . ." she continued.

"Yes?"

"Franz is an official employee. He could not let it be known I had once been married to a Jew. There would have been serious consequences if the party had found out that he had two half-Jewish children living with him."

"He was a Nazi?" Reimer asked.

"Yes. But he was just an ordinary party man. He had nothing to do with the terrible things that you are telling me—all these things we are just hearing about now. He was only the block warden of this block, and he was very proud of that."

When Reimer and Eggart were back in the street, Reimer exploded. "Son of a bitch! He's worried about losing his block warden badge, and she lets her kids get dragged off to Mauthausen! I'll fix the bastard!"

"How?"

"I'm going to put him in the automatic arrest category as a member of the Gestapo!"

Eggart laughed. "You wouldn't!"

Reimer stared at Eggart. "Your ass, I wouldn't! The son of a bitch was a block warden, running his little neighborhood spy service for the Gestapo! It was all these fucking little shits that made the big shit work. 'Franz Hochheimer is suspected of complicity in the roundup and transportation of Stuttgart's Jews.' That bastard is going to sweat in Kornwestheim for a while!"

Eggart suddenly became aware that he had not realized the depth of Reimer's feelings. Reimer would do exactly as he said.

XII

On Friday, the 13th of July, General Eisenhower dissolved the Supreme Headquarters of the Allied Expeditionary Force. The tapestry of cooperation the Allies had woven during the war was starting to unravel. The next day was the anniversary of Bastille Day, the first since the liberation of France. At the invitation of Madeleine Roche, Eggart drove to Lindau to attend the celebration.

Lindau was an island resort town dating back to premedieval times, and the French had chosen it for one of their headquarter cities. The French officers in their dress uniforms were magnificent, especially the North Africans, who could have stepped out of a nineteenth-century ball. Eggart, wearing an officer's uniform with captain's bars, felt drab amid the color. Madeleine was dressed in a wine red evening gown with a silver bodice. It was the first time Eggart had seen her looking feminine. The orchestra played mostly waltzes and foxtrots. She told him she had wanted to wear an off-the-shoulder gown, but had been unable to find a strapless bra.

"You might have tried a braless strap!" he suggested.

"Guillaume!" She deliberately gave his name the French pronunciation, and pretended to be angry. "Be careful!" But her eyes twinkled as she looked up at him.

The ballroom was decorated with red, white, and blue bunting, and there were red and white carnations and roses in blue vases. The food was overwhelming: platters of stuffed and glacéed suckling pigs decorated with fruit, frog legs Provencale, chicken Marchand de Vin, and for dessert, crepes suzette and a six-foot obelisk of ice cream molded in the shape of the Eiffel Tower. Champagne flowed from a fountain.

Despite the cooling of French-American relations, Eggart was treated warmly. Toast after toast was proposed, until bubbles streamed before his eyes. It was not until the fireworks display that, drinking black coffee, he had a chance for respite. As rockets burst against the stars, twinkles of reflected light drifted in the Bodensee.

Afterwards, they returned to the ballroom. It was about midnight when she said, "Now, Guillaume, you will take me sailing—yes?"

"Sure," he replied, thinking she was joking; but a few minutes later they were walking toward the waterfront. The boat she directed him to was a large dinghy, more than ten years old and badly in need of paint. His head was swimming as they stepped aboard.

"This is ridiculous," he said. "You can't go sailing in an evening gown."

"Of course not," she replied. "Help me take it off."

"Sure," he agreed. "What do I do?"

"There is a zipper. You pull it."

He pulled the zipper and the dress split open to the waist. She wriggled out of it. Underneath she was wearing a bathing suit.

"My God!" he said. "You really mean it. You've been prepared all along."

"Contingency planning? Yes?" From a small bag she had brought along she took a pair of slacks and a top, and slipped them on.

"You know," he said, "this won't be the smartest thing you've ever done!"

"You have never lived dangerously, Guillaume?"

"Oh, hell yes!" he replied without conviction. "I'm very tight. I'm not even sure which direction is up, much less where north is!"

"My poor Guillaume!" She took off his coat and unbuttoned his tie. "Kneel down," she ordered. He obeyed. She took a firm grip on his head, plunged it into the water, and held it under.

He came up spluttering, surprised at her strength. "For Christ's sake! You don't have to drown me!"

"Now, you are ready to sail?"

They settled themselves in the dinghy and then, gliding between the other boats, slowly moved out to open water. The air stirred scarcely at all. It was a lazy boat whose canvas luxuriated like a cat as Eggart nosed out past the statue of the Bavarian lion at the harbor entrance. On the smooth water of the Bodensee, Eggart could simply wrap his arm around the tiller and let the boat skate over the water. For a long time Madeleine sat perfectly still with her arms around her drawn-up legs and her chin on her knees. Her eyes were riveted on the wavelets that plat-platted against the hull. After a while she blew up an air mattress and lay on it, her head propped up on a life preserver at the stern of the boat. He sat down beside her. The lights on shore blended into the stars at the curve of the horizon and almost imperceptibly became fainter. There was no sound. The only observable movement was the slight to-and-fro motion of the triangular sail against the stars. They were alone in a world without time and without place.

He turned toward her and kissed her. Her eyes were open and her lips slightly parted. He kissed her again. Her hands wandered through his hair, and he felt the faint touch of her tongue on his lips. He kissed her eyes, her neck, the hollow of her ear. Their lips met again, and their tongues crossed each other wet and warm. She unbuttoned his shirt. Her fingers were antennae exploring his back, moving over his chest and around his neck. He removed the shirt from her shoulders, then slipped the straps of her bathing suit down over her arms to expose her breasts. They were like the breasts of a pubescent girl—soft, and only slightly mounded. When he kissed the nipples they hardened under his touch. Their lips met again, their arms wrapped themselves around each other's backs—bare chest touching bare chest so that each could feel the rapid beating of the other's heart.

His throat dry, he fumbled with the buttons on her slacks. The waistband loosened. His hand slid along the cool, smooth skin of her legs and passed over the slick of the bathing suit. He probed the vortex of her navel. His fingers passed beyond and shivered at the contact with the triangle of hair. In three or four minutes she was naked, and so was he. They undressed each other. Tingling whenever he touched her, he kissed her and kissed her.

The air in the mattress sighed; the blood cascaded through his head; her fingernails dug deep into his back. They lay together, legs intertwined, arms wrapped around each other, the boat still moving silently in rhythm with the stars.

He felt something wet on his shoulder and he looked up. Tears were streaming down her face. His spirit dropped. "I'm sorry," he fumbled for the words. "I didn't mean . . ." He shook his head.

"Oh, no!" She was laughing through her tears. "I am crying because I am laughing—no, that's not right, is it? I am crying because I am happy!"

She laughed and cried simultaneously, and finally the tears stopped. He separated from her, and for the first time his eyes took in all of her body. Her skin held the starlight, and despite the gentle curves of her bosom and hips, she seemed more feminine than any girl he had ever known. "My God!" he exclaimed. "And the first time I saw you I thought you were a boy!"

"You see, Guillaume!" She put a finger to his lips and laughed. "Flat-chested women make the best lovers. There are no obstructions."

He took down the sail, and they used it for a blanket. They dozed. They made love. The horizon turned orange, and the sun rose like a flaming eye. When the air turned warm, they plunged naked and gasping into the cool water of the lake. Returning to the boat, they lay baking in the sun.

"We should be diplomats," he said.

She looked at him.

"We've sure made a dramatic improvement in French-American relations."

He had no idea where they were, but the current was carrying them west-northwest. As the sun rose higher, they discovered that they were thirsty and famished. Turning his attention to sailing the boat, he directed the bow to the northeast. A short time later, even though the shoreline was still a blur, they heard the faint ringing of church bells. It was Sunday. At one o'clock he nosed the boat to shore at the east end of Friedrichshafen.

After eating at a Gaststätte, they cast off to sail back to Lindau. Now there was a good breeze, and, as the boat slapped briskly through the water, he had to pay attention to the sail and the helm. Later in the afternoon, as they neared Lindau, the breeze subsided. He furled the sail and put out the sea anchor. Drifting along, they kissed, they touched, they made love.

The sun spun over the water like a huge orange sunflower whose petals have been plucked. The rays leaping over the surface made her eyes seem cobalt blue, and animated the pupils as if the lake were flowing through them. He buried himself in her like a marmot seeking a nest. He felt warm and secure, and at the same time freed—when he closed his eyes in the swaying boat, it was as if he were soaring in the sky. He didn't want to leave her.

"Couldn't we just go back and forth on the Bodensee making love?" she asked. "No one would ever see us again except when we loomed out of the fog. We would become a legend, like the Flying Dutchman!"

It was a pleasant reverie, and darkness had already fallen when they touched land again at Lindau.

XIII

Under pressure from America to "get the boys home," the United States occupation of Germany was turning chaotic. Barentz reported to Eggart that Siegfried Niehbar had 22 message centers in operation and that 120 men and 40 women were active in the Ibex organization. Recruiting was going well, and Niehbar was optimistic. He bragged that at least a dozen members of Ibex had infiltrated the French and American military governments.

Toward the end of July, the CIC launched Operation Lifebuoy for the purpose of scrubbing hundreds of Nazis out of the posts they were occupying. An attempt was made to seal off the American zone to prevent the escape of war criminals and to inhibit the movement of resistance members. Another operation, Tally-Ho, uncovered caches of radio transmitters, weapons, hand grenades, and dynamite. Fifteen hundred persons were arrested.

These activities only scratched the surface of the resistance, however, and, because of the Nazi infiltration, Eggart did not even trust his fellow agents. His only confidant was Peter Reimer. True to his word, Reimer had had Franz Hochheimer arrested and placed in Kornwestheim Internment Camp, halfway between Stuttgart and Ludwigsburg. Liselotte Feuerstein continued to occupy Reimer's room in the villa. She was practically Reimer's ward. All the Americans in the house took a paternal interest in her, and no one would have suggested that she be evicted. They waited on her, they gave her presents, and they provided her with the best food available from American supplies and the black market. She was blossoming, and had a beauty that was haunting. If it had not been for Madeleine, Eggart would have envied Reimer—though of course Liselotte was little more than a child.

Eggart had helped Albrecht Willach obtain work with an American Military Government War Damage Assessment team. Albrecht did not know that his brother Otto was working for the Americans—either under his assumed name of Bergauer for the Food Administration, or in his covert role for Eggart. After Otto visited his family in July, Albrecht asked Eggart for advice. Albrecht suspected that Otto was mixed up in some shady activity, and concerned that failure to report Otto's role in the SD and Otto's visit to Stuttgart might endanger his own job with the military government.

Eggart reassured Albrecht: "You've told me what you know. Now it's my responsibility."

Otto Willach reported to Eggart that Siegfried Niehbar had taken a room above the Bürgermeister Strauss, a tavern in Esslingen, a few miles southeast of Stuttgart. The operator of this *Wirtshaus* was a Nazi and a resistance sympathizer. Niehbar planned to make the *Wirtshaus* his headquarters in the Stuttgart area. He was talking about having girls bring GI's there, plying them with liquor, and seducing them so that they could be photographed and compromised. Their identification papers and passes would be stolen. Niehbar had given Willach a hundred thousand out-of-date French francs and asked him to try to exchange them for valid currency. The sum, he indicated, was but a small portion of the funds available to him.

"There is one thing that concerns me," Otto Willach said to Eggart. "I met Niehbar's courier, an SS Scharführer, Johannes Barentz, for the first time. Barentz is very suspicious."

Barentz had asked Willach about his status in the Nazi party, his work during the war, and his current occupation in the Food Administration. Willach had tried to cut off the questioning by replying that it was not up to a Scharführer to interrogate his superior, but Barentz had replied that the security of the organization demanded that everyone be able to prove his past record and loyalty. Barentz had then gone to Niehbar and suggested that Niehbar should be wary of Willach, for Willach seemed to have a great deal of freedom and authority for a food administrator, and did not act at all concerned about discovery of his past or present activities. Willach was in contact with American officials every week, and there was definite danger that they might obtain information on Ibex from him, either accidentally or by design.

"How did you find out what Barentz told Niehbar?" Eggart asked Otto.

"Niehbar told me," Willach replied. "I complained to Niehbar that Barentz was insubordinate and asking too many questions. In the SD, a primary rule was that no man should know more, or seek to know more, than was necessary to perform his own job."

"Did Niehbar seem to take Barentz's suspicions seriously?"

"No. He joked about them. He said that perhaps Barentz had overstepped his bounds, but Barentz was a well-trained SS man, and if Germany had had a hundred thousand like him the war would not have been lost. But it is a good thing, Captain Eggart, that I have Niehbar's full confidence."

"Then what are you concerned about?"

"Coming under suspicion is always unpleasant, if not dangerous," Willach answered. "I must wonder if Barentz does not know something. Perhaps he was in the Gestapo, or perhaps he has learned something from someone. He comes into contact with more people in the organization than anyone else. You know that Ibex has agents in the military government, and it is possible that there is a leak. We must be careful, Captain Eggart. I know these men. They are ruthless."

Having one of his agents cast suspicion on the other was slightly unsettling to Eggart. Nonetheless, he chuckled. Evidently, both were performing well, and neither had an intimation of the other's role.

* * *

When Eggart met Barentz two days later outside Kirchheim, Barentz presented him with a pleasant surprise: a copy of the Ibex organization table. Niehbar's plan, Barentz said, was to work for war between America and Russia, and then propose the formation of a new German government. This government, based on National Socialist principles, would rally the German people to the side of the Americans.

Niehbar hinted that, to help implement the plan, he knew of a *sonder waffen*, a special weapon that had been developed but never employed during the war. From the way Niehbar spoke, Barentz believed that there was a connection between this weapon and a secret SS arms depot in Meersburg, a town on the Bodensee.

"Do you have any idea what this weapon consists of?" Eggart asked Barentz.

"No."

"Do you think Niehbar has access to it?"

"I'm not sure. But I don't believe so—at least not right now," Barentz replied. Niehbar seemed to be in contact with someone more important; probably he was the man known as the Werwolf, the head of the entire organization.

XIV

Eggart told Barentz to find out what he could about the secret SS arms depot in Meersburg, and they arranged to meet in Ravensburg on the morning of August 18. Eggart had already made plans to spend part of the week before that in the Black Forest with Madeleine. Then he would drive her back to the French Security Agency and go to pick up Barentz.

The Germans put great value on the curative powers of the mountain air. During the chilly nights, Eggart and Madeleine huddled under the great quilt in the cabin. He kissed her eyes. She nibbled at his ears. They warmed each other's faces with their breaths. Her fingers on his back were like the paws of chipmunks running over him. A clock on the wall cuckooed the proper number of times for each hour.

"The next time he does that," Madeleine said, "I'm going to get him!"

At midnight she darted naked across the filtered moonlight and grabbed the cuckoo after only its third call. After admonishing it in French, she leaped back into bed. Eggart caught her and kissed her.

"And now," he said, "I'm going to get *you!*"

He adored her. He enjoyed her. She said she loved him. They hiked the mountain paths beneath the towering cedars and pines. She told him of her childhood. Although she came from a middle-class family, the house in which she lived had not had electricity until she was twelve years old, and it still did not have a hot-water heater. He had never thought of his family's 1,500-acre ranch in California as big, but to her it seemed an estate. "If you lived in France, you would be a *comte*," she said, and made him tell her stories of vacuum cleaners and electric milking machines as if they were tales from the *Arabian Nights*. "Is everything electric in America?" she asked.

"Yes," he replied. "But I haven't yet told you about the most miraculous invention of all."

"What is that?"

"Electric kisses!"

On the last day of their sojourn, Eggart obtained a horse cart. On a logging trail ascending a ridge, the animal moved steadily but leisurely, like an old campaigner. Even with a bright sun in the sky the forest was dark and moist, wrapped in cathedral silence.

"I still find it hard to accept," she said.

"What?"

"That there is no danger. Sometimes we would go into the forest. The Germans would try to follow. Perhaps one or two from our group would have to stay behind to harass them. Often we never saw them again."

Near the top of the ridge, Eggart tied the horse to a tree. Taking a hamper from the cart, he and Madeleine climbed to the crest, then went a little farther down the opposite side until they reached a small clearing. Far beneath was a green-blue lake. Beyond, as far as they could see, were mountains of trees packed so closely together that their tops were woven into a tapestry. Here and there the trees gave way to a dale or a meadow into which a farmhouse was squeezed.

Madeleine asked Eggart if he knew the future could be predicted by the shape of the clouds. He said he didn't. They tried for a while visualizing animals and objects, but he had little success.

"The clouds just aren't very shapely today." He kissed her. "I think I would do much better predicting the future by your shape."

The warm sun and the wine they had been drinking generated a delicious drowsiness. Stripping to their waists, they let the sun's rays and the light breeze chase each other across their bodies. He kissed her bare skin, her nipples, her navel, her lips.

"I think you are getting warmer," she said. "What shall we do?"

He suggested they take off the remainder of their clothes. A few minutes later she said, "Now I am getting warmer."

Afterwards, they cooled off lying naked in the sun. Plucking a yellow-petaled flower, he stuck it in her hair and brushed his lips across her cheeks. They had become not only lovers but friends. Her fingers slid across his chest and lazily curled one of the few reddish-brown hairs. He took her hand and kissed her palm. A cloud shaped vaguely like an elephant plodded across the sun. An odd thought came into his mind: if by the shape of the clouds one could anticipate the future, why could one not also predict the past? Strange there had never been a Nostradamus of history, someone who could have written a biography of Homer, cleared up the mystery of the Etruscans, or traced the footsteps of the lost Virginia Colony. It would take years for him and Madeleine to catch up with each other's pasts, and there was much, perhaps, that they would never know. He turned toward her, looked into her eyes, and kissed each one in turn.

XV

At Oberndorf, a Black Forest town on the road from Freudenstadt to Ravensburg, Eggart stopped at the Mauser factory. Madeleine knew the French officer in charge of production, and through an exchange of six bottles of scotch, four cartons of cigarettes, and twelve Hershey bars, Eggart obtained a small automatic and a handcrafted rifle that was far more accurate than the American M-1. A technician mounted the rifle with a sniperscope Eggart had picked up before the goods from the Heidelberg optical institute had been shipped to the United States.

After dropping Madeleine off in Ravensburg, Eggart met Barentz, who reported that he had found out the Meersburg arms cache consisted of weapons and explosives assembled from the Friedrichshafen tank works, the Dornier airplane factory, and chemical plants along the Bodensee. Barentz had obtained a good description of the house, had gone to Meersburg, and believed he had located the cache.

"What are the chances of getting into the place?" Eggart asked.

Barentz replied that the house was old and looked abandoned; however, there was a modern double lock on the door, so if the door were not to be broken down, an expert locksmith would have to pick the lock.

Eggart went back to the French Security Agency headquarters. He did not want to involve Madeleine, and the duty officer informed him that Captain Rettemond would have to authorize the request for a locksmith.

Captain Rettemond was almost surely at the Buchhornerhof in Friedrichshafen.

A half hour later, after dropping Barentz off on the
outskirts of town, Eggart arrived at the Buchhornerhof,
where he found Captain Rettemond seated in an armchair
in the lounge of the officers' club. Drinking black coffee and
cognac, Rettemond greeted Eggart enthusiastically.

"An excellent report, Captain Eggart," he said in
German. On the low table in front of him Eggart saw a
jumble of magazines and official papers. Among them was
his report of ten days before. Across the top was stamped
SECRET.

Eggart explained his need for a locksmith. He would
have to be a French army man with security clearance.

"No problem," Rettemond responded, getting up from
the chair. "I'll put in a call to Lindau."

Eggart was uneasy. German girls were walking about
on the arms of French officers. A known member of the
Ibex organization, former SS Hauptscharführer Hinsheid,
worked as a waiter at the hotel. A German waiter appeared
and inquired the *Herr Offizier's* pleasure. Eggart ordered
coffee. According to the description Barentz had given him,
the waiter could be Hinsheid. Eggart felt a troubled
tingling as he watched him walk away.

After the waiter disappeared into the kitchen, Eggart
shuffled the papers so that his report was lost from view.
Although the code names Grosse Käse and Achilles were
substituted for Barentz and Otto Willach throughout the
reports, it would be possible for someone in Ibex to
unscramble their identities.

When Captain Rettemond returned, he informed
Eggart that the locksmith would arrive within the hour.
After the waiter who brought the coffee had left, Eggart
tried as diplomatically as he could to question Rettemond's
practice of bringing secret material to the officers' club.

Rettemond, however, dismissed his concern. "The
Germans we have, they have been housebroken," he said.

The locksmith, a corporal, was driving a jeep. Eggart
told him to follow the Mercedes. At the edge of town,

Eggart picked up Barentz. The drive along the Bodensee to Meersburg took less than a half hour. To reduce the chance of attracting attention, Eggart had the corporal park the jeep off the highway outside town and climb into the Mercedes.

Meersburg was an ancient town that had prospered on fishing and trading. Its name meant "town on the ocean"—to the early residents the Bodensee had seemed as vast as a sea. The town was dominated by its church, the old stone castle that had served for refuge and protection, and a handsome four-story baroque palace. Every plot of land was built upon. Linked wall to wall, the rooftops of the four-story houses presented a solid decking, seemingly leaving no space for streets.

Eggart steered the Mercedes through the arch in the old stone tower. The street was barely wide enough to accommodate the car, and the walls of the houses rose up like the sides of a canyon. Here and there covered passageways bridged the streets from the upper story of one house to another. The street descended toward lake level, where the stone walls of the old fortress towered sixty feet high. Portions of the walls were screened by thick vines and branches and a few huge gnarled trees. Nestled among these, its age-darkened facade half hidden, was a small house. Eggart let Barentz and the corporal off, then drove on and parked the car about fifty yards away.

The house was unoccupied; and when Eggart returned the locksmith was already at work. Eggart was concerned that someone might see them and call the police. The vegetation, however, provided some screening, few people were abroad, and twelve years of Naziism had conditioned people to ignore whatever might be happening around them. The corporal needed only five minutes to pick the first lock, and half that time for the second. Eggart let the door creak open a few inches, then slid his hand along the top and the sides to check for booby traps. There were none.

The three men slipped inside. The room was less than a hundred square feet. The floor was rotted, and patches of earth showed through. A foul, musky odor pervaded. The two small windows, coated with dirt, allowed only a sepulchral light to penetrate. The furniture consisted of two rickety chairs and a chest pushed against the far wall. A ladder led up to the second story. Gingerly, Eggart climbed up. The second floor was completely bare.

The corporal picked the lock on the chest, then opened it. It contained three moldy SS uniforms, two SS daggers, several hundred-mark bank notes, a box of medals, and a number of Nazi party manuals—scarcely an impressive cache.

Barentz, however, exclaimed, "Look! Behind the chest!"

They pushed the chest out. In back was a stone archway about three and a half feet high, apparently once part of the castle wall. A wooden hatch was bolted in place. Since there was no way to obtain a grip on it, Eggart returned to the car for a tire iron. Inserting the iron into a crack between the hatch and the wall, Eggart pried the hatch loose. Stooping low, he and Barentz carefully made their way through the arch. The wall was about four feet thick. Beyond it was a chamber in which the foul, damp odor of the air was almost overpowering. Only a dim patch of light entered through the archway, yet it was possible to see—perhaps more to sense than to see—that the chamber was stacked with crates. Using the tire iron, Eggart broke open the crate nearest him. Two long barrels of heavy aircraft-type machine guns became visible.

It was impossible to stay in the chamber for more than two or three minutes. Eggart and Barentz backed out. Eggart returned once more to the Mercedes in order to get a flashlight. Wrapped in thought, he did not know what made him glance up. A few trees and bushes partially obscured the buttresses of the castle walls and a high bridge, but Eggart caught the hint of a movement amid the vegetation. At the same time, there was a glint of light, like a reflection from binoculars. Returning to the house, he walked unhurriedly, as if he had seen nothing.

Once inside, Eggart told Barentz that he suspected someone was watching them. He instructed Barentz to go out and walk toward the Mercedes in order to attract the attention of the observer. Eggart would use the opportunity to slip out and slide up the stairs along the wall. Barentz was to start the car and cut off the man's escape through the town. Eggart advised the French corporal to wait at the house for half an hour. If neither he nor Barentz returned, the corporal was to lock up the house and drive the jeep back to Lindau.

Eggart delayed until Barentz was halfway to the Mercedes, then edged out the door. Ducking toward the castle wall, he reached it, apparently without being seen. He was within fifty feet of the buttress when the hidden observer bolted.

In the pursuit up the long flight of steps, Eggart, the .38 in his hand, gained on the man step by step and yard by yard, so that by the time he reached the top, he had made up half the distance. Straight ahead was the decommissioned waterwheel of an old mill. Jumping across the gap, the man caught hold of the wooden scoops, and used them like steps to clamber to the top. Just beyond the top, he leaped across the gap on the other side to the road. Following him, Eggart landed on the cobblestone pavement just in time to see a puff of blue smoke from the exhaust of a motorcycle.

Less than thirty seconds later Barentz arrived in the Mercedes. Eggart took the wheel. They flashed down the road to Freidrichshafen in pursuit of the motorcyclist. Although Eggart had not seen the man's face, the motorbike rider was of the same build as the waiter at the Buchhornerhof. Eggart asked Barentz to describe Hinsheid once more, and when Barentz complied, Eggart was certain that Hinsheid was the waiter who had brought the coffee.

Within twenty seconds, Eggart had the speedometer of the car quivering at one-hundred-and-twenty kilometers (seventy-two miles per hour). On the narrow road he could not drive faster, but the Mercedes steadily closed in on the motorcycle. Had Hinsheid continued toward Friedrichshafen, Eggart would have caught him before he reached the town. But a mile beyond Immenstaad, Hinsheid swung off the main highway into the low-rolling uplands rising from the lake. Here the roads were winding ribbons, sometimes unpaved and often little more than one lane wide. Hinsheid had all the advantage of maneuverability. Eggart took chance after chance to keep up. He right-angled around the corners of buildings into villages, twisted between a farm-house and its barn, and left chicken feathers flying in his wake.

Hinsheid roared past an approaching farm wagon. Eggart, careening half along the shoulder of the road, passed the wagon so closely that pieces of straw ticked his cheek. Ahead he saw a kilometer marker centered squarely in the hood ornament of the Mercedes. To miss it, Eggart swerved so sharply that he clipped the rear wheel of the wagon. The Mercedes took the blow in stride. The wagon wheel, however, shattered—through the rearview mirror Eggart could see pieces of it pirouetting through the air and the wagon tipping over.

They sped through Ailingen, Tettnang, and Tannau. "Eglofs," Barentz said, and it was evident that despite the twists and turns, Hinsheid's course was toward Eglofs. Eggart told Barentz to get the Mauser from behind the back seat.

"Hit the cycle!" Eggart instructed Barentz.

Barentz seated the barrel on the top of the windshield and fired. He flipped the bolt back to eject the shell, then pushed it forward to insert a new cartridge into the chamber. He fired again. Hinsheid suddenly swerved off the road and leaped the cycle over a ditch. He headed diagonally across an open field patched with white—Eggart had the impression it was snow, although in summer that was impossible.

"You've got to get him now!" Eggart shouted at Barentz, and skidded the Mercedes to a halt. At that moment the patch of snow rose into the air—it consisted of hundreds of gulls. Hinsheid seemed to disappear among them. Barentz fired. A flash of red erupted from amid the white. Smoke plumed from the cycle. Barentz had hit the gas tank. As the curtain of gulls lifted, Eggart saw Hinsheid vault from the burning motorcycle and dash across the field toward a barn about 150 yards away.

Eggart and Barentz went after him. Barentz, handicapped by his leg, ran with a hobble. Eggart, however, was much faster in the open field than Hinsheid. By the time Hinsheid disappeared into the barn, Eggart was less than fifty yards behind him. The barn was typical of the structures along the Bodensee—large, with a sharply pitched roof terminating in a wide overhang. Revolver in hand, Eggart charged in behind Hinsheid.

A few seconds passed before Eggart's eyes accustomed themselves to the dusk of the interior. On one side were stalls for cows and horses. A low divider marked a pigpen. On the other side were a fruit press for making cider, two large wagons, a plow, a reaper, harnesses, an anvil, a grindstone, and a multitude of tools and agricultural devices. Eggart spotted a couple of ducks. Numerous chickens were clucking about.

When Barentz arrived, carrying the Mauser and breathing heavily, Eggart told him to back off from the barn so that he could watch the doors, the windows, and the hayloft opening on the side. If Hinsheid tried to escape, Barentz was to shoot him.

Hinsheid, lying in wait in the gloom, definitely had the advantage. Eggart's heart pounded as he stalked after him. He went along the stalls, then past the wagons and stacks of filled sacks. Careful not to step among piled-up tools and materials where he could be trapped, he searched the ground floor, then climbed the ladder to the hayloft.

He wound up by the loft's opening, which looked out across the expanse of fields. The motorcycle was burning itself out. In the distance he could see the Mercedes parked cockeyed along the road. Directly below the opening was a huge mound of steaming manure, twelve to fifteen feet in diameter and about the same height.

Eggart's heart hammered. His body felt like a taut drum. Darkness would descend in a little over two hours, and then the odds would be all in favor of Hinsheid. Eggart considered: if he continued searching the barn by himself, he had a good chance of getting himself killed. If, on the other hand, he and Barentz probed the barn together, Hinsheid might slip out and make a run for it.

A third alternative was to set fire to the barn. Eggart

was mulling over that possibility when a dark form detached itself from the shadows. Eggart caught a vision of four steel tips driving at him. To swivel the revolver and try to fire would be futile. Even if he pulled the trigger in time, he would be impaled by the pitchfork. There was only one way out and he took it, plunging like a diver through the loft's opening into the manure pile below.

He landed flat against the sloped pile, his knees and arms breaking the impact and partially embedding themselves in the dung. Momentarily he struggled to free himself, then rolled over. Hinsheid was in midair, the pitchfork in his hands aimed at Eggart's chest. The manure gripped Eggart like mush. Only his quickness saved him. He slithered aside just enough so that the prongs missed his body. One of the tips pierced his left foot, half buried in the dung. Eggart did not realize that he had been spiked until Hinsheid, up to his knees in the pile, tried to pull the pitchfork out of the manure. Eggart's foot and leg were jerked up. As the pain shot through him, he screamed. Instinctively, he pulled the trigger on the Smith and Wesson he still held in his right hand. As if in slow motion, Eggart saw the bullet, which hit Hinsheid in the upper right arm, emerge from Hinsheid's shoulder with an eruption of flesh and bone. In the same instant, the pitchfork spun loose from Eggart's foot. Eggart pulled the trigger of the gun again, but the hammer, fouled by dung, did not even click.

Hinsheid locked his legs around Eggart's body. His left arm curved around Eggart's neck. Eggart's fingers gouged at Hinsheid's eyes. Rolling over and over, they grappled in the manure. The dung slid up Eggart's pants and down his shirt; it lay hot and damp against his body. It was entangled in his hair. It filled his mouth and his nostrils. His sight misted. From beyond the veil of his tear-filled eyes came a blurred motion. A thud jarred Hinsheid with such force that Eggart felt the shock transmitted to his own body. Hinsheid went limp. Barentz had slugged him across the back of the head with the stock of the Mauser.

A few seconds later Eggart stumbled from the manure pile to the side of the barn. He threw up. Again and again his stomach heaved. Around the corner of the barn was a barrel of rainwater. Eggart plunged his head into it. He washed out his eyes, his ears and his mouth, and rubbed his hands and arms clean as best he could.

Ten minutes passed before he returned to the manure pile. Hinsheid was lying face down in the dung. Barentz, wielding the pitchfork, was digging a trench in the middle of the pile.

"What's that for?" Eggart snapped.

Barentz lifted another forkful, then turned toward Eggart. "Hinsheid," he replied matter-of-factly.

"He's dead?"

"If he is not dead, he is beyond the living," Barentz replied and returned to his task.

"What do you mean by that?"

Barentz, motioning toward Hinsheid, shrugged. Eggart knelt beside him. Hinsheid's skull was cracked open and smeared with dung. Sticky, half-coagulated blood covered the back of his head and his neck. Eggart lifted Hinsheid's head. His face was masked with manure. From his partly open mouth a glob of dung protruded like a half-eaten apple. If the blow had not killed Hinsheid, he had asphyxiated.

Eggart's stomach heaved again. He dropped Hinsheid's head. Searching through Hinsheid's pockets, he found nothing.

Eggart looked up. Barentz, sweating, had completed his task. What Barentz was suggesting was obviously the sensible course. Every minute they remained by the barn increased the chance of their being discovered, and a subsequent investigation might well destroy Barentz's usefulness. Still, Eggart hesitated.

"Let me tell you!" said Barentz, reading his mind. "When I was in the East, there was a Jew assigned to clean the cesspool. One day a Scharführer pulled out his pistol and told the Jew to jump in. He had to jump. He was up to his neck. The Scharführer fired a shot a few inches from his head and yelled, '*Kopf unter!*' When the Jew didn't react quickly enough, the Scharführer pulled the trigger again. The Jew had to dunk his head into the shit. When he came up, the Scharführer shot closer and again yelled, '*Kopf unter!*' Every time the Jew came up to take a breath, the Scharführer fired closer, until he shot his ear off. Finally, the Scharführer tired of the game. The Jew went under; he came up; and the Scharführer shot him between the eyes."

Eggart felt as if he had been hit in the groin. In a cold sweat, he helped Barentz lift Hinsheid, and they dropped him face-down into the trench. Barentz piled the manure high on top of him. He would decompose quickly. When the farmer eventually uncovered him, all that remained would be a skeleton.

Dragging the burned-out motorcycle back to the car, Eggart and Barentz hauled it up to the rear bumper and tied it on; after dark, Eggart pushed it into a ravine. A drive of a few miles took them to a brook near Laimnau. Eggart stripped, stood in the cold water, and scrubbed himself for twenty minutes. The pitchfork's prong had entered his foot just behind the division between his small and fourth toe. The wound throbbed, and he sprinkled it with sulfa powder.

Barentz, too, was filthy. After Barentz washed, Eggart gave him a set of khakis from the several changes of clothes that he carried in the car. As Barentz stood there, looking Chaplinesque in pants several sizes too large for him, he and Eggart burst into laughter. But the tension and horror of the past few hours were too strong—their laughter died almost as soon as it had begun.

Darkness was settling. The French corporal must have reported to Captain Rettemond by now and peaked the curiosity of the Security Agency. Eggart's foot was burning, but he decided he had better go back to Ravensburg. Since he did not want to involve Barentz with the French, Eggart left him behind. In the morning, Barentz's own clothes, which he had washed, would dry, and he could pedal back to Stuttgart.

When Eggart arrived at the French Security Agency headquarters, he pretended to Captain Rettemond that the German who had been spying on them in Meersburg had escaped. Eggart would have liked nothing better than to return to the house in Meersburg by himself to examine the find, but that, in French territory, was impossible. His foot was swelling dangerously; nevertheless, when Rettemond inquired about his limp, Eggart shrugged it off as a sprain he had suffered in the pursuit.

At first light Eggart accompanied a detachment of French Security Agency personnel to Meersburg. The job of hauling out the crates of guns and ammunition through the small opening lasted well into the afternoon. The French issued exclamations of astonishment and appreciation as the boxes were broken open: there were enough weapons to outfit two thousand men. Eggart was praised warmly.

He, however, more and more feeling the after-effects of his battle with Hinsheid, had little interest in the arms. He was hoping to come across some clue to the strategy of Ibex, to the identity of the Werwolf, or the nature of the special weapon—the *sonder Waffen*—referred to by Barentz. When the chamber was about two-thirds empty, Eggart found a strongbox filled with documents that he managed to spirit to the Mercedes without attracting the attention of the French.

As Eggart headed the Mercedes for the American zone, his throbbing foot was swollen so badly he could not remove his shoe. His throat was parched and aching, and his eyes were bloodshot and teary. He still felt nauseated. He gripped the steering wheel as if it were the bar of a roller coaster. As the car leaped up and down the hills and swerved around the sharp curves of the roads in the Black Forest, Eggart seemed more to be hanging on than driving. Branches reached out for him; spectral figures whooshed over the hood and vanished on the windshield as he ducked; a giant cuckoo mockingly swooped low and made him look over his shoulder; Hinsheid's skeleton rose steaming out of the dung.

Mile after mile, Eggart sped on. Turning the steering wheel almost by instinct, he tried to keep from plunging over the cliff of hallucination. It was a journey through a nightmare that did not end until he reached the Seventh Army hospital at Heidelberg some time past midnight.

XVI

During eight days in the hospital, Eggart absorbed enough penicillin, sulfa, and tetanus antitoxin to return a platoon to action. After limping out of the hospital, he drove across the river to the CIC offices, where he sat down to examine the contents of the strongbox.

What Eggart discovered totally perplexed him. The box contained the main patient register of *Funkstelle*, "radio installation," *Grafeneck* for 1939 and 1940. There was the copy of an order from the office of the Führer (Adolf Hitler) authorizing the referral of certain persons to the *Gemeinnützige Stiftung*, "public utility," for determination as to the applicabilty of "Special Action 14 f 13." At the bottom of the strongbox were scores of yellowed lists containing a total of nearly eleven thousand names. All had been referred to Funkstelle Grafeneck with the same notations: "special treatment" or "special healing procedure." The lists all carried the signature of Dr. Rudolf Riessel, an Obersturmbannführer in the SD who had been head of the public health service in Stuttgart. The only connection that Eggart could discern between Funkstelle Grafeneck, Meersburg, and Ibex was that on a list of personnel employed at the radio station in 1940 the name of a Rottenführer (corporal) Augustus Hinsheid appeared.

Eggart's initial reaction to the contents of the box was that they were a product of lunacy. As best as he could figure, Hitler had authorized a public utility to select thousands of ill people to be sent to a radio station for treatment. The involvement of the public health service in Stuttgart seemed to indicate that a communicable disease was being dealt with. But what kind of treatment could have been prescribed? Nothing, apparently, had been beyond the realm of eccentricity and queer thinking in the Third Reich. Still, this would take some unraveling.

None of Eggart's fellow agents in Heidelberg were able to provide any clarification. A couple of them suggested that Eggart drop the contents of the box into File 13— whatever the papers referred to, they didn't seem to have any connection with CIC's task of counterintelligence. Searching the maps in the office, Eggart was unable to discover a Grafeneck anywhere in the vicinity of Stuttgart. Driving to Ludwigsburg, he checked there and in Stuttgart to see if any of the people listed as being employed at Grafeneck in 1939 or 1940 might have been arrested.

When he showed the list to Peter Reimer, Reimer pursed his lips: "We might have one."

"Who?"

"Dietrich Togler," Reimer replied. "When the French were here, they made a hell of a wreck of the SD headquarters. But a few days ago some of the boys decided to give it another going over. They didn't find anything. But they came across an old guy squatting in the ruins of the building. When we questioned him he did a lot of babbling. Most of it didn't make much sense. But one thing was odd as hell."

"What's that?"

"He mentioned that he'd been at this Funkstelle Grafeneck. That didn't mean anything to us. He wouldn't tell us what he did there. Finally he mumbled that he'd always been cold, and that it was only by sleeping on top of the ovens that he'd kept from freezing. We didn't get anything else out of him. Now can you tell me what the hell a bunch of ovens was doing at a radio station?"

Dietrich Togler was fifty-five years old, gray-haired and balding, with watery blue eyes. His right hand trembled slightly. Eggart offered him a cigarette and had coffee brought in. In questioning most Germans, Eggart had learned he could achieve results by assuming the paternalistic mantle of a stern but benign authority. The lower- and middle-class Germans had been conditioned to accept authority no matter by whom it was wielded; it was transferred from the father to the schoolmaster, and from the schoolmaster to the officer. The fact that Eggart represented the authority of a different army was almost irrelevant.

As Eggart shuffled through a large stack of papers on his desk, Togler eyed them apprehensively. Although most were random forms and reports, Togler assumed they contained information vital to his future.

"Now, Togler," Eggart said. "I have many documents. *Funkstelle* Grafeneck—that was merely a cover for an SS operation, was it not?"

"*Ich weiss nicht*," Togler mumbled.

"Here is a list of people who worked at Grafeneck. Your name is on it. So are the names of many SS men. Why were they there?"

"*Ich weiss nicht.*"

"Were you not a member of the SS, too?"

"*Ich weiss nicht*," Togler intoned once more. He used the response "I don't know" for protection, like a turtle crawling into its shell.

"Togler!" Eggart shouted, crashing his fist down on the desk. Startled, Togler jumped halfway up, and a look of fear crossed his face.

"I am tired of your refusal to cooperate!" Eggart continued. "We are preparing to put criminals like you on trial. If you cannot prove your innocence, we shall hang you! We shall *hang* you, Togler, if you refuse to answer my questions!"

Togler stammered, and a bit of froth appeared on his lips.

"Here is a list of patients, Togler!" Eggart spoke roughly as he turned one of the yellowed sheets of paper so that Togler could see it. "What happened to the patients at Grafeneck?"

"*Ich weiss*—" Togler started to say, then stopped. "The patients?" he repeated.

"The patients, Togler!" Eggart snapped.

Togler expelled the air from his chest, and his head wandered from side to side on his shoulders. "The patients came to Schloss Grafeneck to be treated. The brothers cared for them."

"*Castle* Grafeneck? Not *Funkstelle* Grafeneck?"

"Yes."

"What brothers?"

"The Samaritan Brothers."

"What were the Samaritan Brothers doing there?" Eggart asked, astonished.

"The castle was theirs. They ran the Heil und Pflege Anstalt, 'Welfare and Nursing Institute.'"

Eggart was taken aback. The tale was producing one unexpected turn after another. "What were the patients there for?"

"For the head." Togler made a motion with his finger to his forehead and mimicked the behavior of a feeble-minded person. "Idiots!"

"It was an institution for the mentally retarded?"

Togler did not answer, as if he were absorbing the question. Then, after a moment, he nodded.

"What was your job?"

"I was an orderly. A medical orderly."

"You helped the doctors?"

"Yes."

"You lived at Schloss Grafeneck?"

Togler nodded.

"You slept on top of the ovens?"

Togler hesitated. "That was later."

"What do you mean—later?"

"Later, when the war came."

"Aren't the tops of ovens a strange place to sleep, Togler? Why did you sleep there?"

"I was cold. It was the only warm place."

"Were the ovens always burning?"

"They were burning. Yes."

"What was burned in them?"

"*Ich weiss nicht.*" Togler fell back to his standard response.

"You slept on the ovens, but you don't know what was being burned in them?" Eggart's eyes impaled Togler.

Togler shrank back. His lips formed a silent "*Ich weiss nicht.*"

"You're lying, Togler!" Eggart pounded at him. "There was no Samaritan Brotherhood. There was no Heil und Pflege Anstalt. There was only the SS doing their dirty work. And you were part of them!"

Togler half rose in his chair. *"Ich weiss nicht! Ich weiss nicht!"* His words were like a stifled scream. His eyelids fluttered, his eyeballs rolled upward, he sucked air in like a panting dog.

"You will tell me!" Eggart strode around the desk and put his hands on Togler's shoulders. Togler, trembling, tried to disappear into the chair. Eggart's fingers dug into his bones. Togler's mouth opened wide. A shudder ran through him.

"I will tell," he whispered.

With that, Togler became like a huge boil that has suddenly been lanced. In October 1939, he said, an SS officer had appeared at the Heil und Pflege Anstalt and announced the SS was taking over. The brothers had been ordered to leave, but most of the lay workers had been told they could stay on. Togler, who had no place to go, had been grateful. New doctors had come in. A short time later, Togler had noticed that there was a great increase in drugs being administered to patients—at first mostly orally, then by injection. One of the doctors explained that these were recently developed drugs designed to improve the mental condition of the retarded. Then, however, the inmates had started dying. Togler was in charge of the burials. First he buried three or four people a week, then a dozen, then twenty. He had spent all his time supervising the digging of graves, which was carried out by the inmates, many of whom died a week later themselves.

Togler, though he had not understood what was going on, had been terribly disturbed. One Sunday, without telling anyone, he had slipped away to seek other employment. A few days after he registered at the employment office in Stuttgart, he had been picked up by the Gestapo.

At the Hotel Silber, the Gestapo headquarters, he had been told he faced charges of dereliction of duty and disloyalty to the Reich. Unless he returned to Grafeneck, the best he could hope for would be confinement in a concentration camp. Of course, he had returned. Signs had been erected that said EPIDEMIC—DANGER. Watch posts surrounded the entire complex. He had been warned that Grafeneck had been designated a secret installation, and been made to swear that he would divulge nothing of what he learned during his duties.

Within a few weeks, all of the 200 feebleminded housed at Grafeneck had been killed. Then buses, each carrying 25 or 30 new "patients," had started arriving. A crematorium had been constructed to dispose of the bodies.

Most of the new arrivals had been children. After Togler undressed them, a doctor had given them a one-minute physical examination. Then they had been given an injection.

"What was the result?" "Eggart asked.

"In the morning I collected them."

"They were dead?"

"Yes."

"You carried them to the crematorium?"

"Sometimes. Sometimes I took them to the cellar."

"To the cellar? What for?"

"For examination."

"You mean for autopsies? Dissection?"

"Yes." A shudder ran up and down Togler's body.

"What's the matter?"

"Then I had to pick them up again."

"They were not a pleasant sight?"

"They had been cut open. Many of them no longer had heads."

"Their heads had been cut off?"

"Yes."

"What was done with them?"

"They were filled with some kind of fluid."

"To preserve them? They were embalmed?"

"Yes."

"Then what happened to them?"

"They were packed in crates and shipped off."

"How?"

"On the railroad."

"Where to?"

"I don't know. Once or twice I saw an address. It was Berlin, I think."

"Was this done for the purpose of experimentation?"

"I don't know."

"But there were experiments going on?"

"I think so. The doctors were all the time trying new things. They wanted to see what would kill people the quickest. More and more people kept arriving, and they could not kill them quick enough. That was the problem, they said. Often the bodies we loaded on the wagon to take to the oven were still warm. Sometimes they moved. But we put them in and burned them anyway. The doctors said it couldn't be helped. So they were all the time trying new ways to kill people faster and surer."

"These new ways—the experiments—did they succeed? Was some new, deadly way of killing people developed?"

"I don't know, but I think so. Yes. There were bodies in the cellar."

"What do you mean?"

"Bodies that were not to be burned. It was said they were being used to grow something—" Togler, who had only a sixth-grade education, groped for a word. "Germs."

"What happened to the bodies?"

"They were shipped off. The doctors became very excited and said it was too dangerous to keep them anymore."

"Because of the bacteria that were growing in them?"

"I think so."

Eggart felt sure that the special weapon referred to by Siegfried Niehbar was associated with the bacteriological experiments mentioned by Togler. Togler, however, had been only a flunky, and he knew little more. Tracking down Dr. Rudolph Riessel, the Württemberg public health director, was the next task.

Rudolf Riessel, Eggart discovered, had been arrested two months before while driving his car. Not only were Germans banned from driving cars without special permits, but possession of a car was presumptive evidence of association with the Nazis. When Eggart went to the Kornwestheim Internment Camp, however, he was told that Riessel had been released two weeks before. Riessel had explained that he owned the car because he was a doctor, a cursory check had indicated he was telling the truth, and there had been no other information on which to hold him.

Riessel lived along the *zahnradbahn*—the cog street railway that ascended the steep Stuttgart hills. In the company of two other agents, Eggart went to Riessel's house and took him back to Ludwigsburg for questioning.

Eggart did not tell Riessel why he had been picked up again, and Riessel, who supposed the new interrogation was related to his previous arrest, pretended outrage. Eggart let him talk as much as he wanted. Riessel, florid-faced, complained that his money and watch had been stolen during his detention by American MP's. For days he had been held with more than a hundred other people in an outdoor compound, and finally they had been moved into barracks previously occupied by foreign laborers. The wooden bunks were covered only with straw. The straw was dirty, and the barracks were alive with bugs.

"As a doctor, I must protest these abominable conditions," Riessel declared.

"I can understand your concern," Eggart answered, "but foreign workers lived in the same barracks for years."

"Yes. But after all, they were Russians."

Eggart stared at Riessel.

Riessel cleared his throat, then continued. "They were used to such things. They had never known anything else."

"Nor, I suppose, had the French, the Danish, the Czechs, and the Greeks. Men, women, and children— stacked in slave worker camps like cordwood."

"But what had I to do with that?"

"I was under the impression, Dr. Riessel, that you were head of the public health service in Stuttgart."

"Yes. However, I—" Riessel stopped. The aggressiveness slowly slid from his eyes as if a cloud were blotting out the sun. His pupils retreated and shifted anxiously from side to side.

"I am fully aware of your position, and your activities, Obersturmbannführer Riessel," Eggart punched in.

Riessel started to answer, but his voice failed. A glint of

perspiration appeared on his forehead. Finally he rasped, "I am a medical man. I have done nothing wrong."

"Then you have no cause for concern, *Herr Doktor*," said Eggart, pulling out the transportation lists for Grafeneck. "As public health officer for Württemberg, you were familiar with Schloss Grafeneck?"

"Schloss Grafeneck?" Riessel pretended bewilderment.

"The Heil and Pflege Anstalt operated by the Samaritan Brotherhood. Surely the name is not unfamiliar to you."

"*Ach Ja!* Schloss Grafeneck." Riessel gave a small nervous laugh. "It was not an important installation."

"Not until it turned into *Funkstelle* Grafeneck. Correct?" Eggart placed the lists in front of Riessel. "Would you tell me about the people you committed to the *Funkstelle, Herr Doktor?*"

"I?" Riessel shook his head. "I had nothing to do with that."

"But the lists were all signed by you. Ten thousand six hundred and fifty-four people were consigned to Grafeneck in a period of fourteen months."

Riessel blanched. "It is true, I signed them. But it means nothing."

"It is your signature. But it means nothing?"

"No. Most of these people did not originate in Württemberg. They were merely in transit. But someone had to take responsibility. I was forced to do so."

"Grafeneck, Dr. Riessel, is in Württemberg. That was their destination. How could they be merely in transit?"

Riessel swallowed, unable to find a reply.

"They were in transit, were they not," Eggart continued, "because from Grafeneck they disappeared. They were *vernichtend!*" Literally translated, *vernichten* meant "to turn into nothingness," and Eggart found the word peculiarly appropriate.

"It was an order that came directly from the Führer," Riessel attempted to justify himself. "I was merely a functionary. Württemberg Police Commissioner Christian Wirth controlled the operation."

"What, precisely, was that operation?" Eggart demanded to know.

"The aim was to relieve the Reich of people who could not possibly have a useful existence. The mentally afflicted. Freaks. People of that sort."

"Including children?"

"Well, yes. If they were *Ausschusskinder*."

"Garbage children?" Eggart looked incredulously at Riessel.

"One could call them 'committee children' just as well," Riessel cleared his throat. "In any case, their lives were of no practical account."

"So for that reason they were exterminated?"

"They were not needlessly left to suffer but were granted mercy deaths."

"But in the process, experiments were conducted on bacteriological weapons. Right?" Eggart asked.

"That was entirely out of my jurisdiction!" Riessel exclaimed.

"Whether it was in your jurisdiction or not, that's what happened, isn't it?"

"Well, there were some people, including the Führer, who thought that as long as they were going to die anyhow, their deaths might as well be used for scientific investigation. That is how the experiments came about."

"All right, Riessel. I know about the toxin that was developed. I want you to describe it for me."

"I know nothing about a toxin."

"You keep saying that you know nothing, but it's obvious that you're lying. What it comes down to, Riessel, is how much you're willing to tell me in order to save your skin."

"I would tell you—willingly!" Riessel pleaded. "It was a secret project in which I was not directly involved. So how could I have information!"

"As head of the public health service in Württemberg, weren't you concerned about the danger of a new strain of highly toxic bacteria?"

"Of course. I am a responsible man." He thought the matter over, hesitated, then continued. "It was, in fact, due to my protests that the experiments with the toxin were, after a few months, abandoned."

"It turns out, then, that you had more influence than you thought," Eggart observed sarcastically.

"Well, naturally, I did what I could, but it was not primarily due to my objections," Riessel retreated.

"What *was* it due to?"

"Well—" Riessel stopped, started again, then back-tracked as if trying to find his way through a maze. "All I know is rumors, things that I heard second and third hand."

"What kind of rumors?"

"That something better had come along. Or that, perhaps, they were combining the germs with a nerve gas, a combination that multiplied the effectiveness of both components."

"What sort of nerve gas?"

Riessel shrugged. "Honestly, captain, I have no idea. The gas was not something that would have been tested at Grafeneck. You must be aware that Grafeneck ceased operating in less than a year and a half."

Eggart knew Riessel's last statement was true. Though Eggart continued the interrogation for several hours more, he failed to elicit anything else of importance from Riessel.

Still, what Eggart had discovered was alarming. The SS had been deeply involved in the development of germ warfare. The link between the Meersburg cache and Grafeneck indicated that the Werwolves probably had access to the bacteriological weapon that had been tested. In that case, they would have the ability to wreak havoc.

When Barentz next reported to Eggart, he related that Niehbar had been furious when he learned the French had discovered the Meersburg depot. Niehbar guessed that the French had learned Hinsheid's true identity and had been able to torture the information about Meersburg from him. The only good thing about developments, Niehbar had commented, was that the *sonder Woffen*, "special weapon," had not been stored there.

The Americans, Niehbar declared, were mama's boys—only interested in going home. For a few months they had had the advantage, but now things were changing. American security and background investigations were so slipshod that former SD and SS personnel were having little difficulty gaining employment in the American military government and police. In Württemberg Nazis held positions as high as district president, and in Bavaria they were scarcely barred from any position, no matter how high. Pipelines were being laid into the internment camps so that Ibex knew within a few days the names of people who were arrested, whether they had been interrogated, and what they told the CIC. At the Ludwigsburg internment camp, a female member of Ibex worked at the X-ray station. A pastor, who had been an SS Obersturmführer during the war, made the rounds of the camps on the pretext of holding Sunday services and hearing confessions. Once a week Niehbar received reports from everyone.

Any Ibex member interrogated by the occupation authorities and providing information would be automatically *ausgesiedelt*, Niehbar told Barentz. Niehbar had already directed Friedrich Mussgay, the former Gestapo head in Stuttgart, to liquidate three members who had been arrested and then released. Mussgay intended to make the killings look like the work of one of the bands of displaced persons roaming the woods. But everyone within the Ibex organization would know the truth. "We will tolerate no *Spitzeln!*" Niehbar had shouted.

"How can Mussgay operate so freely when he is on the automatic arrest list of the Americans and the French?" Eggart asked Barentz.

"He has very good false papers. He uses the name Mosemaier."

"Moses Maier?" Eggart exclaimed, astonished.

"No. Mosemaier. That is the family name. The Christian name is Sigmund."

Eggart had the uneasy feeling that while he was setting traps in the Ibex network, Niehbar was burrowing around and behind him. Because of the limited number of CIC agents and the paucity of catalogued intelligence, the SS men were experiencing no great difficulty in reestablishing subversively the organization that formerly had operated openly. Despite temporary setbacks, Niehbar was becoming more and more confident.

Eggart needed to know more about Niehbar's background, and he was not satisfied with the information Otto Willach had provided so far. Two days after talking to Barentz, Eggart met Willach and lit into him. "How come you didn't tell me that Niehbar ordered the execution of three of his own people?"

"That is Mussgay's department," Willach replied, as if by doing so he was answering Eggart's question and absolving himself of responsibility.

"Your job is to tell me everything you know and everything that goes on. I warned you, the moment you start holding out on me, I'll ship you off to France."

"Please, Captain Eggart. I have tried to tell you everything of importance. You would not want me to relay every small detail—"

"You're damn right I would! I want to know what Niehbar eats, where he eats it, the hours he sleeps, whether he snores, if he talks in his sleep, and what he says; whether he brushes his teeth at night, what kind of toothpaste he uses, the hour and minute he takes a shit, and—if I order it—you will bring me a specimen of that shit! Do you understand?"

Willach blanched. "Let us be reasonable, captain."

"I am being reasonable, Herr Standartenführer. I want to know right now everything you have not told me. And why you have not told me."

Willach licked his lips. "Sturmbannführer Niehbar's hours of going to the lavatory are irregular. Sometimes he complains of constipation. He brushes his teeth with soap—you see, even in the days of the Third Reich there was a shortage of toothpaste . . ." Willach trailed off and looked at Eggart expectantly, almost hopefully.

"All right," Eggart suppressed a smile. "You will make it your business to find out precisely what Niehbar did during the last six years. I want especially to know who his associates were."

XVII

Eggart spent the next few weeks systematizing the information regularly reported by Barentz and Otto Willach. He built a master file of names and stuck pins into a map of southern Germany to mark the location of Ibex cells. It was the kind of unexciting, unglamorous routine of which nine-tenths of intelligence work is composed.

Reimer, in the meantime, was working with the American Military Government to establish a new civilian administration purged of Nazis, and simultaneously attempting to cope with his unofficial guardianship of Liselotte. Looking at her, Eggart had difficulty recalling the childlike, desperate girl who had arrived on the bus a few weeks before. She was filling out like the creation of a sculptor who day by day adds clay to the skeletal framework. The toughness and maturity that the horrors of the concentration camps had developed in her masked the fact that she was only sixteen, but she no longer conveyed the haunting quality that had originally struck Eggart. Only her eyes remained like a violet veil behind which unfathomable images constantly shifted.

Though the practical knowledge Liselotte had acquired made her an adult several times over, her formal education had ended when she was ten, and she needed instruction in such basics as arithmetic, writing, and spelling. She learned rapidly but since she had little patience for lessons that she considered juvenile, she sometimes slammed a book down and stalked out. Reimer was fortunate in finding a young woman, Theresa Hadler, who took an interest in her and tutored her several hours each week.

Theresa was a twenty-eight-year-old brunette of medium height whose green eyes lingered defensively behind her glasses. She was intelligent and interesting, though not particularly pretty. A full bosom emerged from a straight waistline. Since she spoke excellent French and fair English, she had worked as an interpreter for the French, and the American Military Government had absorbed her into its administration as a matter of course.

Her father was a well-known professor of history who had taught at the Stuttgart Gymnasium, the classical high school, and had never been a member of the Nazi party. Since the books used in the schools for the past twelve years had been vehicles for Nazi propaganda, the Allies faced a mammoth task of expunging, rewriting, and reprinting. As a cover for his CIC operation, Eggart was passing himself off as an educational consultant. When Eggart met Theresa, he suggested to her that her father might be well suited to participate in the rewriting of the history texts.

Theresa replied that she would be glad to introduce Eggart to her father, but that he had not been well since the great air raids on the city the previous year. On some days he was perfectly lucid, but on others his mind seemed to wander through the volumes of history. "There is no telling how he will be at any given time," she explained.

Theresa lived with her parents in a well-kept three-story house in one of the older sections of Stuttgart. Storm shutters flanked the windows and the figure of an angel guarded the door. Although the house was at the edge of the area of devastation and the outside walls were pockmarked with hits from small bomb fragments and antiaircraft shrapnel, the structure was essentially undamaged.

Professor Hadler was a slight man, three or four inches shorter than his daughter. His voice was so subdued that Eggart could recognize only a few of the words he spoke in his nasalized Württemberg accent. He was muttering, as if giving directions to himself as he led the way through a hall into the "salon," a dark room with brocaded drapes curving around the windows. Several bookcases were filled with leather-bound books. Porcelain figures dignified the shelves of a glass case. Around the walls were displays of old coins, helmets, sabers, and medals. The room was like a small museum.

"My daughter has told me of your mission," the professor said suddenly and clearly after they were seated. Eggart, surprised at the change in his voice, thought he would continue, but the professor was staring as if he saw something behind Eggart.

Eggart was acutely uncomfortable. After a minute of stark silence, Eggart said, "I had hoped that since your experience in education goes back to the time of Kaiser Wilhelm, you could provide some insights for the revision of textbooks we are working on."

"Revisions are not necessary. Revisionists are the problem." The professor spoke clearly again. "Bismarck devised for Germany the most advanced social and economic system in the world, and revisionists—ever since the destruction—they have sought—geopolitically fragmented . . ." He lapsed into unintelligibility.

Eggart, with Theresa's help, attempted to continue the conversation for a few minutes; however, the only comprehensible statement Professor Hadler made was, "In the Thirty Years' War they killed people, but not cities. Now they kill the cities, too."

"I am sorry," Theresa told Eggart. "Some days he is better than others. Today is one of his bad days."

They left her father and went into a sitting room. Frau Hadler, a pleasant, healthy-looking woman who was slightly taller than her husband, brought in a tray with a silver coffeepot, demitasse cups, and cake. Theresa explained that her father had been traumatized when nearly twelve hundred planes had dropped tens of thousands of high-explosive and incendiary bombs on the center of the city on the nights of July 25 and 26, 1944. After the all clear had sounded on the second night, he had gone out, intending to record for history his observations. From dozens of broken gas and water mains jets of flame and water had soared upward and cascaded down in brilliant iridescence. The city's historic buildings had melted like carved wax candles. Professor Hadler had found four of his students welded to the charred barrel of an antiaircraft gun. For two days he had wandered through the streets as ashes had rained down upon the city. When he returned home, he had begun to write. But his mind, unable to absorb all he had seen, had become like a kaleidoscope of history in which the pieces constantly rearranged themselves.

"You see," Theresa said, "my father is a German through and through; a German of the old school who believes in order and logic. The universe, he always thought, is rational, and the rationality of the universe manifests itself in the existence of nations and the lives of people. If order is destroyed, a chain reaction results and chaos sets in. The individual pieces are forced from their places and lose their functions. The mechanism runs wild. My father has been more and more bewildered by developments, and as a result of the bombings he finally lost his place in the scheme of things."

"In other words," Eggart suggested, "your father was overcome by the irrationality of the Nazi era."

"Yes, to an extent, but that would be an oversimplification," Theresa continued as her mother, taking no part in the conversation, refilled Eggart's cup. "Hitler was not the source of the irrationality; that started with the end of the war in 1918 and the signing of the Versailles Peace Treaty the next year. Hitler was the consequence. Hitler was inevitable, my father said, once the victorious powers at Versailles subverted the traditional order and imposed an illogical peace."

"That almost makes it sound as if your father believes that history is preordained."

"Not necessarily preordained," Theresa qualified. "But he does think that history is the product of circumstances."

"In what way?"

"Like a chemical reaction. It is possible to obtain different compounds by mixing sodium and chloride, but it is not possible for the product to be sugar. In the same way, the course of history is restricted by the elements that are compounded."

"Are you saying that your father thinks Germans had no—or very little—free choice in what happened?"

"There was a choice, of course. But it was limited. The French, British, and American policies after the First World War could only lead to economic disaster for Germany. That was one of the elements in the historical compound, and with the ingredients that were mixed together, the result was bound to be either Communist dictatorship or National Socialist dictatorship. Most Germans would have preferred neither, but we did not have a choice, because we had no control over the elements we had to work with."

It was a viewpoint of history that disturbed Eggart because, if it were true, individual accountability was much less a factor than he had always believed. "Should not a person be held responsible for his actions if he knew they were morally wrong?" he asked Theresa.

"We Germans have always been perfectionists and idealists." She smiled slightly. "We like to think that everything is precise, like mathematics. Even our language is that way, so unlike French, where everyone can read in his own nuances. But the world is not perfect, idealistic, or precise."

"That didn't answer my question."

"Perhaps not," she continued, "but it is relevant. Because the Americans are now saying that the Germans should have acted as if the world were perfect and precise. And that was not the world in which we lived."

"But everyone was—and is—faced with the same problems."

"Exactly!" There was almost a note of triumph in her voice. "Let us consider just one example."

"Yes?" He was puzzled.

"Thousands of people were killed in the bombings. Indiscriminately. Supporters of Hitler, opponents of Hitler, men, women, old people, children, infants. This bombing was entirely contrary to the Geneva convention and the rules of warfare—"

"But it was the Germans who initiated the bombing of civilians," Eggart interpolated.

"That may be so. But it has never been recognized that one murder justifies another. When you start falling back on causation to explain an action, you become imprecise and imperfect."

He tried to speak again, but she went on. "An airplane is shot down. Two or three airmen survive and are brought through streets where people are still digging for the broken bodies of their children. In their grief and anger, the people attack and kill the airmen. Now the Americans want to try for murder the guards who were escorting the airmen."

"The airmen had the right to be treated as prisoners of war."

"As soldiers, yes. But as killers of civilians, they were murderers."

"The killing of civilians was an unfortunate by-product of the bombing of industrial targets."

"The killing of civilians was an unfortunate by-product of the resistance of Warsaw and Rotterdam," she said, deliberately provoking him. When he started to protest, she shut him off. "Who is to say what the motives were? Who can separate the precise truth from the imprecise rationalization? Were the airmen to demand a detailed accounting of every mission and refuse to fly if it was not to their satisfaction? You know that a soldier cannot make moral judgments for himself—if he did, the whole conduct of the war would break down. Perhaps that would be all to the good, but it is not how nations look at the matter. If the guards are guilty of allowing the civilians to kill the captured airmen, then the airmen are just as guilty of killing the civilians, the commanders of the airmen are guilty of ordering the bombings, Churchill is guilty of making the strategic decision, Hitler was guilty of provoking Churchill, the German people are culpable for allowing Hitler to attain power, and Clemenceau and the other Allied leaders and bankers were responsible for establishing the climate in which Hitler could develop and flourish."

"The chain is endless and almost impossible to disentangle—is that what you're saying?"

"You're an apt pupil." She smiled. "As you will readily

see, everyone's choice was limited by the circumstances in which he operated. The guards had to choose between protecting the airmen who had just killed their countrymen—and in protecting them do more injury to their neighbors—or of abandoning the prisoners and letting the people vent their anger. The airmen had to choose between carrying out the mission, and thereby killing civilians, or disobeying orders. In both cases the choices were imperfect and imprecise, and, given the circumstances under which they were made, obvious."

"You're making a persuasive case that right is wrong, and wrong is right," Eggart said wryly.

"Often it is difficult to differentiate between right and wrong. One may be forced to choose between two wrongs. What can seem right at one time or in one circumstance will be looked on as wrong in another."

"And you think we aren't making allowances for that in our approach to Germany." He halted momentarily. "Why then are you working with the military government?"

"Because we are all subjects of circumstance, are we not?" She cocked her eyebrows quizzically. "I want to help. I don't want to see the errors of the past repeated."

"Do you think there's danger that they will be repeated?"

"If the Allied policy is to be one of revenge—and not of reform—yes. If there is to be no consideration of the circumstances under which people acted—yes. If judgments are to be based on abstract and unrealistic precision and perfection—yes. If Germans are to be punished for the same acts committed by the Allies only because the Allies are the victors and the Germans the losers—yes."

"Everything cannot be pinned on circumstance," Eggart objected. "The killing of children, the murder of Jews, the abominations of the Gestapo—"

"No. Of course not. But the conditions established by the occupation will determine whether the German people will be turned in new directions or forced into resistance once more. For example, take the trial that is to be held in Nuremberg—"

"What about Nuremberg?" Eggart asked sharply.

"Everyone knows what the outcome will be. The Russians were just as bad as the worst of the Germans. But the Germans are on trial, and the Russians will be the judges."

"Göring, Kaltenbrunner, and the rest—they ought to be allowed to go scot-free? There should be no accounting at all?"

"No. They should be lined up and shot. People would understand that. The Reich leadership was responsible for millions of deaths—Germans, Jews, French—what does it matter? But it is casuistry to try generals for war or diplomats for signing treaties that were broken. These things have been going on for thousands of years. It was not a crime yesterday, and it will not be a crime tomorrow. If you make it a crime today, the German people will look on it as hypocrisy. They will have the feeling reinforced that they are being singled out for persecution. Subjecting the German people to the humiliation of a show trial will serve no good end. Far better the Reich leadership be done away with quickly and summarily, and the book on Hitler closed."

XVIII

That was unquestionably the passionate desire of the Germans—to forget! If they were forced to remember, if the past were going to be held against them, a renewal of resistance would follow—that was the implication Theresa Hadler left with Eggart. Although official American policy was to purge Germany of Nazi influence and chastise each Nazi according to his culpability, in practice the military government administration bordered on the chaotic.

Niehbar, Barentz reported, was initiating a widespread forgery operation. He had obtained paper, ink, a mimeograph machine, official stamps, and an American typewriter. Two printers were cooperating. Ibex would furnish people with new papers, and would then be able to control them, for Niehbar would be in a position to denounce them at any time. "The Americans think they are calling the tune, but Germany has always led the world in composers," Niehbar rhapsodized to Barentz.

As the chill of autumn stripped the leaves from the trees, the dreariness of defeat and devastation became pervasive. The shops were empty. There was little food. German money was all but worthless. The shortage of coal was so severe that scavengers pecked like birds through the railroad yards. People lived in caves that had been burrowed into the ruins; and smoke rising from invisible pipes leading through the debris gave the wreckage the appearance of an active volcano. *Stümmelmen* followed GI's around to snap up discarded butts, the tobacco from which they worked into new cigarettes—the most valuable medium of exchange. Children stole the garbage from American mess halls, ate some of it, and sold the rest. The fondest wish of many families was to have a daughter become the fräulein of a GI. The soldiers were enjoying the life of conquerors. Huge PXs sold goods at bargain prices. Liquor cost $.50 to $1.50 a quart, and men went on duty with canteens full of scotch and cognac. Germany's poshest resorts were turned into rest and recreation compounds where all-inclusive vacations cost $1.50 a day.

While a mood of sullen noncooperation spread over the land, sparks of resistance flashed here and there. Former Hitler Youth, singing Nazi songs, goose-stepped through the streets. Germans working for the occupation were threatened with death. "Filth belongs to filth" was smeared on the homes of girls who went out with GI's. German POWs threatened a general strike.

"The situation is explosive," Colonel Campbell said at a meeting of CIC agents. Contingency plans had been drawn up to deal with a major outbreak. Reprisals would be taken against the civilian population: houses would be razed, hostages held, buildings from which the underground was suspected to be operating would be bombed.

"For Christ's sake!" Eggart swore half under his breath. The Nuremberg trial was to begin November 20, less than three weeks off, but the United States was preparing to employ some of the same methods used by the Nazi leadership. For Eggart, Theresa Hadler's warning took on added meaning.

"To nip anything in the bud," Colonel Campbell continued, "we'll launch Operation Doublecheck on November 18." It was expected that seventy to eighty thousand people would be picked up for interrogation.

The agents responded with a collective groan. It would be like a cattle roundup. Any intelligent culling out of suspects would be impossible.

One German who had succeeded in adapting himself completely to the occupation was Otto Willach. Like a chameleon, he took on the coloration of his environment, and Captain Josephs, in the Food Administration, spoke highly of him.

"We've got a hell of a problem," Josephs told Eggart. "Stuff is pouring into the black market. We've got no control at all. Otto Bergauer's given us a few tips. He seems to know what's going on, so I put him in the anti—black market unit."

Eggart thought that, in view of Willach's record in France, appointing him as an investigator of black marketing was like making a bear an inspector in a honey factory. For obvious reasons, Willach had not mentioned his new assignment to Eggart.

Eggart, conversely, could not tell Josephs the truth without blowing Willach's cover. "Don't you think you're taking a risk in trusting Bergauer?" Eggart asked Josephs. "What's to stop him from getting involved in the black market?"

"Hell! What's to stop anybody? Half the army's into it!" Josephs retorted.

Farmers were supposed to produce enough food to provide each displaced person with 2,000 calories daily and each German with 1,550, but the farmers had little incentive to ship their produce to market. They did not want to accept German marks, for there were no industrial goods to buy. They wanted cigarettes, chocolates, canned food, soap, army blankets and uniforms, gasoline, liquor, sulfa and penicillin—the things the American army could provide. GI's bought cigarettes for five cents a pack and sold them for the equivalent of ten dollars. Supply officers and sergeants showed up at depots with requisition slips for units long after those units had been deployed to the United States. Truck convoys left a supply depot with a hundred tons of supplies and arrived at their destination with fifty. Boxcars were shunted to sidings and never seen again. The only people to whom marks were of value were GI's, for they could exchange the marks for dollars. Many men sent two thousand dollars a month back to the United States, and a few netted ten times that amount. Hundreds of thousands of dollars changed hands in poker and crap games.

To replace the military policemen who were being shipped home, the military government hired displaced persons, mostly Poles, as guards. Before long, twenty-six

thousand men were in the "Polish guard" companies. The
DPs lived under the most wretched conditions—in the
barracks of former labor camps, in lean-tos, in shacks made
of wooden crates with tarpaulins for roofs. The Germans
did not provide the food they were supposed to, and the
DPs were hungry and had no money. Many of the guards
cooperated with fellow DPs in hijacking goods. The camps
flourished as black market interchanges.

"We can't trust the Krauts with guns," said Captain
Josephs, "so we've got to have the DPs. But we can't trust
the DPs with the goods. So we need a Kraut to keep an eye
on the DPs."

"Like the wolf, the rabbit, and the cabbage. Who's
going to watch whom?"

"That's right," Josephs agreed. He related that Willach
had been responsible for uncovering a large black market
meat ring. Willach had also provided information that had
enabled military police to catch several Polish guards and
their German confederates as they unloaded boxcars at a
siding. "A really valuable man," Josephs concluded.

Otto Willach laughed when Eggart brought up his
successes. "Captain Eggart," he said, "when one is standing
on an anthill, no matter in which direction one goes, one
will step on ants. The quartermasters, they are all being
sent back to America. They are supposed to leave behind
huge depots of canned goods, petrol, blankets, clothing,
meat, flour, beans, chocolate, cigarettes, but they say it
does not make sense to them. Why should they go home
and leave behind all these things that nobody will ever
use?"

"You sound as if your sympathies were with the black
marketeers. But Captain Josephs says you're doing a good
job exposing them."

"Ach, Captain Eggart! If I were not an honest man! I
will tell you. The DPs and the Germans, they are the ones
who are being caught and punished. But the corrupters—
they are the Americans! It is the Americans who are making
the big money. Shall I tell you who the American racketeers
are?"

"That's not my concern. Why don't you tell Captain Josephs?"

"But I would have to start with Captain Josephs' secretary. She is running a wholesale black market in petrol coupons, transportation passes, and official forms. There is a smuggling ring in art objects. The chief collector is a colonel. Do you want to arrest a colonel, captain?"

No, Eggart thought. Sergeants don't arrest colonels.

Willach interpreted his silence. "An army is an army— yes, Captain Eggart. Or, as we say in German, orders are orders, and schnapps is schnapps."

Willach related that Niehbar was pressing him to take a trip to Bavaria. Ostensibly, it was because Niehbar's wife was ill. Niehbar was so insistent that Willach had agreed to reorganize his schedule, and had made up a story to tell Captain Josephs. "Of course, I would not go without your permission," Willach observed.

Eggart had no objection. Whatever business Niehbar had in Bavaria would probably be of interest.

When Eggart saw Willach on the following Tuesday, Willach's report exceeded Eggart's expectations.

Willach had first driven Niehbar to Landshut, where Niehbar had visited his wife. Afterward, Niehbar had revealed the real reason for the trip: it was a meeting in Bad Tölz, the site of a former SS officers training school, south of Munich. Niehbar again had Willach park near the Isar River bridge, as he had previously.

As before, Niehbar disappeared up a side street. Heeding Eggart's instructions, Willach followed him. Unexpectedly, Niehbar headed through the wooded section on the north of the town and began climbing a hill. After a hike of about a quarter mile, Niehbar reached a twin-steepled church that overlooked Bad Tölz. From a distance Willach watched him go in.

After waiting a few minutes, Willach went after him, and cautiously entered the church. From just inside the door, Willach could see Niehbar sitting in a pew near the back with another man. Bent over prayer books, they were speaking in low tones, as if reciting verses. Willach was, of course, unable to hear them, but the conversation seemed to be punctuated at times by animation, even anger.

"Could you identify the man who was with Niehbar?" Eggart asked.

"No. I saw only the back of his head and shoulders."

"How was he dressed?"

"Nondescriptly. He had on a gray sweater."

Willach had watched briefly, then slipped outside again and waited in the nearby woods until Niehbar emerged. The other man had not come out with Niehbar, and Willach had been forced to hurry back to the car. He barely had had time to catch his breath before Niehbar returned.

"Did Niehbar give any indication who he'd met?" Eggart questioned.

"Yes and no. He was in a bad humor. He complained about *Schreibtischleute*, 'desk people,' who keep saying that all the facts have not been taken into consideration and weighed before making decisions. If there had been fewer decisions and more action, Niehbar groused, Germany would not have lost the war. All the *Schreibtischleute* keep thinking about is why something should not be done and the possible consequences if it is done."

"The thrust of the conversation was that he was anxious for more action, but was being held back?" Eggart asked.

"Yes."

"So that whomever he was meeting was his superior in Ibex?"

"I believe that would be correct."

"Could it have been the Werwolf himself?"

"Quite possibly."

"Did he say anything to make you think so?"

"Not directly, but I gained that impression because he started reminiscing about his experiences in Russia. He told me he had attended the *Einsatzkommando* training school at Pretsch in May 1941 and afterward had commanded an extermination squad in the Ukraine. He bragged of sitting on the edge of a ditch and shooting people until his weapon had become so hot it disintegrated. He said he had once killed thirty-five people while smoking one cigarette. But there had been too many people, and the weapons the *Einsatzkommando* had been given were not adequate. It

was at that time he had learned about a bacteriological
sonder Waffen that could have wiped out the entire
population. But there was always a Brigadeführer Schreib-
tischmann (brigadier general bureaucrat) in Berlin too
squeamish to use it."

"So it's your impression that he was equating the
Brigadier general bureaucrat with the Werwolf?"

"In general, yes. He complained that the Brigadeführer was always talking about the right opportunity and
the right time. But, he said, men of action make their own
opportunities—Hitler had proved that—and though the
Brigadeführer might be reluctant to employ the *sonder
Waffen*, he himself was not."

"If he had it?"

"If he had it. Correct."

"What about the Brigadeführer? Did Niehbar indicate
whether he was in possession of the weapon?"

"Niehbar seemed to think he has access to it. If he is
not in possession of it, he probably knows where to get it."

"You're positive you didn't know the man Niehbar was
with?" Eggart asked intensely.

"No."

"From your own knowledge and experience in the SD,
couldn't you make a guess?"

"I could give you perhaps thirty or forty names. He
might be one of them. He might not. Would that really be
of help to you?"

It probably would, Eggart thought. The more information one has, the greater the possibility some of it will turn
out to be useful. That Niehbar's superior was a man of
caution was something to be thankful for. If the Grafeneck
weapon came into Niehbar's hands, the result could be
catastrophic.

After leaving Willach, Eggart drove to the American
Military Government documentation center in Frankfurt.
Hundreds of cases of Nazi party records had been discovered. The file of the SS Race and Settlement Office
turned up by the Ninth Army in the Harz Mountains
contained detailed background and genealogy information

on a half million SS men who had applied for permission to marry. The SS officer file discovered by the Third Army in the Tyrol held the names of fifty thousand individuals, from Untersturmführer to Reichsführer SS. But the condition of the records was chaotic, and the documentation unit was hampered by the same attrition of personnel as the other American forces. Some records were in Munich, some in Frankfurt, some in Nuremberg; others were in transit to Berlin.

None of the documentation people had any idea who the Brigadeführer described by Eggart might be. Eggart himself looked at a stack of files on Brigadeführers and quickly realized that they would help him little. The search was made more difficult because the Brigadeführer evidently had not been a troop commander, but a faceless bureaucrat. Was it possible for such a man to be the leader of the Werwolves? Why not? It had been talent for organization that had propelled the unprepossessing Himmler to the top, and the Reichsführer SS had made his mark in the early 1920s by administering the arms caches secreted from the Inter-Allied Control Commission all over Bavaria.

When Eggart returned to Stuttgart, Albrecht Willach, who was working for the American Military Government War Damage Assessment team, told him that two French investigators had been to the apartment to inquire about Otto. Otto, Albrecht said, stayed away from the Alexanderstrasse apartment, but kept his family supplied with food and money. Glancing inquisitively at Eggart, Albrecht wondered aloud whether the French or the Americans would ever catch up with Otto. Otto had always been an opportunist, Albrecht philosophized. He had done well in the Nazi system without ever believing in National Socialism, and in the end he might do just as well under the Americans.

"That is his great advantage," Albrecht said. "He is not troubled by morals or philosophy."

XIX

Eggart was beginning to ask himself whether the atrophy of morality was not an occupational hazard for an intelligence agent. One of the two French investigators who had questioned the Willach family was, not surprisingly, Madeleine, and she managed to track Eggart down in his office in Ludwigsburg. Her trip was strictly official, she said, but in the line of duty a woman sometimes had to make great sacrifices. Since Eggart was a very difficult subject to question, she would have to seduce him to extract information. She expected it would take at least three or four days.

Usually he put out of his mind the conflict created by his love for Madeleine and his exploitation of Otto Willach. He tried to think of it as an unfortunate adjunct of their jobs and the different goals they were pursuing. Still, he was being dishonest; he couldn't kid himself about that. It was an imperfection in their relationship, and in a way it made him love her all the more.

He took her to his room in Heidelberg. She made him close his eyes while she changed. When he opened them, she was standing there in a silky black nightgown she had obtained from Paris. The scent of Chanel floated across the room. Pretending to be a femme fatale, she moved about seductively, well out of his reach. He watched her for a half minute, then started laughing.

She stopped, then pouted. "I thought you would be a raging lion, roaring for your mate. But you are a hyena!"

"I'm sorry." He smiled. "But you do look like a twelve

year old trying very hard to act grown up in your mother's things."

"You're insufferable!" she cried. "What do you want me to do?" As if to answer her own question, she tried pushing out her chest like a feminine ninety-seven-pound weakling enrolled in a Charles Atlas course.

He doubled up in laughter. An object whizzed by his ear. He grabbed her. "I've always had passion for little girls. What could be better than a little French girl I picked up in the German woods?"

She nuzzled against him in bed, the tip of her tongue tickling his neck damply like the nose of a puppy. Stroking her hair, he drank in her perfume—their loving was languid and rhythmic, almost as if suspended in a trance. Later he opened a bottle of wine and cranked up the phonograph that had been left behind by the German family. He put on a waltz, and they danced in the dark room, she in her black nightgown and he in a pair of army shorts. He could not help thinkng of the family who had lived there and hailed Hitler. It was a scene they would never have envisioned.

She always seemed to find security with him. As cool and efficient as she was on the surface, sometimes at night she had fits of shivering. Once, when he had gotten out of bed and she had awakened alone in the darkness, she had screamed. Perhaps because Eggart's room was still filled with the ambience of the German family, it made her uneasy. After she went to sleep she thrashed about, muttering and shouting. Once she let out a terrible scream and caught Eggart on the chin with her fist. He still had a red spot there in the morning. When, puzzled, she asked him about it, he replied, "I ran into a French nightmare."

But she could recall nothing.

In the afternoon they hiked up the Heiligenberg, which rose to 1,400 feet behind the town. It was a cold, damp day, and in her heavy, loose sweater she did, in truth, look like a child tramping through the woods. He felt overwhelmingly protective and loving.

A few hundred feet below the summit the Nazis had carved a massive stone amphitheater where, by the flame of torches, thousands upon thousands had attended neopagan festivals to recall the spirits of the Druids and incarnate the Norse gods of Wagnerian opera. At the very top, like a counterpoint, were the ruins of a ninth-century basilica that had served as protection against pagan Saxons.

Perching themselves on one of the walls, Eggart and Madeleine looked down at the intricate skeleton of hall-ways, cells, courtyards, and towers. The tall trees on all sides made a lake of the gray sky. In the dark shadow of the ruins an occasional squirrel or other small animal stirred a stone, vivifying the spirits of those who had occupied the place centuries before.

Madeleine was pensive and almost downhearted. When he asked her what was the matter, her response made it clear that she did not want to talk. Finally, kicking her leg toward the amphitheater, she said: "The good is in ruins. The evil flourishes."

"The amphitheater isn't exactly flourishing," Eggart noted.

"No. But it wouldn't take much to make it go again. I have that feeling everywhere in Germany." She flicked a pebble down. "You know, what bothers me even more than the guilty ones is the complicity."

"What do you mean?"

"Otto Willach, for example. I have the feeling that he's always just around the corner, yet every time I look beyond, he's gone. The family are decent people. But I'm sure they're protecting him."

"Why?"

"They're evasive. Even Albrecht! You'd think that after spending five years in Dachau, he'd tell the truth."

"Still, they *are* brothers."

"All the Germans are brothers. No matter what they've done, the Germans will protect each other—because they're Germans! If it weren't for that, I would have caught Willach by now!"

"How can you be so sure?"

"I know. Willach always was, in American words, an 'operator.' He is keeping his family well supplied. My intuition tells me he is involved in the black market."

"What if you don't catch him?"

"I will. I won't leave Germany until I do."

"Good!" He tried to be jocular. "I hope it takes you a long time."

"Damn you!" she cried angrily, completely unresponsive. "This isn't something you can joke with me about."

"I'm sorry. I didn't mean—"

"Will you help me?" she asked suddenly.

His heart jumped. "How?"

"If he is mixed up in the black market, he must have some connection with the Americans. You could check with the Food Administration and see if you can find a lead."

"What about you? Haven't you done that already?"

She grimaced. "I'm French. And I'm a woman. A lot of your American friends don't take me seriously. They try to date me, but they don't give me information. Of course," she continued after a moment, "I might try to spread the word about my talent for seduction."

"That *would* lead to trouble." Now it was he who didn't appreciate the joke.

"Then you will help me?"

He felt like a live turkey turning on a spit. Theresa Hadler's thesis kept coming back to him: everyone's actions are restricted by the framework of circumstance. Morality and ethics are imperfect and imprecise.

As much as he loved Madeleine, this was one thing about which he couldn't be honest with her. He picked his words carefully. "I'll do whatever is in my power," he said.

But he was not happy with himself.

XX

Nor, as Eggart discovered once more, could he be satsified with Willach's veracity. Barentz revealed that during Willach's trip to Bavaria with Niehbar, Willach had stopped in at the Swiss consulate in Munich. This was a detail Willach had forgot to mention to Eggart.

"Why did he do that?" Eggart asked Barentz.

"It was connected with his relationship to the baroness, Nadja von Leithorst."

"Who?"

"The Baroness von Leithorst. She is Swiss. But she is the widow of a director of the Robert Bosch Works, and Willach has moved in with her."

Eggart gave a low whistle. "Nice going," he muttered under his breath. The Bosch Works was a huge enterprise, second in size only to Mercedes Benz in Stuttgart. "Where does the baroness live?" he asked.

"She owns a château near Gaildorf. But she has a Swiss passport, and she also spends a lot of time in Zurich. During the war she worked in Amt III G of the SD."

"Is she a member of Ibex?"

"Not as far as I know."

"What is Niehbar's reaction to Willach's liaison with her?"

"At first he didn't like it at all," Barentz answered. "He worried that Willach's loyalty to Ibex might wane, but I think Willach convinced him that through her he can establish a Swiss connection for Ibex. That's why he went to the consulate—to try to get some papers for himself. If you were to meet Willach in person, you would see that he has a facility—you could put him in a room with Satan at one end and the Angel Gabriel on the other, and he could talk to both simultaneously and make each believe he is on his side."

That was Willach! He would always look out for Otto, and anything else was incidental. At least Eggart didn't have any illusions about him.

Otto, however, was not the only person who had acquired feminine companionship. Barentz confessed that he, too, had obtained a girlfriend. The woman was Gertrude Schlenck, a telephone operator for the American Military Government in Stuttgart. Formerly with Amt VI of the SD, which controlled the operation of agents in foreign territory, she was now one of Niehbar's informants. She had told Barentz that she had been raped by Moroccan troops. When she had come to the French Security Agency headquarters in Ravensburg to complain, she had been placed in custody as a material witness. She had been well treated and given plenty of food and wine, she confided to Barentz, but every day one or more officers had gathered "evidence" from her. This had gone on for weeks, she said, until she had become pregnant, and the French had released her so she could come to Stuttgart for an abortion. While she had been held at Ravensburg she had been able to gather much information, and had even compiled a picture file of French Security Agency personnel, which she had smuggled out via other German girls. She had gone back to Ravensburg since, she recounted, and the French had greeted her warmly. They liked her because she had been a "good sport!"

"I am concerned about Fräulein Schlenck," Barentz said.

"I am, too," Eggart retorted.

"No. I speak in a different sense," Barentz continued. "On the one hand, she drinks too much and she talks too much. On the other, she asks *me* questions: What am I doing? Whom do I see? What is Siegfried Niehbar doing? Once she said she thought there was something suspicious about Niehbar's operation. She mentioned especially that he spent a great deal of time with this man who worked for the American Food Administration, and that I should watch him and not trust him. Then again she blurted out that we should go to the American Military Government and tell everything. That way we would be safe."

"Do you think she's testing you?" Eggart asked.

"I don't know. One time it will seem as if she is pumping me for information, the next as if she is trying to warn me, and the third as if she is upset and frightened. She believes Germany's loss of the war is the vengence of the Norse gods on the people for having adopted Christianity. Before we go to bed she has a ritual of dedicating her body to Frigga."

"Why Frigga?" Eggart asked.

"Frigga is the goddess of marriage, who also has knowledge of the world's fate," Barentz answered. "Gertrude is very worried about what will happen. She keeps nagging me to visit a fortune-teller with her."

"That's not so strange, is it?" Eggart responded. Germans were speaking of a "miracle" to deliver them from their plight. Fortune-tellers were doing a booming business as people flocked to hear their futures unveiled.

"Perhaps not," Barentz agreed, "but I have a feeling that something is going on."

Four days later, on Monday, December 3, Eggart met Barentz again. They rendezvoused at the Adlereiche, the "eagle's nest" on the north side of the Pfaffensee, a lake southwest of Stuttgart. While waiting in the brisk but sunny weather, Eggart found a few crumbs in his pockets and fed the squirrels.

When Barentz arrived, he was out of breath; it had been a long and hilly bike ride from Stuttgart. He and Eggart started walking along the footpath in the park. Barentz used the bike to support himself and ease the pressure on his bad leg.

He told Eggart that he had accompanied Gertrude to the fortune-teller. A sign outside a side door of the apartment house on Olga Strasse advertised fortune-telling in the evenings. They had entered. A jangling bell announced their arrival. There was an anteroom, but no receptionist. When Gertrude knocked on an inner door, a voice invited them in. Drapes covered the windows; the room was dark. A lighted, iridescent globe placed on a table provided the only illumination. Behind it sat a woman with a kerchief around her head and large, ruby-studded gold rings in her ears. Shimmering in the rubies, the light from the globe was like a thousand tiny hypnotic crystals, but it illuminated only the bottom half of her face. Gertrude was even more nervous than usual and spoke deferentially to her. The fortune-teller asked Barentz to sit down at the table.

She began, in the usual way, by describing Barentz's family and early life. She told him that his father was dead and that his mother had worked hard to raise him. She was obviously perceptive. There were some things that Barentz wondered how she could know, but her recounting was not so out of the ordinary as to be psychic. Then, however, she began to relate how Barentz had joined the Waffen SS, how he had been assigned to the Wiking Division, and how he had fought on the Russian front. She knew when and where he had been wounded. She told how he had been recuperating at Hohenlychen when an SS Gruppenführer had singled him out for a heroic mission. She then went on to predict that he would distinguish himself on this mission and play a vital role in the resurgence of Germany. She spoke all the time as if she were deriving the information from the crystal, in which some kind of mechanism made the colors change continuously. The iridescent globe and the gold and ruby earrings created a hypnotic mood, and Barentz went into a kind of trance as she carried him back over his life.

"It was some time before I realized," Barentz said to Eggart, "that she could not possibly have known many of these things unless she had access to firsthand information. Siegfried Niehbar does not know the details of my stay at Hohenlychen. But she does. She knows precisely the instructions I received, almost word for word. I could draw only one conclusion."

"You mean that she is in contact with someone who was at Hohenlychen?" Eggart asked.

"Yes. Someone who had been close to Gruppenführer Prützmann, someone intimately connected with the organization of the Werwolves. Someone who spoke to Prützmann about his meeting with me and knew the instructions he gave me."

"Then Gertrude Schlenck took you to her by design—not so that she could tell your fortune, but so that she could meet you and recount your past," Eggart deduced, excitement surging in him.

"I came to the same conclusion," Barentz agreed.

"If that's the case," Eggart conjectured, "your girl friend may have been her agent all along. Gertrude was thrown into your path deliberately so that she would establish a liaison with you and bring you under the fortune-teller's influence."

"I have been compromised," Barentz said, chagrined.

"Well," Eggart retorted, "you may have been screwed. But you haven't been compromised. At least, not yet. What's the point, though? You could hardly be more involved with Ibex than you already are."

"Maybe they want to impress me," Barentz ventured.

"Right." Eggart nodded. "To impress you and establish their legitimacy with you. That's why they chose this method—letting you know that they have greater access to the secrets of the SS and the Reich Central Security Office than Niehbar does." Eggart thought back to Niehbar's meeting in the church with the Brigadeführer and the Brigadeführer's fear that Niehbar would act precipitately. For the Brigadeführer, Barentz would make a valuable informant. "Unquestionably, there's something they want from you," Eggart conjectured. "Something that might require you to be disloyal to Niehbar. Then you'd be in the same position as your girl friend. No wonder she's neurotic!"

"But Gertrude provides Niehbar with information weekly," Barentz said.

"Yes. But why can't Gertrude also tell the people in Stuttgart what Niehbar is up to? For that matter, hasn't she been gathering information from you? Who has more personal contacts, who knows the message centers more intimately, who is more constantly on the go than you?"

"You are right," Barentz said. "She's a member of Ibex, so I didn't hesitate to speak to her about the organization."

"Now, however, that's no longer enough for the fortune-teller and her superiors," Eggart surmised. "Gertrude is eccentric and not reliable, so they want to get the information from you directly. Did the fortune-teller put out any feelers, make any advances to you?"

"No. But she did predict that I would return so I could learn more about my future."

"Exactly!" There was a note of elation in Eggart's voice. "Could you recognize the woman if you saw her on the street?"

"No. As I said, the light was very bad. I could not discern her eyes or any portion of her face above her cheeks. But I feel sure she is not anyone I have met before."

After leaving Barentz and driving back to Stuttgart, Eggart walked by the corner house on Olga Strasse, which was part of a block-long apartment complex. In the ground-floor window next to a side entrance was the sign advertising palmistry and fortune-telling daily from 6:00 to 10:00 P.M. The street dead-ended just beyond the house. From there, a long flight of stairs led down to Urban Strasse, the next parallel street. Eggart descended the steps and looked back. A retaining wall dropped straight down from the house to a small garden that was shaded by three large trees. Eggart would have liked to place the fortune-teller's quarters under permanent observation, but that was out of the question. There was no manpower available for such a stakeout.

Ten days passed before Eggart's next meeting with Barentz. Barentz had been summoned again by the fortune-teller. Again she had kept her face, obscured by greenish blue mascara, hidden in the shadows. She no longer attempted to dissemble her connection to the Werwolf organization, but related word for word, as far as Barentz could recall, the orders he had received from

Gruppenführer Prützmann. She described Prützmann and
the hospital at Hohenlychen. She wanted to leave no doubt
in Barentz's mind, she explained, that she was receiving
directions from the chief of the Werwolf organization. He
was a high-ranking officer who had been at Hohenlychen
with Himmler and Prützmann.

"Who is that officer?" Eggart asked.

"She did not say."

As Ibex's chief courier Barentz was a key man in the
obtaining and transmitting of information, the fortune-
teller emphasized. According to reports received by the
Werwolf, Barentz's performance was excellent. The Werwolf had decided, therefore, that he wanted regular, direct
reports from Barentz. These were to be transmitted
through the fortune-teller.

Barentz had pretended to be dense. He said he would
have to inform Siegfried Niehbar and obtain his permission.

"No," the fortune-teller had replied. He must not do
that. He was being promoted to the headquarters network
of the organization. Niehbar was not to know about
Barentz's special assignment.

Barentz protested. If he acceded to the fortune-teller's
request, he would be disloyal to Ibex. Why would the
Werwolf ask him to perform such a mission? And how could
he, Barentz, know that the orders did, in fact, come from
the Werwolf?"

The fortune-teller replied that only someone whose
authority descended directly from the late Gruppenführer
Prützmann would have known what she did about Barentz's
background and his meeting with Prützmann at Hohenlychen. That was why she had gone through the charade of
telling his fortune—to validate her own position.

Barentz had pretended to remain unconvinced. That
might all be true, he said, *if* she were not a fortune-teller.
But if, in fact, she *were* a fortune-teller, then she might
have obtained the information by occult means. In that
case, there was no proof at all that she represented the
Werwolf. He would instantly obey any order from the
Werwolf, but he must know who the Werwolf is. It seemed

very strange that the Werwolf would ask him to go outside regular channels.

The fortune-teller had become angry. She had declared that the Werwolf would not be pleased by Barentz's obstinacy.

Barentz had stood his ground. The most he would agree to for the time being was not to inform Niehbar of the meeting.

"I thought it was the safest position to take," Barentz told Eggart. "No matter whom the fortune-teller represents, I have demonstrated my discretion, caution, and loyalty. If the Werewolf really wants direct reports, surely he will be able to provide documentary proof. Perhaps he will even be willing to reveal himself."

"Beautiful!" Eggart exclaimed.

Neither Barentz nor Eggart had, of course, any doubt that the fortune-teller represented the Werwolf. The Werwolf was re-creating Himmler's chain of command. Himmler had placed deputies directly responsible to him in all of the key administrative centers. The fortune-teller was, in effect, the SS and Polizeiführer of the Werwolf in Stuttgart.

Eggart arranged with Barentz to be informed beforehand the next time Gertrude Schlenck summoned him to a meeting with the fortune-teller. Lying in the Frauenkopf woods in the southwestern part of the city were the remains of a British bomber. Barentz could reach the wreckage in less than an hour. He was to scratch the time and date of the meeting beneath the tail of the plane.

During the following week, Eggart checked the plane twice daily without finding a message. When he returned at noon on Thursday, December 20, he was surprised to discover Barentz himself there.

Barentz explained that he had had no opportunity to leave a mesage. He had met Gertrude at six o'clock the previous night. Gertrude had insisted that the fortune-teller must see him immediately, and that there could not be a moment's delay. After they had entered the apartment, the fortune-teller had ordered Gertrude to go back out into the anteroom, and Barentz had remained alone with the woman. A few minutes later, Barentz had been startled to hear a man's voice address him out of the gloom at the back of the room. He could barely make out the white impression of a face and a reflection of light indicating that the man was wearing glasses.

"Could you tell what he looked like?" Eggart asked, both excited and disappointed.

"Impossible."

"What happened?"

The man had handed several sheets of paper to the fortune-teller, who had passed them on to Barentz. Barentz immediately recognized them as the list he had been required to memorize at Hohenlychen. Another paper contained a letter written to Gruppenführer Prützmann by Barentz's company commander in the Wiking Division. Apparently, in response to an inquiry, the letter had praised Barentz and declared him to be completely reliable. There was no question of denying the authenticity of the documents, and Barentz had said he would do whatever he was asked.

"The man was the Werwolf?" Eggart asked.

"I would think so."

"Go on."

"He was anxious to know everthing about Otto Willach, and his relationship to Niehbar. He asked how Willach had become Niehbar's driver and how much I thought Niehbar trusted him. He wanted to know if Niehbar had full confidence in him, since he works for the American Food Administration. And he asked what I knew about Willach's work in regard to the black market."

"What did you tell him?"

"I related all I knew. I said that I myself had had suspicions about Willach, but that Niehbar had laughed and told me not to worry. I went into great detail about the trips they took together."

"What was the Werwolf's reaction?"

"He seemed satisfied."

"Go on."

"That was about all. Once I agreed to do what he asked, he was very pleased."

"Did he mention anything else? Did he say anything about where he was located, or where you could contact him?"

"No. I'm to make all my reports through the fortune-teller."

"Did he give any indication of what his plans were?"

"No. Except that I received the impression that he intends to take much more of an active part in running the organization than he has before. During the last few weeks, he said, there has been a great clarification regarding Germany's future, and I could be confident that I would be involved in developments that would focus the attention of the world."

Niehbar might have complained of the Werwolf's caution, but it appeared to Eggart that the Brigadier general bureaucrat—if, in fact, he was one and the same man—was not given to understatement. "Do you have any idea what he had in mind?" Eggart asked.

"No. That was the extent of the conversation."

The entire interrogation had lasted no more than twenty minutes. The fortune-teller had made Barentz wait for half an hour after the Werwolf had disappeared into the darkness before allowing him and Gertrude to leave. Eggart had a bitter taste at the thought of how close he might have been to capturing the Werwolf, if only Barentz had been able to get a message through. The fact that the Werwolf had risked coming to Stuttgart, as well as the whole thrust of his approach to Barentz, seemed to indicate that the resistance was entering a new phase.

XXI

Eggart's mind roamed over the developments of the past several months as he drove through the Black Forest toward Hinterzarten, a resort near Freiburg, where he had arranged to spend the Christmas holidays with Madeleine. A light rain was falling that, at higher elevations, was transformed into snow. On the deserted road, he was enveloped in a cocoon of dark silence more accentuated than disturbed by the metronomelike sweep of the windshield wipers and the throaty sound of the engine.

The case was like a jigsaw puzzle for which he first had to find the pieces before he could fit them together. Like most guerillas dispersed geographically, the Werwolves were not a homogenous band but had their factions and quarrels. A Nazi like Niehbar whose goal did not go beyond harassing the occupation forces was much simpler to deal with than an intellectual like the Brigadeführer who directed his activities toward some grand design. The existence of the *sonder Waffen* completely invalidated the CIC's premise that the major dangers to be forestalled were a mass uprising or coordinated sabotage. Such occurrences seemed unlikely. The Grafeneck weapon provided the Werwolves with a far more potent means of attack. A relatively small number of men could contaminate and therefore destroy a single important target, or should they wish they could create chaos among the occupation by scattershot attacks. The only thing Eggart found reassuring was that Barentz had demonstrated his ability to keep on top of events.

It was 4:00 A.M. when Eggart turned the car down the

road into the bowl shielding Hinterzarten. The village
served as his depot in the French zone, and he had rented a
large room on the ground floor of a chalet. When he
unlocked the door, the beam of his flashlight seemed frozen
in the chill air, and at first he did not see Madeleine. Then
he caught sight of her hair streaming over the pillow from
beneath the heavy quilt covering her head and her face.
Undressing virtually in a single motion, he slipped in
beside her and fell asleep.

They awoke with their arms wrapped about each other.
A lacework of frost had formed on the windows, so that the
light from the early-morning sun was golden but subdued.
Her eyes smiled when she saw him, and her face crinkled
into laughter. "My mother would be horrified," she said. "If
she went to sleep alone and found a man in her bed in the
morning, she would jump out screaming!"

"Not in this temperature!" Eggart said.

She laughed. "How much do you think two people
making love can raise the temperature of a room?"

"I don't know. But it's a worthwhile scientific experi-
ment."

He kissed her. She fluttered the lids of her eyes against
his.

"I didn't wake up last night when you came in," she
said, "but I dreamed you made love to me, so I must have
known you were here."

"Are you sure you only dreamed it?"

"I'm sure. But sometimes I ache so much to have you
make love to me I want to wrap myself around you like a
python and squeeze you. Is that shameful?"

"I think it's delightful."

She drew the sheet and the quilt over their heads.
"Now," she said, "we're all alone in a dark cave. Let's be
delightful."

"And shameful."

Neither wanted to get up and light the tiled stove.
Like children on a Sunday morning, they luxuriated in the
warm bed. Noon was approaching and the frosting had

disappeared from the windowpanes before hunger finally drove them out of bed. Smoke rose from the houses, which were clustered in the village and scattered amid the undulating fields beyond. Here and there a ski run cut a white channel through the dense fir trees on the gently sloping hills. Crisp snow covered the ground. Eggart had learned to ski in the California Sierra, but Madeleine was a neophyte. She could scarcely take three steps without toppling over. She folded up sideways, crossed her skis, tumbled head over heels, and tobogganed down a hill on her bottom. At last she became so frustrated that she took off her skis and threw snowballs at him. He countered by kicking snow in her face with his skis. She grabbed him and he lost his balance. They wrestled in the snow.

Before they had left the chalet, he had lighted a fire in the stove, and when they returned he built it up till it roared. They took off their damp clothes and sat naked on a bearskin. Eggart split some chestnuts and roasted them in the oven below the fire pit. Their bodies tingling from the heat, they drank kirsch and peppermint schnapps. She lay down flat on her stomach, and he gave her a massage. "Now," he said, "I should douse you with a bucket of ice water and flay you with a birch switch to really make your blood tingle."

She looked up at him. "You don't have to go to such extremes."

"No?"

"No, Guillaume. Come, lie down beside me."

It was an invitation that was irresistible.

They spent eight days like that. "What a *lune de miel* this would have been," she said, "if we were married!"

"If we were married," he answered, "we'd probably be fighting over which side of the bed each of us slept on."

"Never!"

"Never?"

"Never. We will always both sleep on the same side."

On Tuesday evening, New Year's Day, he drove her back to Ravensburg. He never had had such a hard time parting from anyone. They kissed long and longingly in the parked car. She dropped off into a light sleep with her head resting on his shoulder. Finally it was eleven o'clock. Picking her up gently, he deposited her on her feet in the doorway.

"Parting is not sweet sorrow," she said. "It is a cold bed."

It was a lonely drive back to Stuttgart. He supposed he ought to start practicing French. Laboriously he worked to put together a few of the words he had learned from her. *"Veux-tu—se marier—avec—moi?"* Once he had them, they repeated themselves over and over in his mind like a tune one cannot get out of one's head.

XXII

Not until January 8 did Eggart see Willach again. Willach reported that Niehbar's plan to seduce American soldiers with Ibex girls was paying dividends. One of the girls had gotten a corporal named Rucker drunk at the Esslingen Wirtschaft that was the SS hangout and had taken him to bed with her. He had fallen hard for her and would do anything she wanted. Niehbar reasoned that Rucker would soon be so involved he would be completely in Ibex's power. Ibex could use him to obtain American uniforms, equipment and documents.

"Is Niehbar, in fact, providing people with passable new papers?" Eggart asked.

"Very much so. The quality is not always too good, but that can be masked with grease spots, water stains, yellowing—the ravages of time. Also, he has had a stroke of luck. An Obersturmführer named Bock escaped from the Ochsenfurt POW camp in Bavaria, and he knew where Amt VI F had secreted some of their materials."

"The technical office of the external SD?" Eggart asked.

"Yes. Amt VI F had been counterfeiting foreign passports, identity cards, driver's licenses, and the like. The cache was made up of completed blank forms, as well as the instruments and materials to make documents of all kinds."

"Niehbar has already obtained the materials?"

"Yes. Bock brought them to him."

"Who has he provided documents for? Anyone of importance?"

"I know of no one above the rank of Hauptsturmführer." Willach thought for a moment. "He did hear from the secretary of Otto Ohlendorf. She had been arrested by the British, but was released."

"Gruppenführer Otto Ohlendorf?" Why did his secretary contact Niehbar?"

"Apparently he knows her quite well. He told me he served in Ohlendorf's *Einsatzgruppe* in the Ukraine. When I showed him the newspaper that said Ohlendorf was a prosecution witness at Nuremberg, I thought he would have apoplexy!"

"He was surprised?"

"Shocked! Ohlendorf was one of his heroes, and Niehbar considered him one of the staunchest of men. Niehbar declared that if Ohlendorf betrays Germany, then the Götterdämmerung has arrived. But he is trying to convince himself that it is a trick on Ohlendorf's part and that he will turn the table on the Allies."

Three days later, when Eggart met Barentz, Eggart learned that Niehbar's reaction to the developments at Nuremberg was not only matched but exceeded by the Werwolf's. Barentz was reporting to the fortune-teller weekly, and she told him that the Werwolf regarded the trial as a disgrace to Germany. The Nazi leaders presented such a dismal and abject appearance that the world was receiving the impression that the German nation had been ruled by fools. Robert Ley had hanged himself in his cell and left a testament in which, blaming Germany's defeat on anti-semitism, he had written, "The Jew should make a friend of Germany, and Germany a friend of the Jew." SS General Erich von dem Bach-Zelewsky, the chief of anti-partisan forces, testified that one of the purposes of the attack on the Soviet Union had been the extermination of thirty million Slavs. Dieter Wisliceny, one of Eichmann's deputies, admitted that more than five million Jews had been systematically killed.

The newsreels in the theaters and the loudspeaker trucks blaring broadcasts of the trial were destroying the remnants of the people's self-respect and national pride, the fortune-teller remarked to Barentz. She spoke bitingly of the American prosecutor, Robert Jackson, who just before

Christmas had vowed, "Thousands of others, if less conspicuous, are just as guilty of the crimes as the men in the dock, and will be brought to justice."

The fortune-teller promised that Jackson would never live to implement his threat. The Werwolf had ordered leaflets delivered to all SS adherents through the message centers. The flier was printed crudely, a crudeness that enhanced the sinister impact of its message:

BETRAYED

Loyal comrades of the Schutzstaffel! Once again our sons and brothers are betrayed. We who shed our blood unreservedly for the ideals of the Führer watch with nausea and horror the spectacle at Nuremberg, where those who purported to be our leaders perform like puppets on the strings of the conquerors. While the brave, hard youth of the SS met the enemy hand to hand and ground him into the dust, the deputies in whom the Führer put his trust wallowed in corruption. We now see clearly how those who had given their pledge to the Führer consorted with the enemy. Behind the back of the Führer, the chancellery was turned into a Schweinerei of luxury and treason. We promise you that the betrayal will not go unavenged. The land will be cleansed of the traitors. We will strike a blow that will bring the invaders and their stooges to their knees. Comrades of the SS, prepare yourselves! From the blood-drenched soil of Germany, the flower of our best and bravest will flourish and grow mightier than before!

UNSERE EHRE HEISST TREUE!

DEUTSCHLAND ERWACHE!

After reading the exhortation, Eggart pressed his lips together and stared at the paper. "*Unsere Ehre Heisst*

Treue" was, of course, the SS oath of loyalty. "*Deutschland Erwache!*"—Germany Awake!—had been the Nazi slogan of German resurgence during the 1920s. The pattern of resistance that had followed World War I was repeating itself. Then it had been the Freikorps; now it was the Werwolves.

"What does this mean?" Eggart, indicating the leaflet, asked Barentz. "Is there a plan for action?"

Barentz took a deep breath. "It is the Werwolf's belief that the trial must be brought to an end, no matter what the cost. He intends to deliver a gift to Nuremberg."

Barentz and Eggart were, of course, speaking German. "*Ein Gift für Nürnberg?*" Eggart, puzzled, iterated as he looked at Barentz. What kind of a present could the Werwolf have in mind?

"*Was für ein Gift—*" he started to ask, then halted abruptly, realizing that he had not translated the word *Gift* from German to English. *Gift*, in German, meant "poison."

"Do you mean," Eggart asked Barentz, "that the Werwolf intends to poison the International Military Tribunal?"

"That was my impression," Barentz responded.

"How?" Eggart asked. But even as he posed the question, the probable answer came to him. "Was anything said about the Grafeneck toxin?"

Barentz nodded. "By implication, yes. The fortune-teller remarked that, in the past, Germans had exercised too much restraint in employing the products of their ingenuity against their enemies. But it was clear now that the Allies did not appreciate the restraint and were, in fact, taking advantage of it. She said that Germany is engaged in a battle for survival, and measures, no matter how harsh, must be taken."

"Did she indicate how the poison was to be introduced into the Palace of Justice?"

"No. She did not talk at all about particulars or details. But I was ordered to alert a pharmacist named Hubert Prettkrag, who was associated with Wirth, that he should prepare himself to take an extended trip."

"Was Prettkrag in the SS?" Eggart asked.

"Yes, he was a Hauptsturmführer."

"Where does he live?"

"In Tübingen."

"Does Prettkrag know where Wirth can be found?" Eggart continued.

"I believe so, yes."

"Do you think you could obtain the information from him?"

"No," Barentz shook his head. "Herr Prettkrag is very supercilious. He is one of those German who would never confide in anyone he considers below his station in life."

"Does Prettkrag have a function in the Ibex network?"

"Yes," Barentz replied. "Prettkrag has developed a method for removing the SS blood mark, and Niehbar sends people to him for that purpose. Niehbar keeps saying he can give people new identities, but as long as they still have the blood mark they are like the Jews with the scar of circumcision."

"Is Niehbar in touch with Wirth through Prettkrag?"

"I am almost certain that he's not. Prettkrag belongs to the headquarters network, so he is under the direction of the fortune-teller and responsible to the Werwolf."

Eggart was shaken by Barentz's revelation. The Werwolf had not been exaggerating a few weeks ago when he had told Barentz to expect developments that would focus the attention of the world.

XXIII

Tübingen, where Prettkrag lived, was a university town south of Stuttgart. Rather than arrest Prettkrag and attempt to pry the information about Wirth out of him, Eggart decided to let Otto Willach try his hand with Prettkrag and instructed Willach accordingly.

"But how should I represent myself to Prettkrag," Willach protested, "and what if Niehbar finds out?"

"As a Standartenführer you should certainly carry weight with a Hauptsturmführer. I'm of the impression that you don't lack ingenuity. As for Niehbar, there's nothing he'd like better than to find Wirth. If he should discover what you're doing, simply tell him that you are trying to help him."

"You are placing a heavier and heavier burden on me," Willach sighed, before acquiescing to Eggart's demand.

After attending to Willach, Eggart immediately prepared a report for Colonel Campbell and delivered it personally. Campbell read it in silence, then puffed contemplatively on his pipe for several minutes. Finally, he asked, "What do you suggest?"

It was a question Eggart was unprepared for. He had expected Campbell to make the suggestions. "I'm not quite sure, sir." He hesitated. "There are a number of alternatives."

"What?"

"We could round up Niehbar and everyone we have a handle on. That would blow the organization open. But it's likely we wouldn't get the Werwolf. We couldn't even be sure it would crimp his plans for Nuremberg."

"Go on," said Campbell.

"Or we can wait to see if Willach can track down Wirth. If we get Wirth, we should be able to develop a lot better idea of the nature of the toxin. Failing that, we can continue the current M.O. and not act until we can arrest the Werwolf along with all the other people. In the meantime, we might try throwing monkey wrenches into Ibex here and there; and we'd better make damn sure of the security at Nuremberg."

"Just how would he go about poisoning our people?" Campbell asked. "The scheme sounds right out of Machiavelli."

"I don't think we ought to consider it in the traditional or limited sense of poisoning," Eggart replied. "We're dealing with a bacteriological weapon that could be employed in any number of ways."

"Do you think Barentz's report is credible? After all, he was merely repeating what he'd heard from someone else— and in the most general terms. There's no hard evidence."

"I've always found him completely reliable. He's not given to exaggeration. And circumstantially the pieces fit."

"All right." Campbell repacked his pipe. "I'll forward your report to Seventh Army and to CIC Frankfurt. You'd better stick around. I have a hunch someone will want to talk to you."

At 10:30 on Tuesday morning Eggart received a summons to the office of Major General Albert Brannigan at USFET in Frankfurt.

Eggart settled into the back of the army sedan. He knew very little about General Brannigan, although the general's name came up from time to time in conversations between intelligence agents. The drive to Frankfurt took less than an hour. The headquarters of the American forces in Europe was located in the former I. G. Farben building, a seven-story structure with ten thousand windows, nicknamed the Westchester Biltmore of Germany. Although surrounding blocks had been leveled by bombings, the

Farben building had suffered only minor damage. Rising above the ruins, it glinted in the sun and could be seen from miles away.

An elevator carried Eggart to the sixth floor. Brannigan's suite of offices was behind an unmarked door. Eggart was admitted to the general's office after only a momentary wait. Brannigan was seated, reading, behind a desk on which a multitude of papers was piled in neat stacks. Eggart came to attention and saluted.

"Agent Eggart! Be at ease!" Brannigan looked up. Despite a receding hairline, he had a youthful appearance. Eggart was struck by his eyes, which seemed to photograph Eggart from various angles and store the negatives for future reference. "Sit down," Brannigan gestured to a heavy leather chair. "I'll be with you in a moment."

Three minutes passed before Brannigan looked up. "I've just reread your report. Let me amplify. I have now read the entire file of your reports. You've done a hell of a job!"

"Thank you, sir," Eggart said.

"It's 12:30," Brannigan glanced at his watch. "Why don't we talk about it over lunch." Brannigan rose and Eggart followed him down to the basement of the building where they entered a door designated Generals Only. Eggart found himself in an intimate room. The tables were covered with white linen, decorated with flowers, and set with gleaming silverware. Four tables were occupied. Brannigan spoke briefly to two other generals. It occurred to Eggart that if Niehbar or the Werwolf were aware of this room they might wipe out a good portion of the American brass in Europe with one well-placed bomb.

After Brannigan and Eggart were seated at a table in a corner, Brannigan asked Eggart about his background. He smiled when Eggart related how he had become an agent in the CIC.

"I'll have to see about getting Lieutenant O'Neal as our permanent recruiter," Brannigan said.

Eggart glowed.

"From our point of view," Brannigan continued, "your Ibex friends couldn't pick a worse target. We had to push the Russians damn hard to get them to agree to hold the trial in Nuremberg, instead of Berlin, where they wanted it, so any hint that there's trouble brewing would set them off on a propaganda hayride. And, of course, the occurrence of an actual incident is unthinkable!"

The general halted as a waiter brought a château bottled red Bordeaux and poured it into the sparkling glasses. "We're caught between the Werwolf and the Russians," he continued. "If anything did happen, you and I might as well pack our bags for Leavenworth. On the other hand, to go around shouting 'poison!' would be almost as bad."

Brannigan took a sip of the wine, then urged Eggart to follow his example. "Good wine can't make a bad situation better," he said, "but it can help you look at it more positively."

"I hope so," said Eggart, not entirely convinced.

"Do you have any clues as to whether the Ibex organization has infiltrated the Palace of Justice?" Brannigan asked.

"No, sir. The concept of the attack on Nuremberg only developed in the last couple of weeks."

"What we shall have to do," Brannigan said, staring into his wine glass, "is to make damn sure we've got a secure operation in Nuremberg and at the same time not tip anyone off to the fact that we've got any special concern. That's *my* problem."

Brannigan lapsed into silence for several minutes. To Eggart it was like receiving the first half of a crucial telegram and then having the wire break down.

"Yours isn't quite that easy," the general finally went on. "There are men who would, in my place, say 'Thank you, you've brought us this far, but it's now become too important a matter to leave in your hands. We need a more experienced manager.' But I've seen too many operations fucked up by meddling with the man who's become intimate with the people and the nuances and has the feel. I'm going to let you continue."

"Thank you, sir."

"Don't thank me. I'm putting a load on you that I don't

know I'd want to carry myself. For all practical purposes, you'll be reporting directly to me. I'll be getting a copy of your reports the same day as Colonel Campbell. I have got to know every move Ibex is planning—no ifs, buts, or apologies later!"

"I'll try, sir. But I'm limited by whatever information I get from Barentz and Willach."

"Damn it, Eggart! You won't *try*. You'll do it! You have my total support. Whatever you need, ask for it, and if I can get it for you, you'll have it! But if you screw up the operation, there'll be no hole for either one of us to crawl into. I'm placing my confidence in you. God help you if it turns out I've *mis*placed it!"

Eggart winced, though he didn't let his expression show it. The prudent thing to do would be to tell the general he should, in fact, get someone more experienced to take over. But Eggart's ego wouldn't stand for that kind of cop-out. Besides, since failure was unthinkable, one might as well dwell on success and glory.

"I like that!" Brannigan said.

"What?" Eggart was startled.

"You've got enough sense to wonder whether you should turn me down, but too much guts for your senses. That's an excellent combination. There's one more thing that played a part in my decision."

"Yes, sir?"

"Your opinion that we should go for the whole bag. I wish I were your age, Eggart. There aren't many men in intelligence who have the opportunity you're getting!"

XXIV

Eggart felt like a Japanese pilot just honored by being chosen for a kamikaze mission. It was crucial that Willach find out about Wirth, but for two days Eggart was unable to contact Willach. But when Willach finally returned to his room in Waiblingen, he related triumphantly how he had won the confidence of Prettkrag, and concluded, "Wirth is being sheltered in the Styrian Alps."

"Where?" asked Eggart.

"Somewhere near Leonstein, on the Steyr River."

Looking at a map, Eggart found Leonstein about forty miles southeast of Mauthausen. "Would it be possible to surprise Wirth?" he asked.

Willach shook his head in the negative. "The people in the area are fanatic Nazis," he said. "They have never lost their faith in Hitler. Any stranger would immediately arouse suspicion, and they would warn Wirth to flee. The only way to reach Wirth is to leave a message on a roadside crucifix that has been erected at a place where a child was killed by a swarm of bees. One of the local people checks the place every few days, and the message is taken by a hunter or a herdsman to Wirth's hideout in the mountains."

"Then someone he can trust will have to make contact with him and lure him out of hiding," Eggart observed.

Willach agreed with him.

"I'm going to arrange with Captain Josephs for you to go into the American zone in Austria. You'll drive to Leonstein."

"I?" Willach looked startled. "But how shall I explain to Wirth why I am there?"

"You'll tell him that Niehbar wants to see him about the Grafeneck weapon."

"Captain Eggart!" Willach backed off. "Now you are asking too much! You are placing me in an extremely dangerous position."

"Not nearly as dangerous as the one you'd be in with the French. You *will* do it, Willach!"

"But what if Niehbar finds out? Prettkrag trusts me, but he is asking a lot of questions. If Niehbar were told that I had discovered from Prettkrag where Wirth was and had gone off to Austria without informing him—" Willach shuddered. "*Gott im Himmel!*"

Willach was pale. His skin had a clammy texture to it. For once, Eggart was certain that he was not acting.

Willach's objection was valid. If Wirth were captured and Niehbar discovered that Willach had been in any way involved, it would mean, at best, the end of Willach's usefulness. The mere suspicion by Niehbar of any unusual behavior on Willach's part would put a serious crimp in Willach's operation. And any hint that Ibex had been infiltrated would make Eggart's task inestimably more difficult. It was a dilemma that would take considerable thought and ingenuity to resolve.

"All right," Eggart said. "Something will have to be done to protect you. I'll work on it. In the meantime, you're to let Captain Josephs know where you are every day. That's a command!"

"I don't like it," said Willach, shaking his head. "An intelligence operation that oversteps its bounds is folly."

Eggart slept hardly at all that night, and the next day was as tense as a coiled jack-in-the-box. Every alternative he considered had its drawbacks. Sitting in the CIC office in Ludwigsburg, he jotted down possible courses of action and noted the pros and cons of each. Periodically, he leaned back in his chair, closed his eyes, and prayed for a sudden flash of wisdom. Afternoon passed into evening. The time was nearing 10:00 P.M. Down the hall someone was playing old Nazi records.

Massed voices, the thud of marching feet—it was the

"Horst Wessel Lied," the Nazi hymn. Across the black screen of his closed eyelids Eggart could see the rolling ranks of brown-shirted men, torches held high, advancing to the hypnotic rhythm of the martial music. It was as if Hitler had incarnated a Wagnerian opera and had carried the whole nation off on a flight of blood and thunder, the people not realizing until too late that what they had been swept into was not a romance but a murderous drama in which the most grotesque visions turned into reality.

"Wenn Judenblut vom Messer spritzt," the hand-cranked phonograph was scratching out. "When the blood of Jews spurts from our knives, we will feel the better for it."

A loud knock startled Eggart. As his eyes jerked open, he almost toppled off the chair. Before he had a chance to say anything, an agent appeared in the doorway.

"There's a message for you from Kempten," the agent announced. "They've arrested a German who was carrying papers identifying him as Otto Bergauer, a Food Administration official. He got into a scrape in the French zone, and the French have filed a claim on him. He gave the CIC man there your name, but he wouldn't say anything else. If he's an operator of yours, you'd better get down there!"

"Christ!" Eggart was furious. Kempten was in the Allgäu, near the border of the French zone. What the hell was Willach doing there?

Swinging the Mercedes onto the autobahn, he pressed down on the accelerator. Road markers flashed by almost before he saw them. Wisps of snow lay on the road, but the night was bright and clear. The speedometer registered 150 kilometers per hour as he roared past the few other vehicles on the highway. In fifteen minutes he was skirting Stuttgart, and in another half hour he reached Ulm. Turning off the autobahn he had to slow down to sixty, and it was another hour before he reached Kempten. The clocks were striking 11:30 as he alternately accelerated and braked through the streets.

Willach was being held in the military police compound. Eggart showed his identification to the guard at the gate and was directed to the building that contained the orderly room and reception area. Opening the door, he headed straight for the desk. Several persons, some in French uniforms, were standing, conversing, to one side. Eggart paid no attention to them. He was almost to the desk when one of the figures detached itself and moved to intercept him.

"Guillaume!"

He pivoted at the sound. An uneasy, almost sickening foreboding spread through him. Turning away from the desk, he took Madeleine by the arm. They went over to a corner.

She was excited. "We've caught Otto Willach!"

"How do you know? Are you sure it is Willach?"

She nodded. "I'm positive. I identified him."

"How was he apprehended?"

"There's been a lot of smuggling going on across the Swiss border in the Vorarlberg, so we established checkpoints all along the roads running near the border. This Opel was stopped at Dornheim for inspection. The driver's papers were made out in the name of Otto Bergauer, a German working for the American Food Administration. That only made the inspector more suspicious, and he decided on a top-to-bottom search of the car. When Bergauer saw that he would be unable to bluff his way through, he turned the car around and sped off. We chased him across the mountains to Oberstaufen, and he finally crashed into a roadblock after crossing into the American zone. There was a false compartment in the trunk. It was stuffed with money."

"But how do you know this Bergauer is Otto Willach?" Eggart asked her. "If he is working for the American Food Administration, he must have had a thorough security check."

"I don't know how he managed it. He probably had false papers. After all, they weren't so hard to come by in the SD."

"How did you get involved?"

"Bergauer was first checked out in Immenstadt after he was taken at the roadblock. He has an SS blood mark under his arm. He was in custody of the military police, but our

Security Agency people participated in the interrogation. We have a picture file of the Germans who are high on our target list, and one of our men noticed that Bergauer resembled Willach, so he called Ravensburg. In the meantime, the MPs brought Bergauer to Kempten. So I came here. I've seen him and talked to him. There's no doubt. He is Willach. All that needs to be done is for us to make arrangements to take custody of him."

Eggart took a deep breath. "You're mistaken," he said. "The man is Otto Bergauer. Apparently he has the misfortune to resemble Willach."

Madeleine turned white. "There is no mistake. How can you contradict me! Are *you* an expert on Otto Willach?"

Eggart's head was pounding. He had difficulty putting his thoughts together. "You remember that when I first met you, I was searching for Otto." She was staring at him. The eyes of other people in the room were focusing on him and Madeleine. "I suspected that Willach was a member of the Werwolves," he said.

Her eyes were large and penetrating, and at the same time seemingly unbelieving of what they saw. "You found him," she whispered.

Eggart was utterly miserable. "Let's go outside," he said, and pulled her with him.

They went out of the door and walked about a hundred feet to the edge of the motor pool, where they halted against the side of a three-quarter-ton weapons carrier.

"You lied to me," she accused him.

His mouth twisted wryly, and he shook his head from side to side. "Whatever decisions were made with regard to Willach happened before you—before I fell in love with you. All right, he's a bastard! We both know that. But in intelligence, one doesn't make moral judgments. We needed him. We decided to use him. That's all."

"You betrayed me!"

"Goddamn it! I didn't betray you. There was nothing personal!"

"Not for you. But for me!" She gripped his upper arm so hard that he winced. "But there's no use quarreling. You used Willach for your purposes. Now I'll take him back to France."

He shook his head. "It's no good."

"What do you mean—it's no good?"

"I can't let you take him. We still need him."

She bit her lip hard and long, until tiny drops of blood glistened on it. "You don't mean what you're saying. Willach is a swine. He's totally corrupt. He corrupts everyone and everything he touches!"

"Christ! It doesn't make a damn whether he's corrupt or not!" Eggart's voice was rising. "He's useful. I need him!"

"Then it's true!" she said. "The name Bergauer, his cover with the Food Administration. All were arranged by you!"

"Look! I don't give a damn about Willach! But I've got a job to do. Willach is small fry. But he's essential to *me*!"

"And after he's no longer essential to you, he'll disappear!"

Eggart gestured helplessly. "He hasn't disappeared yet."

"But you're protecting him. You've guaranteed him safety. That's your payoff to him for working for you."

"I haven't guaranteed him shit!"

"Do you think I'm stupid? You think I don't know how these things are arranged? You arrogant bastard! I was fighting for survival while you—you were still galloping your horse in California!"

They were shouting at each other. Her voice was hoarse, and she was crying. They were just beyond the circle of light cast by the bright overhead lamps that illuminated the center of the compound and etched the shadows of the vehicles sharply on the ground. The temperature was several degrees below freezing, and neither of them was wearing a coat. Both were shivering from the cold and the anxiety of the quarrel.

"Willach is not so bad! Willach is not so important! That's what you're thinking!" Her words formed bursts of vapor in the air. "But to me there's no one more important! You say you have a job to do. I have a job to do, too. Willach is *my* job! I've been hunting him since last May. Now, I will take him!"

"For God's sake! Be reasonable!"

"Reasonable?" A laugh wove through her tears. "That's a Gestapo line—be reasonable! When the Gestapo came to our inn, they said they were reasonable men. They sat down and drank some wine. Then they took us in—my brother, my sister, and me. Someone had informed. Who? I don't know. What does it matter?" Her voice became calmer. "The interrogations began. Politely, at first. Then, every day, the pressure increased. The Gestapo told me they knew our inn was a place were information was exchanged, a gathering place for the Maquis. We must know who the members are, they said. Where did they come from? Where did they go? They tried to play us off against each other. Sister against brother. Sister against sister. If one of us talked, they promised, all of us would be saved. The interrogations fell into a pattern. My brother would be beaten and tortured in the next room, and my sister and I would have to listen and imagine what was being done to him. Then I was made to watch while my sister was tortured. They attached the electrodes—"

"God!" Eggart cried out. He wanted to tell her to stop. He wanted to take her in his arms and agree to anything she wanted. But their words had unrolled like strands of barbed wire, and the barricade had already risen between them.

"When the electricity was turned on, my sister's body was shaken like a rag doll's," Madeleine continued inexorably. "She went into convulsions. Her head flopped back and forth on her neck. If one of us did not speak, the convulsions would break her neck."

Eggart thought he perceived a small opening. "What has Willach to do with that?"

"That was when Standartenführer Willach appeared. He said, 'Let me have a little talk with Fräulein Roche.' Let the past be the past, he suggested, and he gave me to understand that I need not betray our old comrades. The future was what counted. In the future I would work for the SD. My brother would be kept in prison, but Willach promised that he would not be killed or sent to Germany.

My sister would be hostage for my performance. Willach himself would take charge of her. His offer seemed generous, almost too good to be true. I thought, Here is a decent German! I cried, and I thanked him."

"You became an informer?" Somehow, the revelation shocked Eggart.

"Yes. I became an informer. I had the choice of sacrificing my brother and sister or turning over to Willach people with whom I was only generally acquainted, for whom I had no personal feelings. It was a game. We all knew the rules, even though no one ever spoke a word about them. I did not betray my friends and old comrades. The ones I reported to Willach were always from other units of the Maquis. They were American and British agents. They were the unimportant small fry. They were suckers. Willach knew what I was doing. He exploited my weakness. He did not care about the Gestapo. He did not care about the Maquis. He pursued his own interests. That he had penetrated the underground raised his stature with Reich Security Headquarters in Berlin and protected his black market schemes."

She seemed exhausted. Eggart hoped she would collapse in his arms. Tomorrow, perhaps . . .

"To protect my family and my friends, I made victims out of strangers. Willach used our inn for his black market dealings. He kept my sister in his brothel. Half the time now she's out of her mind. My brother is crippled."

Tears formed in Eggart's eyes. He could see Willach exactly as he must have been, the bon vivant in his black uniform. He hated Willach—hated him more for being responsible for this confrontation than for anything he had done in France.

"But what was the worst," Madeleine continued, "was that he didn't give a damn about the Nazis. He was doing everything for his own gain, and in the doing proving that we were all like him. He is the one my sister remembers. He is the one who terrifies her! I promised her she would see him dead, so that she need not be afraid of him any more." She swallowed, and her voice, barely audible, came from deep in her chest. "If you love me, you must let me have him."

"Not now," he said, and for some reason the shadow of the machine gun on the weapons carrier seemed to look like the projection of a giant praying mantis. "He isn't worth it."

"What do you mean, he isn't worth it?" she cried out.

"He's wretched, vile. A maggot who fed on the dung of the system. But he's going to help me," Eggart's voice was shaking, "to get some of the designers of that system. And they'll all go to hell together!"

"You goddamn maniac!" she shouted. "You egotistical maniac! You think you can wipe the slate clean all by yourself?"

As she threw the last words at Eggart, she pivoted and ran back toward the military police building. Her words half froze in the night and sounded like faint shouts from the distance. He watched her figure growing smaller, her elongated shadow pirouetting about her, then splitting in two as she was caught between lights.

He found Willach's Opel. The front end was smashed, and there were bullet holes in the rear window. The trunk had been broken open and the interior ripped apart. If he were to get Willach out of military police custody in Kempten, he had to do it before Madeleine mobilized the French machinery. If the French were able to make a cause célèbre out of Willach, or if they succeeded in delaying his release, Willach's usefulness would be at an end.

It was a few minutes past 1:00 A.M. when Eggart drove to the CIC villa in Kempten and placed a call to Colonel Campbell in Heidelberg. It was a damn good thing, Eggart considered, that General Brannigan had given him a blank check. A half hour passed before he was able to reach Campbell and explain the situation.

"You want me to spring him, is that it?" Campbell asked.

"Yes, sir. So far the French have no concrete proof that he is Willach. There's a French lieutenant who knew him personally, but I challenged her identification of him. All his papers are under the name of Bergauer. I propose we bluff it out. We say we did a thorough background check on him, and he's not Willach."

"Isn't that likely to get us into a real donnybrook with the French?" Campbell asked.

"Yes, sir. Especially if Willach is in the middle of it. And eventually we'd be bound to lose. That's why I want to get him out of here right away. If the French can't find him, they can't identify him, and we'll just keep telling them they were wrong. Without a body, they won't have a case."

"That's going to take some doing, Eggart." Campbell did not sound pleased.

Eggart returned to the military police compound. Among Willach's possessions was a box containing stacks of marks, francs, and dollars—nearly twenty thousand dollars in all. When Eggart walked in, Willach was lying on a cot in the detention cell. He started up anxiously, then gave way to the joy of recognition. "Captain Eggart!" he exclaimed. "I knew you would not abandon me!"

"You slimy bastard!" Eggart reacted without thinking. His arm shot out, and the V between his thumb and index finger thrust against Willach's throat. The shock of the blow staggered Willach back and pinned him against the wall. A dazed expression appeared on his face.

"Haven't you ever done anything in your life that wasn't shitty?" Eggart asked as he dropped his hand from Willach's throat.

Willach sat down heavily on the cot. He started to speak, but instead only swallowed.

"What the hell were you doing heading for Switzerland with a trunkful of cash?" Eggart demanded.

"A favor for a friend. I am too easily taken advantage of. He—"

"Balls! Don't give me that crap! You've been playing the black market, and you decided the time had come to cash in!"

"I am sorry that your confidence in me is not stronger . . ."

"Oh shit!" Eggart exploded. He had the urge to pound Willach, to see his body disintegrate like a balloon. It was clear that after their meeting the previous night Willach had decided not to risk an encounter with Wirth but instead disappear to Switzerland. Willach's making a run for it was, of course, in character, yet it was an action Eggart had not taken into consideration. "The bargain was that you would work for us," he said, "and I'd preserve your neck from the French. You busted the bargain!"

Willach's face was the color of a cadaver. "A man can be pushed only so far, Captain Eggart. Everyone has an instinct for self-preservation. You were prepared to sacrifice me for your goals. Perhaps I was not prepared to sacrifice myself."

"In that case, you're useless to us, and the French can have you!" Eggart felt a surge of relief. He could tell General Brannigan that Willach had reneged.

Willach, however, did not let him continue this train of thought. "That would serve neither your purpose, Captain Eggart, nor mine. We would be mutual losers. With what I know about your operation, you cannot afford to have me go on trial. And then, who would supply you with information on the Werwolves? No!" Willach was regaining confidence. "We cannot separate our association so easily!"

"You sure as hell tried!"

"Let us say that it was a mistake. An error due to pessimism, for I am, as you know, a pessimist, Captain Eggart. My philosophy is that politicians come and politicians go; regimes come and regimes go; even occupations come and occupations go. But we as individuals continue— if we provide for ourselves! If we are realistic, we must act according to our self-interest. My flaw is that I am a cynic."

"And a liar, a manipulator, an all-around bastard!"

Except for flushing slightly, Willach reacted not at all. "Your opinion of me does not matter, Captain Eggart. Your motives are not saintly. You have been using me. You haven't the least concern what happens to me when my usefulness to you is exhausted. But this will not do any longer."

"What does the cynic suggest *will* do?" Eggart asked.

"I will help you trap Wirth. Then I must escape—from Germany—from Europe. You will arrange it."

"That is beyond my power."

"But it is *not* beyond the power of your superiors. You are an influential man, Captain Eggart. In the SD we often made arrangements for people who cooperated with us."

"Just where would you go?"

"I speak French quite well. I have always admired the French, and before the war, I spent many pleasant days there. I would be happy in some place with a French atmosphere. Montreal—I have heard many good things about it—although perhaps I would be more secure in Louisiana."

"You have as much chance of sneaking past the Statue of Liberty as Hitler has of getting by Saint Peter!"

"But I will not be me, of course. I could be my brother."

"You would be Albrecht?"

"Yes. A few changes here and there. There would be no great difficulty."

"And Albrecht? He could be Otto—and go to France for trial?"

"You are being facetious. Albrecht will be Albrecht. There will be two Albrechts. One in America, and one in Germany. I will take care of his financial needs."

"You're incredible! Anything can be taken care of! Anything can be fixed!"

"Yes. There were no stricter controls than under the National Socialists. So if it could be done in the Third Reich, it can be done in Germany now. Or in America. It is a question of quid pro quo. You need something. I need something. We make an exchange—that is how free enterprise works, is it not?"

Eggart suppressed his fury. If he were to do what was just, what would enable him to reconcile with Madeleine, he would let the French take Willach. But that would negate the work of months, place the whole operation in jeopardy, and give the Werwolf that much more maneuverability to attack Nuremberg. Eggart could not afford to act in accordance with his intinct. Theresa Hadler's viewpoint that one's actions are limited by the circumstances in which they are taken kept flashing through his mind. Decisions are based not on right or wrong, but on necessity. He was still agonizing with himself at 7:30 in the morning when a teletype arrived from Seventh Army headquarters authorizing the release of Otto Sergauer to Agent Eggart.

Rationalizing that the decision had been taken out of his hands, Eggart spirited Wiilach out the back of the compound and pushed him into the Mercedes.

XXV

Willach's escapade had done nothing toward resolving the question of how to approach Wirth. Eggart wondered whether Willach should tell Niehbar of the trip beforehand. If Willach did, and Wirth were then apprehended, how could Willach be covered? And if Willach refused to continue as an operative once he had completed the Wirth mission, was it, in fact, necessary to provide him with a cover? Would informing Niehbar not risk aiding him to establish his own contact with Wirth?

Not apprising Niehbar had the disadvantage that, if Niehbar found out, Willach would come under suspicion. Yet it had the distinct advantage that, if Wirth could be picked up quietly, Niehbar need never discover what had happened and Willach would not have to provide an explanation.

Eggart decided to send Willach to Austria without having him tell Niehbar about the trip. Eggart procured another Opel, but this time Willach would not have free rein. In order to keep track of Willach, Eggart had a hidden radio transmitter, powered by the generator, installed in the car. When the car was in motion, the transmitter would emit signals so that the auto could be followed from the air.

On the Monday after the incident in the Allgäu, Eggart drove Willach across the Austrian border at Salzburg. Willach was to proceed alone to Leonstein, contact Wirth, and attempt to persuade Wirth to return with him. Willach would cross back into Germany at Braunau-Simbach, then take the lightly traveled route toward Stuttgart through Eggenfelden, Landshut, Ingolstadt,

Donauwörth, and Nördingen. The CIC would have the bridge at Braunau under observation, and Eggart would track the Opel with a spotter plane. If Wirth came back with Willach, he would be arrested along an isolated stretch of the road.

It was midday when Eggart halted the car on the eastern edge of Salzburg and prepared to let Willach continue on alone.

"I trust you to come back," Eggart said, "but if you don't, I'll track you all the way to hell. This time there won't be any reprieves."

Willach nodded, tight-lipped. "We have a bargain, Captain Eggart. I will keep my part. Then it will be up to you to keep yours."

Eggart watched the Opel disappear down the road, then got into the Mercedes, in which an agent had been following. They headed for the Salzburg airport, where a Stinson L-5 observation plane was waiting. A half hour after he left Willach, Eggart and the agent were airbone, and in another fifteen minutes the beeps from the Opel's transmitter were sounding in their earphones. The road skirted the Mondsee, the Attersee, and the Traunsee—elongated lakes lying between the fingers of the Alps. The wind blowing in invisible waves off the mountains made the plane hump like a boat skimming across choppy water. Eggart had a hard time keeping his stomach out of his throat.

They trailed Willach for three hours as he headed south down the Krems River valley and then made the turn north for the short leg on the Steyr. As the sun was setting, Eggart lost sight of the car in the narrow, twisting streets of Leonstein. A few minutes later, when Willach halted the car, the radio signals ceased. The pilot headed the plane for the airport at Linz.

For the next four days, Eggart made two flights daily over the area, but not once was he able to pick up the signals. Increasingly anxious, he was preparing for takeoff on the morning of the fifth day, Saturday, when a message from the checkpoint at Simbach informed him that Willach had arrived there.

By plane and car, the trip to Simbach took a little over

an hour. Willach was waiting for Eggart in a guard hut near the bridge. Though Wirth was not with him, Willach spoke quickly to reassure Eggart.

"I did not fail," he said. "I have seen him."

It had not, he asserted, been easy. Local residents had watched him every minute after his arrival. He had sought out the crucifix and left a message. Four days had passed without a reply. Then, on Friday night at about eight o'clock, a man had come up to him in the Gaststätte and invited him to take a ride. Willach had mounted on the rear seat of a motorcycle. Without turning on the headlight, the driver had roared off. Familiar with every twist in the road, he had maneuvered through the darkness like a bat. The unpaved road had become narrower and narrower. After weaving in and out of forests, they had reached a rock-strewn meadow where they bumped along a footpath. So it had gone for more than an hour. Finally, Willach, his heart beating heavily, had been deposited at a farmhouse, where Wirth was waiting.

"In my whole life I have never been on such a wild ride," said Willach. "It is an experience I would not want to repeat."

It was obvious that Willach had no idea where he had been taken. "What did Wirth have to say?" Eggart asked.

"He was curious as to why I had come. I explained that Niehbar was interested in the Grafeneck weapon and wanted to talk to him."

"What was Wirth's reaction?"

"Wirth is primarily concerned about his own safety. He did not respond enthusiastically. In fact, he was exceedingly closemouthed. He gave me the impression that he was in contact with the Werwolf. Wirth seemed to think that there was a great deal of intriguing going on and that too much intriguing was dangerous."

"You couldn't get him to come with you?"

"No. He is dour and suspicious. I pointed out to him that Niehbar would be able to help him with new papers. That seemed to interest him, and he said he would communicate with me later."

"Were you able to find out anything about the toxin?"

Willach shook his head in the negative. "No," he said. "Wirth would not talk about it at all."

The results of Willach's journey were disappointing. Still, the trip had opened a channel to Wirth. During the drive back to Stuttgart, Willach argued that he had fulfilled his part of the bargain and that Eggart must now help him escape from Germany. Eggart, of course, had not promised Willach anything. All he had agreed to was that, once Wirth was captured, he would speak to Colonel Campbell. Since Wirth had not yet been lured out of hiding, Willach would have to resume his position in the Food Administration and continue with his role in Ibex. Willach protested that this would place him in great danger.

"Why?" Eggart asked. Willach had done nothing wrong from Niehbar's point of view. Eggart consented that, to protect himself, Willach could tell Niehbar that he had seen Wirth during his trip to Austria for the Food Administraton. The contact with Wirth should please Niehbar, and Willach certainly had enough facility for explanation to satisfy Niehbar as to why he had not mentioned the trip beforehand.

Uneasily, Willach agreed to return to the job. Eggart had the feeling that there was something missing; something that, once more, Willach was not revealing. Yet, although he questioned Willach for several hours and went over his meeting with Wirth three times, he was unable to elicit additional information.

Eggart felt disheartened. For the past ten days he had kept his mind occupied with the effort to capture Wirth. But now that he was back in Stuggart, the full impact of his quarrel with Madeleine hit him. He thought about writing her, about driving to Ravensburg to talk to her, but what could he say? He could not refute her accusations that Willach's wartime crimes were being forgiven in return for his cooperation. Eggart would have given much to have been able to reconcile Madeleine's demand for justice with his own deal with Willach. But Eggart was more and more coming to the conclusion that the devil was an interested third party in espionage and intelligence work, and was sitting by, grinning at Eggart's dilemma.

Eggart was lonely, frustrated, and miserable. He met Barentz at the Weilheim crossroad, but Barentz's report was routine. In Stuttgart, Eggart took Theresa Hadler to lunch, and one evening they went to a concert. When he drove her home, she invited him to a chamber music concert at her house the following week. Sure that he would feel out of place, he tried to decline.

"Oh, please?" she said. "You have never heard me play."

"I didn't know you played."

"Yes. The violin."

"All right." He gave in.

Theresa was pleasant. He found talking to her stimulating. But as soon as he left her, his thoughts returned to Madeleine.

A mixture of rain and snow turned the road slippery when Eggart picked up Barentz on Tuesday.

"There is an important new development," Barentz announced.

"What?"

"Willach drove to Austria for the American Food Administration. While he was there, he made contact with Sturmbannführer Wirth. Niehbar was annoyed with Willach for not telling him about the trip, but he is delighted that Willach found Wirth."

Eggart pretended surprise at the news, then let Barentz continue.

"On Sunday," said Barentz, "when I reported to the fortune-teller, I told her what I had heard. She was greatly agitated. I had to recount every detail over and over for her."

"Do you know why she was so upset?"

"She thinks Willach is a troublemaker. She was very suspicious of his trip to Austria and wondered how it was that he had such freedom to go places. She is afraid that if Niehbar is able to establish direct contact with Wirth, the conflict over how to employ the Grafeneck *sonder Waffen* will increase. She said this is a time when great vigilance and discipline are essential, and actions like Willach's are against the interest of the organization. She asked me my opinion of Willach. I responded that I had once told Niehbar I suspected Willach might be an American agent."

"What was her reaction to that?"

"She remarked that whether or not he was an American agent was not as important as the damage he might do if he were cornered."

It was a curious comment. Barentz could provide no clarification, and Eggart pondered over it during the next few days. If Willach's trip had accomplished nothing else, it might at least aggravate the disagreement between Niehbar and the Werwolf. If the dissension became pronounced enough, there was even a possibility that Ibex would break apart.

XXVI

Walking helped Eggart to think, and he often roamed through the bombed-out area of Stuttgart. Sunday morning was cold and overcast as he headed through the ruins until he came to the Hospitalkirche, whose huge Gothic arches stood roofless and naked, like a monument to a destroyed civilization. He thought of his reaction when he and Albrecht Willach had first viewed the city nine months ago. What had impressed him then was the physical ruin, but he now knew that the pulverization was somehow less awful than the lives that had been crushed, the people who had been sucked into the Nazi vortex and spewed out, twisted and sadistic, or broken.

He was angling back through the debris of the narrow streets toward the burned-out Rathaus when a sense of unease overtook him. Feeling he was being followed, he looked back and saw no one, but in the zigzag course through which the streets took him it was impossible to tell if anyone were behind him. He reached the Marktplatz opposite the Rathaus, where the remains of the gabled houses had the charred look of an old campfire. Turning the corner, he flattened himself against a wall. He carried the lighter, more compact Mauser automatic rather than the Smith and Wesson .38, and now, with the weapon cocked in his hand, he waited.

He thought he heard faint footsteps approach, hesitate, then stop.

No one came. After waiting half a minute, he darted back around the corner. The street was empty.

Feeling foolish, he resumed his walk. Opposite the

Königsbau, a jeep with three MPs screeched up. One of the military policemen demanded to see his papers. After Eggart had showed them, the MPs explained that Poles were rioting in one of the DP camps and were fanning out through the city. A few shops had been looted. Germans were being assaulted. American forces had been placed on alert.

As he walked to the CIC office, Eggart wondered whether Theresa Hadler would have to call off her concert that evening. But a cold drizzle discouraged the rioters, and by evening the streets were quiet. Eggart drove over to the Hadler house, and knocked on the door within a few seconds of 6:30 P.M.

In America, people would have drifted in during the next fifteen or twenty minutes even if they were "on time," so Eggart was amazed to see everyone converging on the door within two or three minutes of 6:30. By 6:50, the fifteen guests were settled on the chairs and the sofa in the salon, and the musicians—three women and two men—were tuning their instruments. A good-looking gray-haired man cocked his ear as he drew his bow across the strings of a viola. A small man with metal-rimmed spectacles cradled a cello. A tall, thin woman adjusted the reed on her oboe, and a plump middle-aged woman who smiled a great deal periodically sounded A on the piano.

The pieces were by Bach, Schubert, and Brahms. The salon gathered the notes into a rich, warm tone. Professor Hadler was obviously much taken with the music and seemed more lucid than on the occasion of Eggart's first visit. The guests were evidently his friends and colleagues. Most were over fifty, and aside from Theresa Eggart was the only person in the room under thirty-five. He would have felt uncomfortable were it not for the intimacy generated by the music. None of the listeners made a sound; their attention was total. Some closed their eyes and kept time with slight movements of their heads. Theresa had seated Eggart on the sofa, where he was facing her, and he could see how intently she played. The music seemed to offer relief for emotions she normally did not display.

Shortly after eight o'clock there was a break. Frau

Hadler served coffee, cake, and liqueurs. At 8:30 the concert resumed, and at 9:20 it was over. A few minutes of conversation followed. The guests, however, had to reach their homes before the 10:30 curfew, so at 9:30 there was a general leave-taking. Eggart was glad he had come, and he joined the others in warm thanks to Theresa.

When he reached the Mercedes, he opened the door and put his hand in his overcoat pocket where he thought he had left the car keys. They were not there. He felt through the pockets of his pants. No luck. Closing the car door, he retraced his steps to the house, but found nothing.

Perhaps the keys had slipped out of his pocket while he was in the house. He did not like to disturb the Hadlers, but only a few minutes had passed since he'd left. Theresa responded to his knock. During the concert she had had her hair piled in a bun at the back of her head, but now it was loose and falling to her shoulders. For the first time since he had known her, she was not wearing glasses.

"William!" she said, surprised. There was a slight flush to her cheeks.

Apologizing, he explained that he could not find his car keys.

"Come in, please," she said. "We will look."

They searched through the wardrobe in the hallway where his coat had been hung, but found nothing. "Let us examine the sofa," she said. "It is like a magnet. I have found a little of everything in it—including my mother's wedding ring."

She ran her hand down along the side and the back of the ornate silver-brocaded sofa on which he had been sitting. "Ah," she said. "We may have success. These are yours?" She pulled out two keys on a chain and held them up.

Eggart took them from her. "They sure are," he said.

She laughed and fell back against the sofa with her arms spread wide. Eggart apologized again and started to turn toward the door.

"Oh, William!" she said. "Will you make me get up again right away? Look! I am having a nightcap." She picked up a long-stemmed liqueur glass. "Will you not join me?"

He was planning to go to Waiblingen to check up on Willach. But her eyes were pleading, and after such a pleasurable evening he really could not refuse.

She picked up a carafe and poured the liqueur into another glass, which she set down on the coffee table next to hers. Eggart moved toward the sofa. "Would you not like to take off your coat?" she asked.

"I suppose so," he said, slipping his coat off and laying it over the back of a chair. He sat down next to her on the sofa.

"The music—it is really exciting!" she said. "Schubert I like especially. His music is both masculine and feminine. It is a continuous interchange—like an opera without words."

"You play excellently." He took a sip from the liqueur.

"Not nearly as well as I used to. To play well one must practice every day, and I no longer have the discipline."

"When did you begin to play?"

"When I was six. My father's family has always had musicians. My grandfather was a superb violinist. Even as a child I liked to play, though of course I hated practice. I thought all one had to do was move the bow back and forth and put one's fingers on the strings here and there."

"You did provide me with a new experience tonight," he confessed. "My first chamber music concert. I truly enjoyed it. The others, I suppose, were mostly your parents' friends?"

"Yes." She sighed. "Twice now in twenty-five years Germany has been a land of the old and the middle-aged. That is why I am so glad you could come. You added a breath of youth."

"Good Lord!" he said. "I wasn't alone. You looked as if you'd just graduated from college."

"Ah, William! You flatter me too much." She drank from the glass, her long fingers twining themselves about the stem. "For a woman in Germany today the future is very bleak. Another generation of men have been decimated. We will be lonely—just like the women of 1918."

There was really nothing he could say to that. He took

another swallow of Benedictine. She was right. Although she was fairly attractive, quite talented, and intelligent, young German women greatly outnumbered the surviving men.

"This must be the darkest hour right now," he suggested. "After a while the POWs will be returning, and I'm sure that among them there must be someone who would be pleased to share his life with you."

She took a slow sip from her glass. "The man with whom I would have liked to share my life will not be returning. He was killed in Russia four years ago."

He had no answer to that. She was wearing a black dress with a lace top and a deep neckline. The room was warm and retained within it a residue of the music, lingering like the fragrance of yesterday's flowers. He reached for his liqueur glass, still a quarter full, on the coffee table. As he straightened up with it, he somehow brushed against her bosom. The long stem twisted out of his hand. As he grabbed at it to keep the glass from dropping, the dark amber liquid spilled onto Theresa's chest. A few drops rolled down into the cleft of her breasts.

Eggart, momentarily paralyzed, watched them with dismay. When he looked up, her eyes snared his. He realized that he had been staring. He flushed.

"Oh, William!" she said, impulsively taking his hands. "What does it matter? Are a few drops of Benedictine to come between us?"

Her question was a double entendre. He was not sure, but he thought she repeated her words silently, almost like a faint echo. Now he and she were joined by their hands and their eyes. A moment later, her lips, pliable and feminine, brushed against his. Her hands slipped inside his shirt, climbed up his back, and held him to her. He kissed the Benedictine from her breasts. As she flipped off her shoes, her legs rubbed against his thighs like a sensuous cat. Item by item their clothing fell to the floor. Her legs ensnared him like a vise. It was past 11:30 when she finally let him go.

"I'm glad you came back," she said.

"I have no regrets," he said, smiling.

* * *

He left the window open in the Mercedes as he headed on the road to Waiblingen. The frigid air striking his face shocked him out of his drowsy relaxation. He arrived in Waiblingen at about 12:30 and drove up the winding streets past the ancient Rathaus and the fountain. He parked beneath a tree that formed a parasol over the remaining half of an old tower into whose crescent a bench had been built.

Shutters were closed on the windows as he made his way along the narrow deserted streets toward Willach's room. The stone and mortar houses were drab and peeling. Silhouetted against the sky the *Hochwacht Turm*, "high watchtower," cast its presence over the town from the top of the hill. The earlier drizzle had left a thin coat of ice, and Eggart slipped two or three times.

He entered the passageway running along the old wall. In places he had to duck to avoid the timbers of the framework. The passage was barely wide enough for two persons, and it was like going into a pitch-black tunnel. The beam of his flashlight cut through the darkness, intersecting here and there with rhomboids of gray night light admitted by openings in the corridor. His footsteps echoed loud and hollow from the damp stone walls. He had progressed only a short distance when once more he had an eerie sensation of footsteps behind him.

He stopped. But there was only silence.

He shifted the Mauser to his coat pocket, switched off the flashlight, and started up again. Again he thought he heard a double echo. The corridor angled slightly to the left. Making the turn, he ducked into an opening beyond and kept stamping his feet, pretending he was going on. He waited. He heard nothing. No one came.

Damn! he thought, he was getting spooky. He went on, his left hand holding the darkened flashlight and the fingers of his right curled around the butt of the Mauser. Frequently he glanced over his shoulder. Suddenly, ahead, he caught sight of a shadowy movement in an indentation of the passage. Instinctively, he threw up his left arm. The truncheon hit his flashlight, spinning it from his fingers, and glanced off his forearm.

Eggart's right hand darted out, but before he could aim the Mauser a figure leaped at him. The shot went off wildly. Eggart never saw the face of the man who launched himself from the darkness. As the man's body thudded against his, Eggart's left arm hooked around his assailant's right. Eggart gave the arm an inward twist and simultaneously drove his knee into the man's groin. There was a sharp crack. Doubling over, the man dropped the truncheon.

When Eggart tried to disengage himself, the attacker clamped his teeth down on Eggart's right wrist. As Eggart emitted a yell of pain, the man sliced his left hand up underneath Eggart's right armpit. Eggart's arm went numb. The automatic dropped from his fingers.

The assailant dashed for the low wall that separated the opening in the passageway from the steep embankment and the brook beyond. Eggart leaped after him. The man had the upper portion of his body over the wall when Eggart caught him around the middle with his left arm. Since his right arm was still numb, Eggart swung his right leg over the wall to brace himself and haul the man back.

Too late, Eggart discovered that the top of the wall was slick with ice. The man slung his legs over and carried Eggart with him to the other side.

Entwined like wrestlers, the two of them were launched into the darkness. Eggart had a nightmarish sensation of falling through a void, followed by a jarring shock as they hit the embankment. Ricocheting, they plunged into the brook. As the freezing water fountained into Eggart's face, he gasped, as if someone had struck him in the stomach, and his breath was sucked from him.

Eggart's overcoat billowed about him and momentarily buoyed him to the surface. Then, with a sudden tug, his assailant pulled him under. Eggart's left hand shot into the face opposite him, and his fingers found the man's eyes. Feeling was returning to Eggart's right arm, and he crooked it around the back of the man's neck. Never before had he had the sensation that if he lost he would die, and the thought generated an adrenal anger. Pushing with his left hand, he kept arching the man's neck back until he felt the bones snapping. Then, as if in a dream, Eggart was splashing up through the surface of the water. The man floated limply against his arm.

Eggart tried to disengage himself, but his water-soaked overcoat was like a leaden shroud. As he struggled to disentangle his arm from the body of his assailant he seemed to have no power over his muscles. He was gasping. A whirlpool roared in his head. It was as if he were dreaming, and he was drowning in his dream.

Then, spinning violently, he felt himself floating through space. He crashed to the ground, and the bruising jar made him want to cry out. Someone was pounding on his back with a sledgehammer. He opened his mouth to yell *Stop! Damn it! Stop!* Instead, a sickening mixture of water and bile belched out.

When he jerked back to consciousness, he was lying on his stomach, his head turned to one side on the freezing ground. Someone was pushing on his back.

"Get off!" he gasped, and struggled to get up. As his eyes swam into focus, he caught sight of someone kneeling by his face. It was Madeleine.

Utterly disoriented, he thought he had been attacked by members of the French Security Agency. Then, Madeleine and Henri Pittard, who had been applying artificial respiration, were helping him to sit up. He was shaking uncontrollably; he had never been so cold in his life.

Willach! As the thought struck him, he tried to push himself to his feet. "Where's Willach?"

"That's what we want to know," Madeleine retorted.

"You were following me?" The words rattled out through his chattering teeth.

She nodded. "Yes."

He wondered if he should dissemble. But he had to get to Willach—if, in fact, Willach was still in his room. The problem of how to keep Madeleine from taking Willach could be dealt with in turn.

With Madeleine and Pittard's help, he stumbled to his feet. Once up, he felt stronger. Crossing the bridge and passing beneath the tower that projected upward from the old wall, the three of them entered the passageway from the opposite direction. In the darkness, Eggart groped for the door to Willach's room, and pounded on it when he reached it.

The latch slipped loose. The door opened a few inches.

The beam of Pittard's flashlight probed around the floor and the walls of the dark room. Clothing, books, and papers were strewn about, the doors of the wardrobe stood open, and the bureau drawers had been pulled out. As Eggart moved toward the bed, Pittard's flashlight focused on the white flesh of a naked man lying faceup with a pillow over his head.

"Willach!" Eggart called out.

There was no answer.

The beam flicked over the fat and hairy body, mottled with brown spots here and there. Eggart pulled the pillow aside. Willach stared at him, his lip curled back from his teeth in a half grin, half snarl.

He was dead.

Madeleine was hidden in the shadows behind the beam of the flashlight. Eggart wondered what she was thinking. Would Willach's death satisfy her, or would she continue unforgiving? Someone would have to remain in the room and someone else inform the CIC of what had occurred. Shaking, Eggart suggested that he stay, while Pittard and Madeleine drove to Ludwigsburg.

Madeleine remarked that Eggart was in no condition to be left alone. Pittard proposed that Madeleine drive Eggart to Ludwigsburg, but Eggart was determined not to leave the room until he had searched it. So Pittard agreed to go, while Madeleine remained with Eggart.

Pittard retrieved Eggart's Mauser from the corridor, and Madeleine lighted the kerosine lamp. After Pittard left, Eggart stripped off his dripping clothes. Madeleine pulled the quilt off the bed, spread it on the floor against the wall, and taking off all but her underwear pushed herself up against Eggart. Sitting with their backs against the wall, they wrapped two blankets around themselves. Eggart's body temperature was two or three degrees below Madeleine's, but gradually his shivering subsided. The halolike light from the lamp made the room seem like a black and white sketch, almost surrealistic in its disorder. Willach's body looked waxen and occasioned neither pity, revulsion, nor dread in either Eggart or Madeleine. They might have been paid sitters at a wake.

"I had never expected to meet anyone like you," Madeleine said. "The war had turned us hard and bitter, and I doubted that there was anything left in the world except cynicism and selfishness. You were fresh, idealistic, affectionate—you rekindled my faith. I guess I should have known you wouldn't stay that way—that the more you learned, the more you would become like us."

"It's a lousy environment and a lousy job," said Eggart, his teeth still chattering a little. "But it's fascinating. And it's had one compensation."

"What?"

"You."

"I don't know, Guillaume. I hated you for what you did to me. But when I was hating you I began to think only that I would never love you again, and then I was so miserable . . ."

She began to cry.

He kissed her tears one by one as they wandered down her cheeks. "I don't think perfection exists," he said. "If it did, it would be very dull. Maybe it's because we don't really know how much we want what we have until we dont' have it any more. I love you, Madeleine."

Laying her head in the crook of his neck, she ran her hand over his chest. "It was just one more rotten thing in all of Willach's rottenness—that he should have been the cause of our quarrel."

"I don't know. You could look at it the other way and be grateful to him."

"Why?" She reacted sharply.

"If it hadn't been for him, I might never have met you in the first place."

"You're right." She managed a smile and kissed him lightly on the lips.

It did not seem at all incongruous that they were huddled naked beneath two blankets, a Mauser and a Beretta within reach and a dead man lying a few feet away. The secrets of a few weeks before were secrets no longer.

They could talk frankly now, as if they had been acquainted a long time and shared the same experiences. They had found imperfections in each other, but the crisis had passed, and there was a new bond of tenderness between them.

He had been dozing about an hour when he was jerked awake by the sound of heavy footsteps in the corridor. It was a few minutes after five o'clock. Madeleine, scrambling to her feet, put on her clothes and unlocked the door. A half dozen men from the CIC and the CID (Criminal Investigation Division) flooded into the room.

Pittard brought a dry uniform for Eggart, and Eggart dressed beneath the blanket. His eyes blinked at the popping flashbulbs as the CID photographer shot pictures of the room from every angle. A doctor was examining the body. Eggart himself joined in the search of the room, now a hive of activity. The disarray became accentuated. But nothing of any consequence turned up.

Willach had been dead about five hours, the doctor said. Except for two or three welts and bruises, he was unmarked. Apparently he had been held down and smothered with the pillow.

It was still dark when Eggart left the room at seven o'clock in the morning. Madeleine had to return to Ravensburg to make her report on Willach. Eggart was exhausted and aching; his body felt as if it had been put through a rolling mill. After examining him and listening to him wheeze, the doctor prescribed penicillin and bed rest to ward off bronchitis or pneumonia. On reaching Ludwigsburg, Eggart went to bed and did not awaken until eight o'clock that evening.

XXVII

When Eggart opened his eyes, Peter Reimer was sitting in the room. Groaning, Eggart propped himself up on his elbow. He was famished. Gradually, he recalled that he had not eaten in more than twenty-four hours.

"Maybe I can dig up a can of worms," Reimer suggested.

"I don't know why the hell everybody's been trying to make a fish out of me lately," Eggart complained. He pushed himself to his feet. "I think we can do better," he said.

There was a black market restaurant operating not far away, and while they were waiting for their pork roast, Eggart told Reimer what had happened. Barentz's words repeated themselves in his head. What had the fortune-teller said? Whether or not Willach was an American agent was not as important as the damage he might do if he were cornered.

"There's something Willach knew that I never got out of him," Eggart grimaced. "I had the feeling he might tell me whatever it was on the day I got him aboard a ship or a plane."

"You have no idea what it was?"

"No." Eggart shook his head. "He could have had some documents. The people who killed him were sure as hell looking for something in that room."

"Do you think they found it?"

"I doubt it. Willach was too cagey to have kept anything important with him." Eggart lapsed into thought.

Suddenly he looked up. "Pete! We've got to get out to Gaildorf! The château of the Baroness von Leithorst!"

"In the morning!" Reimer answered. "In the immortal words of Brer Rabbit, 'The race is not to the swift, but to the swallow.' So eat your *Schweinbraten*."

Eggart, Reimer, and two additional agents arrived at the château, a structure out of a nineteen-century novel, in midmorning. A circular driveway led up to a large rectangular double-winged building. Gothic archways and windows accentuated a facade bracketed by slender towers. Leafless trees ensnared by vines framed the house in a Medusalike tangle of branches. A sagging wrought iron fence surrounded the grounds.

No one responded to the agents' knocking on the door of the château. Finally, at a nearby cottage, they roused a peasant woman who had the warm, milklike smell of a cow. She informed them that madame, the baroness, had left several days before with her two personal servants. She did not know where madame had gone or when she would return. While madame was gone, the woman said, she herself, together with her husband and daughter, cared for the place.

Eggart asked the woman if madame's friend—Willach—had been a frequent visitor, and she replied yes. But in response to Eggart's request to be admitted to the house, the woman indignantly ejaculated, "*Nein!*" Only when it was emphasized to her that she was dealing with American "police" and that they would arrest her unless she complied, did she shrug her shoulders and produce a key.

From the door of the château a hallway ran almost the length of the house. At the far end, paneled double doors opened onto a banquet room, which was arranged perpendicular to the hall. The walls were lined with armor, shields, halbreds, and knightly instruments of war. Not counting the kitchen, pantry, wine cellar, bathrooms, and utility areas, the house contained twenty-six rooms, ranging in size from large to huge. The rooms were furnished with carved Empire-style bureaus, chests, armoires, wardrobes, dressers, cabinets, and desks containing hundreds of drawers. Shelves of leather-bound books reached to the ceiling along three walls of the library. Some of the furniture was covered with sheets.

"We need a platoon to search this place," Reimer suggested.

Eggart questioned the woman and her family regarding the presence of a safe and of possible secret hiding places, but they answered that they knew nothing. While Reimer started in the library and the other two agents turned to pulling out drawers, Eggart had the woman direct him to Willach's room. After spending an hour there without finding anything, Eggart went to the library, where Reimer was just finishing his search of the desk.

"I suppose if we were real detectives we'd check those fucking books page by page," Reimer said, "but I'd be a bibliophobe before I got through with half a wall."

The rain that had started falling earlier was pouring down, and a heavy wind played through the towers with a high-pitched eerie sound. The house was without electricity, and dusk seemed to descend at noon.

By the second night they were overwhelmed by the immensity of their task and all in bad humor. Drinking wine, they sat around morosely and speculated on the ghosts inhabiting the house. The next morning was not much better. Shortly after noon, however, as Eggart was rummaging about in the bottom drawer of a cabinet, he discovered a leather-bound photo album. On its cover were runic symbols and two swastikas. When Eggart opened the album, he found himself staring at the smiling face of Otto Willach in his black SD uniform.

The picture must have been taken about ten years before, and the entire album presented an SS gallery of the carefree days before the war with Russia: the sardonic Reinhard Heydrich striding toward the camera with Willach by his side; a smiling Heinrich Himmler decorating Willach; Willach riding in Paris with a Brigadeführer, evidently Max Thomas; Himmler and a group of SS officers, including Willach, dressed in Lederhosen, receiving flowers from two comely girls at an Alpine resort; Adolf Hitler, in his baggy pants, pointing with his riding crop toward a flight of German bombers overhead, with Willach faintly visible in the SS entourage behind. Some of the pictures had been personally inscribed. It was the photographic record of Otto Willach's career in the SS from the early 1930s until 1941 or 1942. But that was not what struck Eggart.

"Look at this, Pete!" he said, showing Reimer the album.

Reimer was fascinated by the pictures, but Eggart interrupted him. "A picture has been lifted here," Eggart pointed out, and flipped from one leaf to another. "A second here." He continued through the album. "About a dozen in all. Missing! Why?"

Reimer shrugged. "Willach must have taken them out."

"Why would he do that?"

"They incriminated him."

"That doesn't make sense. Why would they incriminate him any more than the pictures he left in? If he were worried about being incriminated, why didn't he destroy the whole album?"

"I don't know."

"Because the pictures didn't incriminate *him*! They pointed the finger at someone else. At the other people who were in those pictures!"

The search took on new specificity. When darkness fell, the agents lighted kerosine lanterns and candles and worked on until nine o'clock. At daybreak, they resumed. Eggart discovered various letters to the baroness, including some from SS personnel. They made interesting reading, but revealed nothing further about Ibex. Reimer found papers that were apparently rough drafts of reports the baroness had prepared for the SD during the war.

Late in the afternoon, Eggart was going through a secretary in a sitting room on the second floor. He had just about finished when he noticed that the top drawer did not pull out as far as the other two drawers. Sliding his hand to the back of the second drawer, he felt the bottom of the top drawer. A piece of wood gave beneath his fingers. The false back of the top drawer flipped open.

A large envelope filled the small compartment. In it were numerous stock certificates for German and Swiss firms, as well as deeds of land—most of them made out jointly to Willach and the Baroness von Leithorst. There was also an agreement signed by Willach and the baroness indicating that Willach had an interest in other holdings. Evidently, Willach and the baroness had had not only a personal but an intricate business relationship.

If anyone knew where to find the information Eggart was seeking, it would be the baroness. The servants insisted they did not know where the baroness could be reached. Sometimes, they shrugged, she went to Zurich.

On Friday, Eggart and Reimer returned to Stuttgart, and Eggart prepared to drive to Switzerland. When he left the CIC villa a few minutes after eight the next morning, a huge rainbow spanned the hills. He was not a believer in omens, but it was the first rainbow he had seen in months. Perhaps it was a good sign.

Eggart drove rapidly along the familiar route: the autobahn to Ulm, the river road to Memmingen, and then across the mountains to Lindau and Bregenz. He reached Zurich at noon. Baroness von Leithorst was not listed in the telephone book, but when he went to police headquarters and identified himself, he was directed to a sunny villa on the lake, the antithesis of the Gaildorf château. A maid ushered him into a sitting room, and a few minutes later the baroness appeared. A woman in her early fifties, she looked her age but was still attractive. Eggart explained that he wished to talk to her about Willach.

"When did you see Otto?" she asked.

"A few days ago. Late Sunday night."

"I saw him two weeks ago," she related. "He did not look at all well. I expressed my concern, and he said that he was experiencing some difficulties. He told me it would be safer if I left Germany until he was able to arrange matters."

"Unfortunately he was unsuccessful," Eggart said. "He's dead."

She stared at him; then she excused herself. After

seven or eight minutes she returned to the room. Eggart could see that she had been crying, but she was again perfectly composed. "I had ordered tea prepared earlier," she said, "but it is the housekeeper's day off, and I wanted to make certain the maid did not forget to put the rum on the tray."

Eggart had expected to thoroughly dislike her. Instead, she had an air of graciousness that made it easy to establish a rapport. Talking about Otto Willach helped her overcome the shock of his death. She soon realized that Eggart must be an American intelligence agent, but for her the war was over, and it did not matter.

She had met Willach ten years before, when he was an ambitious SD officer in Stuttgart. After the start of the war and the death of her husband, Willach had recruited her for intelligence work. Since she was a Swiss citizen by birth, she was able to travel as a neutral, and had become an agent in the German intelligence operation in Switzerland. She was having financial difficulties trying to maintain the properties left her by her husband, and after Willach was posted to France in 1940 he offered to help. They came to an agreement that she would invest money for Willach in Swiss and foreign securities and banks in return for the interest and a portion of the capital. Periodically, Willach had made trips from France to Switzerland, and he had always brought large sums of money with him.

Eggart did not feel it was the appropriate time to point out to the baroness that these were ill-derived gains. He needed her help, and he explained to her his suspicion that among Willach's papers and possessions there might be a clue to his murderers. She said she was anxious to help in any manner she could. Otto did not have many things in the house, but Eggart was free to check through them.

"Of course," Eggart said, "you are also keeping valuables and documents for him in a safe-deposit box."

"Yes," she said. She was.

Eggart found nothing among Willach's things in the villa. He and the baroness had dinner together. The following morning he met her at the four-story block-square building housing the Schweizerische Kreditanstalt on the

Paradeplatz. A bank official ushered them into the safe-deposit vault, and the baroness unlocked the box. It was a large box, and the official carried it to a table for her.

The baroness started taking out the papers, looking at them, and handing them to Eggart. They were mostly securities. Near the bottom of the box was a large brown envelope. Eggart asked the baroness if she knew what was in it. "No," she replied. It was among some things Otto had given her a few months ago with instructions to put them in the Swiss bank.

Eggart took the envelope. It was sealed. Eggart asked permission to open it, and she nodded assent. Ripping the end, he reached inside with his fingers. A set of photographs slid halfway out. Eggart caught a flash of SS uniforms, glanced at the top halves of the next two or three pictures, and knew he had found the missing photos.

"That is what you wanted?" she asked, interpreting his expression.

"Yes."

"You may take them."

"Thank you. May I drive you back to your house?"

"No." She said she would need to spend some time at the bank and had other business to attend to downtown.

Eggart raced to the Mercedes. He wanted a quiet place where he could examine the pictures. Dodging streetcars, he drove as rapidly as he dared through the residential district until he reached the open country and found a spot where he could pull the car well off the road.

He removed the photos from the envelope. There were fourteen in all, varying in size. In the topmost picture three men in SD uniforms were standing together, engaged in conversation. Eggart recognized the first two men immediately: Heydrich and Willach. The third, an Obersturmbannführer, he did not know. The second photo showed five high-ranking SS officers standing alongside an armored column on a snowy plain—Eggart guessed the location was Russia. Of the five men, Eggart recognized only one: Himmler.

When he pushed aside the second photo and his eyes

met the third, Eggart felt as if the icy water of the Waiblingen brook were once more splashing into his face.

He stared and stared at the picture, a three-quarter portrait. On the left side was the same Obersturmbannführer who had been standing with Heydrich and Willach in the first picture. To his right, her arm linked in his, was a smiling Theresa Hadler.

Eggart's breath expelled with a rush. He went rapidly through the pictures. Theresa was in five of the fourteen. She was sitting on the back of a motorcycle whose driver was the Obersturmbannführer. Goggles were perched on their foreheads, and they were looking at an SS Oberführer (senior colonel) who was standing to one side with an approving smile. In a third picture she was sitting at a café table with the Obersturmbannführer. In a fourth she was in a bathing suit, an Alpine lake in the background. She and another woman were standing legs akimbo and arms outstretched while a third woman balanced acrobatically on their shoulders. In the fifth she stood solemnly opposite Heinrich Himmler. Watching were the Obersturmbannführer and a civilian.

In another picture Eggart recognized Siegfried Niehbar—he was with two high-ranking SS officers Eggart did not know. A different photograph showed Christian Wirth alongside Heydrich and an officer unfamiliar to Eggart.

Eggart pulled out a pencil and did a quick tally on the envelope. Theresa appeared in five of the photos; the Obersturmbannführer in five also; Willach was in three; Wirth in two; Heydrich in three; Himmler in two. Those were the men Eggart could identify; but there were many he could not.

He shot the car back into the road. So much for the security check on Theresa. As an intimate of the SS hierarchy in Württemberg and an acquaintance of high-ranking Nazis, she was no doubt a member of Ibex. Eggart was glad that he had stayed away as much as possible from the military government offices. He wondered how long he had fooled her with his cover. She might have had suspicions from the start. She evidently had known Otto Willach, and it would not have required great deduction on her part to conclude that Otto might have turned into an American agent.

Christ! Eggart clenched his teeth. She had invited him to her chamber music concert to make sure he would not be in the way when Otto Willach was killed. She had pilfered his car keys, and then she had seduced him. That should have given the crew in Waiblingen time enough to deal with Willach, but evidently they have been delayed, and Eggart had been intercepted by the guard.

As for Willach—what a clever bastard! He had always provided enough information to tantalize and never so much as to be definitive. He might have strung Eggart along that way forever in order to retain a refuge for himself against extradition to France. It was probable that Willach had known the identity of the Werwolf all along and that if Eggart had concentrated on questioning Willach and had broken him, Ibex and the Werwolves would have come unraveled. But Eggart—and for that matter, Colonel Campbell—had been seduced by the prospect of Willach's usefulness as a penetrating agent. Still, what was it Campbell had said? "There's only one way to get experience in this business, and that's on the job. It's do or die." And Eggart was still alive.

On his way to Heidelberg, Eggart stopped off in Stuttgart to warn Reimer about Theresa Hadler. Reimer was alone in his room at the villa when Eggart appeared and spread the pictures on a table.

"Good God!" Reimer exclaimed and began pacing up and down, halting occasionally to stare at the pictures. "She's so goddamned clever," he said, referring to Theresa. "She started off in the French occupation administration, had no trouble getting herself taken over by the American Military Government, gained my confidence by volunteering to tutor Liselotte, and then ensnared you too. While we've been infiltrating Ibex, she's wormed herself right into the core of the CIC."

"The way you put it gives me a great feeling," Eggart said.

"Hell, it's mainly my fault!" Reimer tried to shoulder the blame.

"You haven't been nearly the sucker I have," Eggart contradicted him. Eggart had not revealed to Reimer that Theresa had seduced him the night Willach was killed.

"My inclination would be to lock her up and charge her with murder," Reimer said. "But of course you've got other considerations. Still, I wouldn't sleep easy with her on the loose."

"The question is, how much *does* she know," Eggart asked half rhetorically.

"She knew enough to murder Willach. What's worse is that she apparently has you tabbed. If she'd found out enough to link you and Willach together, she may have unraveled the entire operation."

"No," Eggart shook his head. "That doesn't figure. For one, Niehbar apparently was not informed about Willach. Two, Barentz is still in the clear, so she doesn't know about him. Three, why did she have Willach killed when she must be aware that by doing so she's tipping us off that our operation has been compromised!"

"I don't necessarily buy your premise about Barentz. For all you know, Barentz might be a double agent."

"And Liselotte might be Mata Hari!" Eggart shot back. "If I can't trust Barentz, I'll cash in my chips." He thought for a minute or two. "Look at it this way. Willach and Theresa were acquainted for a long time. That means Willach probably knew a lot about her, and she was aware of Willach's character and inclination for double dealing. That's why he placed these photographs in the safety deposit box in Zurich. He could use them either to blackmail her or to ensure his own safety. Maybe both. But it didn't work, because when I put the heat on him, Theresa was afraid he'd crack, and had him eliminated. So what it comes down to is the relationship between Willach and Theresa. It doesn't necessarily mean that she's put her finger on the pulse of what we're doing."

"It sounds logical," Reimer agreed, but there was a note of doubt in his voice.

Eggart and Reimer had been so engrossed that they

had not noticed that Liselotte had come into the room. Standing by the table, she had her eyes riveted on the pictures.

Reimer was the first to see her. "Liselotte!" he said. When she did not react, he walked over and touched her. She shuddered.

Thinking that it was the pictures of Theresa that disturbed Liselotte, Reimer tried to reassure her. "We've only just discovered that Theresa was associated with the SS," he said. "Of course we won't allow her to tutor you any more."

Tears began streaming down Liselotte's cheeks, great silent tears that seemed to spring from a well deep within her. It was the first time that Eggart and Reimer had seen her crying since the day of her return to Stuttgart. Except for an occasional remark, she had said little about what had happened to her during the years she had spent in concentration camps. But the pictures of the SS clearly triggered a strong emotion. After three or four minutes, she said, "It is not Fräulein Hadler. It is the officers."

Sitting in a chair and taking occasional sips from the coffee Reimer brought her, she recounted hesitantly what had happened to her. At first she and her brother had been sent to the model concentration camp at Theresienstadt, Czechoslovakia, where she slept in the attic of a barrack and worked in the fields. After a year and a half at Theresienstadt, she was assigned to a transport destined for Ravensbrück, a women's concentration camp near Berlin. At Ravensbrück, Liselotte worked twelve hours a day, six days a week sewing uniforms for the SS. Since the barracks were infested with lice, fleas, and rats, the women were disinfected monthly with a chemical. At these disinfections they had to appear before the *Oberaufseherin*, the female overseer, and the officers of the SS staff. As they were paraded by, the SS conducted "selections." Some inmates were picked as subjects for medical experiments. Others, who were old or ill, had their cards pulled from the files and were never seen again. The younger and prettier women were sometimes ordered from the ranks and separated from the rest of the prisoners. The officers went down the line, inspected the girls minutely, and often pinched their flesh. Joking as if they were attending a slave auction, they ultimately chose a handful of girls. Some went as servants to the officers, and others were placed in the SS brothel.

"One day," Liselotte said, "I was among the group that was held back. A Hauptsturmführer named Keller ran his hands over me, and after he had felt me he said, 'Yes, you still have a good body. With a little flesh you will do very well.'"

Two other teenaged girls had already been working for Hauptsturmführer Keller, Liselotte related. Most of the time Keller left them alone, but once or twice a week he got drunk and took one of the girls to bed with him. "They always came back bruised and crying," Liselotte continued. "I was terrified thinking about the first time he would pick me. I thought that perhaps I would not go or would try to run away. But the other girls argued that no matter how bad it was, it was our only chance to survive. If I was sent back to Ravensbrück, I would be placed in the punishment detail, and no one lasted more than a week on that. So when the time came that I was summoned by the Hauptsturmführer, I went. It was not a pleasant experience."

Reimer's eyes were glistening, but neither he nor Eggart knew what to say.

"I didn't ever want to tell you," Liselotte whispered, not looking at Reimer, "but I had to. Sooner or later you would have found out." The tears had started from her eyes again, and her voice was like a dying breeze stealing through the trees. "After all the bad things, you found me, and I thought you were a miracle. I wanted so much to have you love me. But how can you love me now?"

"Oh my God!" Reimer choked out, and dropped to his knees beside her. "Nothing you ever did could keep me from loving you."

"Even though you know the truth?"

"There isn't any truth. There are only lies and horror on the one side and you on the other." Softly he kissed her cheek.

Eggart had become invisible. Gathering up the photographs, he slipped silently out of the door.

* * *

Eggart drove to Heidelberg that night and the next morning went to see Colonel Campbell. Explaining the source and significance of the photographs Eggart identified the people whom he knew. He told Campbell about Theresa Hadler and her evident involvement in Ibex.

Campbell was able to make one further identification—Gruppenführer Otto Ohlendorf. "We'll see if we can get the rest of the people cleared up tomorrow," he said. "I'll ask the 970th to send us an identification expert from the documentation center first thing in the morning."

The expert from the 970th CIC detachment at Frankfurt arrived at 10:30 A.M. He had no difficulty identifying most of the people in the picture. The man with Siegfried Niehbar and Gruppenführer Otto Ohlendorf was the late Gruppenführer Hans Prützmann. But the expert could not recognize the Brigadeführer in the photo with Heydrich and Willach. Eggart suggested that it might be Max Thomas, and the expert agreed it probably was.

That left two key figures unidentified. One was the Obersturmbannführer. The other was the Oberführer who was smiling at him and Theresa when they were on the motorcycle. The expert was examining the photos with a magnifying glass.

"You can see him again here," he said, pointing to the photograph of Himmler, Ohlendorf, Prützmann, Thomas, and a fifth man, all standing on the snowy Russian steppe. "In the other picture he is an Oberführer. Here he has become a Brigadeführer."

The expert said he would take copies of the pictures back to Frankfurt. He was sure he would be able to come up with identifications on the unknown men, but it would take a few days.

"Sir! May I suggest something?" Eggart asked Colonel Campbell.

Campbell nodded.

"Ohlendorf appears in two of the pictures. Niehbar indicated that he was acquainted with Ohlendorf, and Ohlendorf must know the rest of the people, too. If you could get me an appointment to see him in Nuremberg, that might be the speediest way to obtain an identification."

"Eggart," Campbell replied, "by this time, you have me convinced I could get you an appointment to see Adolf Hitler in the netherworld. Consider it done."

XXVIII

Eggart spent the next day engaged in research on Ohlendorf. Shortly after five o'clock, he received word from Colonel Campbell that arrangements had been made for him to interview the Gruppenführer at 1:00 P.M. on Tuesday.

Eggart reached Nuremberg at midmorning. The city had been bombed and fought over, and more than half of the buildings were damaged or destroyed. Rubble clogged the river. The structures that remained standing were encrusted with centuries of smoke and grime. The blue-faced people plodding through the streets and working amid the ruins in their worn, dark clothing seemed in perfect harmony with the somber city. No wonder, Eggart thought, that Hitler had chosen this place for his gigantic spectacles—they must have made all the more impression on a citizenry so devoid of color and life.

The Palace of Justice was situated in a residential area where the damage was much less severe. Some houses across the street from the palace were bombed out, but others were hardly touched. The palace itself was an immense complex, at the heart of which was a rectangle of seven-story buildings composing a courtyard. Above the entrance to the building where the trial was being held, life-sized classical nudes were seated back to back. Parts of the grounds were surrounded by a stone wall and parts by a high wrought iron fence. It seemed to Eggart that the building—and especially the second-story courtroom—was terribly exposed.

When Eggart presented his papers at the checkpoint

in the fence, he had to wait fifteen minutes before he received clearance and was issued a pass. At the third checkpoint he was met by the lieutenant who was to be his guide. The interior of the complex was bustling with people. German women were scrubbing the corridors, and other German personnel operated the tailor and barbershops, the cafeteria and post office, and even a souvenir shop. Eggart was appalled. Security seemed totally inadequate. Considering the ease with which Ibex had penetrated the military government, it would be surprising if there were not already members of the resistance within the complex.

The lieutenant led Eggart down a corridor past rows of heavy oak doors and ushered him into a room containing a massive table and two chairs in the center. He was asked to wait.

While waiting, Eggart reviewed what he had learned about Gruppenführer Otto Ohlendorf. Ohlendorf, the head of the internal intelligence section of the SD, had testified for the prosecution. He was one of the most important witnesses, a brilliant man. His "Reports from the Reich," prepared two or three times a week for Hitler, Himmler, and the Nazi leadership, had presented facts and unvarnished assessments; he had stood almost alone in daring to speak the truth. From June 1941 unti June 1942 he had commanded Einsatzgruppe D and supervised the shooting of at least ninety thousand people.

Eggart was nervous and agitated. He felt almost as if the roles were going to be reversed and he was about to be interrogated by Ohlendorf.

At precisely 1:00 P.M. Ohlendorf was brought into the room. A military policeman stationed himself at the far side of the room near the window. Ohlendorf, despite his diminutive figure, stood straight, aristocratic, somehow elegant even in the dyed army fatigues he was wearing. He gave a slight bow, and Eggart reflexively bowed back.

Eggart had decided to be completely candid, for Ohlendorf had cooperated fully with all investigations and would probably see through any subterfuge. Eggart handed him the photo of Theresa Hadler seated behind the

Obersturmbannführer on the motorcycle and asked Ohlendorf to identify the officer.

Ohlendorf looked at the picture sharply for a moment,
then replied unhesitatingly, "That is Obersturmbannführer
Klaus von Brechenbusch. The woman with him is his wife,
Theresa."

"Where is Obersturm—" Eggart halted. He had not
really been listening to the second half of Ohlendorf's
answer because he had not asked the question. When
Theresa had said that the man whom she had wanted to
share her life with had died in Russia, Eggart had assumed
she was referring to a fiancé. But there was no reason it
could not have been her husband!

"Obersturmbannführer von Brechenbusch was killed
in Russia?" Eggart asked.

"Yes. By partisans. In the spring of 1942."

"And his wife—was she involved in SS activities?"

"Not directly."

"How was she involved indirectly?"

"She was studying medicine at the University of
Munich. She was an assistant to Dr. Dietrich Steinbruck."

"What was Dr. Steinbruck's connection with the SS?"

"He was engaged in experimental work."

"To develop a bacteriological weapon?"

"Yes. That was Dr. Steinbruck's speciality."

"So Theresa von Brechenbusch assisted Dr. Steinbruck. Can you give me a description of the toxin they
developed?"

"I am not a doctor. The work was performed under the
auspices of Gruppenführer Joachim Mugrowski. He is a
professor of bacteriology and was chief of the SS Health
Department. You would have to ask him."

"Was the serum ever employed?"

"To my knowledge, no. It was scheduled for use on one
occasion, but the opportunity did not present itself."

"What occasion was that?"

"The Führer assigned Dr. Walter Schellenberg the
task of eliminating Otto Strasser."

"Schellenberg was your counterpart in the Ausland
SD?"

"Yes."

"And Strasser had been one of Hitler's associates in the founding of the National Socialist Workers' Party?"

"Correct."

"When was this occasion, and what occurred?"

"In April 1941. Dr. Schellenberg went to Lisbon on the Führer's personal order. Strasser was believed to be there. Dr. Schellenberg carried with him a small vial of the serum."

"Why was the serum chosen as a murder weapon?"

"Because of its instantaneous effect, as well as the fact that it left no trace. Dr. Schellenberg, however, was unable to find Strasser."

"Why was the serum not employed again?"

"Because of its extreme potency."

"More potent than similar bacteriological weapons?"

"Infinitely more so."

"Can you give me an indication?"

"I was told that a vial of this size—" Ohlendorf lifted his small finger, "would kill more than ten thousand people."

"Who made the decision not to use the toxin?"

"Naturally, the Reichsführer SS made the decision. However, he was influenced by Frau von Brechenbusch."

"When?"

"In October—or November—1941. Sturmbannführer Wirth requested use of the toxin for his special program in the eastern territories. The Reichsführer SS directed Dr. Steinbruck to prepare the toxin in quantity, but Frau von Brechenbusch appealed to the Reichsführer. She asserted that the toxicity of the serum was so great that there was no certainty of control. She feared the possibility of a general plague that might spread to our soldiers on the eastern front."

"Nevertheless, some quantity of the serum was in existence?"

Ohlendorf acquiesced.

"What happened to it?"

"That is beyond my knowledge. It was the responsibility of Dr. Steinbruck and Frau von Brechenbusch.

Eggart half stood up, leaned across the table, and handed Ohlendorf another picture. "As you see, Dr. Ohlendorf," he said, "that is a photograph of you and the Reichsführer—taken, I assume, in Russia. Could you identify your companions for me, please?"

"Yes. Gruppenführer Hans Prützmann, Brigadeführer Dr. Max Thomas, and Brigadeführer Dr. Eugen Grossbach."

"Thank you," Eggart said. Grossbach, the previously unknown man in the picture as well as in the other photo with Theresa and her husband, was unfamiliar to him. "What position did Brigadeführer Grossbach occupy?"

"He was a deputy director of Amt VI, with specific responsibility for Amt VIc and the Sonderreferat VIcz. However, since his principal concern at first was economic intelligence, he maintained a close liaison with Amt IIb, as well as with me."

Eggart knew that Amt VI was the Ausland SD. He thought subsection *c* dealt with Russia, but he was not certain, and he had never heard of the Sonderreferat. "Could you please amplify on the designation of Dr. Grossbach's duties?" he asked.

"If you wish. Like myself, Dr. Grossbach is an economist. He was first involved in the eastern territories as director of the Aktion Wieland—"

"Excuse me," Eggart interposed. "What was the Aktion Wieland?"

"The complete inventorying of resources in Galicia and the Ukraine, and the systematic search for new raw materials. This activity led to the broadening of Dr. Grossbach's duties, and he eventually had general supervision also of the Wannsee Institute."

"What work was conducted at the Wannsee Institute?"

"The study of the Russian problem."

"Who engaged in it?"

"Our own experts on the East, as well as Russians recruited by us."

"Dr. Grossbach, then, was concerned with intelligence on Russia?" Eggart queried.

"You are correct," Ohlendorf acknowledged. "Specifically, his area of concern was southern Russia, but the limits were not well defined."

"Would you please explain the nature of the Sonder-referat VIcz."

"It was the special section organized for the commission of sabotage in the Soviet Union. Toward the close of the war, it embraced also the *Überrollen lassen*."

"German agents who were left behind in the Soviet Union?"

"Yes. They were Russians who were ideologically committed to us. Many had collaborated with us during our occupation."

"So Dr. Grossbach was in charge of these agents also?"

"Yes."

"What was Dr. Grossbach's relation to Klaus von Brechenbusch and Frau von Brechenbusch?"

"Obersturmbannführer von Brechenbusch was assigned to Brigadeführer Grossbach's section for some time."

"Where is Dr. Grossbach now?"

"I do not know. I saw him last with the Reichsführer SS at Hohenlychen—except for a brief meeting at Admiral Doenitz's headquarters in Flensburg just before the armistice."

"Did Dr. Grossbach have a residence in the vicinity of Bad Tölz?"

"Many SS officers vacationed in the mountains near Bad Tölz. It was fashionable because of the location of the Junkerschule."

"You are familiar with the Werwolf organization?"

"I am familiar with the plans that were made, yes."

"Was Dr. Grossbach a part of those plans?"

"He was assigned responsibility for *Unternehmen Bundschuh*."

"The establishment of an intelligence network behind Allied lines?"

"Yes."

"After the suicide of Gruppenführer Prützmann, do you know if command of the entire Werwolf organization devolved upon Dr. Grossbach?"

"I do not know."

"Would you consider it likely?"

"I would consider it a possibility, yes. Dr. Grossbach was a man with imaginative plans and stategy. He is of the genre of men who are perfectly content to issue orders, but he does not like to involve himself personally in any action."

Eggart detected a note of sarcasm in Ohlendorf's voice. Ohlendorf's description of Grossbach was consistent with Willach's account.

"Your opinion of Dr. Grossbach is based on knowledge of his role in the Russian campaign?" asked Eggart.

"Dr. Grossbach successfully resisted all suggestions that it was the duty of every SS officer to participate in the action on the eastern front. He was a dedicated bureaucrat. Like the Reichsführer SS, he had a feverish and fertile brain, but an uncertain stomach. He was reluctant to see how his orders were actually carried out."

Looking at Ohlendorf—the carefully groomed, punctilious intellectual who had never admired Himmler—Eggart had difficulty understanding how he could have commanded an *Einsatzgruppe* in Russia.

"But you, Dr. Ohlendorf, did not flinch before the hard tasks Himmler placed on the shoulders of the SS in the east."

"Obergruppenführer Heydrich enunciated the principle that no commander should order a man to perform a task he would not willingly execute himself. To my mind, whether one is personally involved in the execution of an order is immaterial in the chain of command. The highest officer must share responsibility with the lowest soldier for the action that takes place in the field."

"Is that why you are testifying at Nuremberg?"

"I am here because it is important that a clear record be left of the activities of the SS and the SD. The calumnies and slander must not go unanswered."

"You regard the activities of the *Einsatzgruppen* as having been positive?" asked Eggart, astonished.

"Positive—yes. More than positive, they were necessary."

"So you approved of them. You participated in them."

"That is not correct. I strongly disapproved. I made my position clear at RSHA headquarters in Berlin and in the training camp at Pretsch. The entire rationale for the *Einsatz* action—that one people or race is inferior to another—is without scientific foundation and is totally fallacious."

"But if you disagreed so strongly, why did you participate—not only participate, but lead men in these acts of terror?"

"It would have been cowardly of me not to."

"It would have been cowardly to refuse to engage in murder? You did not recoil, even, from killing the children? They too were enemies?"

"Had the children been allowed to reach revenge-minded adulthood, they would have been a greater menace to Germany than the parents. In any event, they could not have survived by themselves, and we did not possess the resources to care for them. The correctness of our policy was demonstrated by the fact that when the children escaped, they became auxiliaries for the partisans. Since the partisans were everywhere aided by civilians, especially the Jews, we were justified in regarding these elements of the population as combatants."

"But Dr. Ohlendorf, the civilized world long ago rejected the mass killing of populations in warfare. Even if you believed these people were aiding the enemy, once you had rounded them up, they were your prisoners, and as such they were under the protection of the Geneva Convention."

"You are in error. The Bolsheviks cannot be considered to belong to the civilized world. The partisans did not fight according to the rules of warfare of the Western world. In such guerrilla actions, the Geneva Convention does not apply. It was the SS that attempted to maintain the standards of warfare. The SS can not be blamed for what happened when the bandits refused to abide by the established rules."

"You contend that all warfare and resistance not conducted by regular army units is illegal?"

"Beyond question."

"In that case, should not the Werwolf movement be classified as banditry, also?"

"Precisely. That is why I opposed the Werwolf concept from the very beginning. The SS was created with the highest ideals: the revitalization of chivalry in the modern world. Such an organization cannot stoop to the under-handed and underground methods of partisans. I do not want the record of the SS denigrated. The SS should not be permitted to engage in banditry when its reputation was established in the battle against outlawry."

As Eggart drove back to Heidelberg, he kept thinking about how the pieces of the Ibex puzzle were falling into place. When Gruppenführer Prützmann had committed suicide, leadership of the Werwolves had devolved upon Brigadeführer Grossbach. But with Grossbach holed up in the Alps, Niehbar had run the Württemberg organization pretty much as he pleased. Willach had known both Grossbach and Theresa Hadler von Brechenbusch, and his reports on Niehbar's meetings with Grossbach had been a combination of omissions and half-truths. He had known the identity of the Werwolf all along, but it had been in his interest to titillate Eggart and to keep him in the dark. The less Eggart knew, the longer Willach had been able to assure himself of his own usefulness.

Theresa's friendship—or acquaintance—with Gross-bach had resulted in the establishment of an independent Ibex cell in Stuttgart that was not under the control of Niehbar. Eggart felt certain that the fortune-teller was, in fact, Theresa. Even odd bits, which at one time had seemed to mean nothing, were part of the pattern. Gertrude Schlenck had arrived pregnant in Stuttgart from Ravensburg. She had been directed to Theresa, and Theresa, with her medical training, had probably been the one to perform the abortion.

Both Theresa and Grossbach had resisted Niehbar's efforts to obtain access to the Grafeneck weapon; four years earlier, Theresa had dissuaded Himmler from allowing Wirth to employ it. Yet Theresa and Grossbach believed that the damage the Nuremberg drama was inflicting on the

German image was such that the time had come to stage a Hitlerian Götterdämmerung. They would risk an epidemic in order to destroy the trial.

On reaching Heidelberg, Eggart spoke immediately with Colonel Campbell and received permission to hand carry his report to General Brannigan. He drove to Frankfurt the next day, and after a wait of about an hour was received by Brannigan.

"Intriguing!" Brannigan said after reading the report. "I look forward to meeting Brigadeführer Grossbach."

"Providing I can deliver him to you."

"I haven't any doubts, Eggart. You're progressing nicely."

"Even though I fucked up the Willach operation?"

"Eggart—let others criticize you. Don't do it yourself. In school, you need a grade of 95 to make Phi Beta Kappa. But in baseball, you can win the batting title with an average of .333. In intelligence work, all that matters is who's ahead at the end. You can strike out nine times in a row, but if you get the big hit on the tenth go-around, that's what counts. Informants like Willach are run-of-the-mill— they feed you what they think you want to hear, not what they know. They're expendable. Willach did more of a service to us by getting knocked off than if he had stayed alive."

"Yes, sir," said Eggart. "But I'm now reduced to one informant. Frankly, after seeing the Palace of Justice, I've got no confidence that the people there could prevent an Ibex coup."

"There's no way the Germans are going to get to the prisoners—or to the Military Tribunal." Brannigan was emphatic. "So far as the food and drinks are concerned, we've got safeguards that would enable us to feel confident if we were eating in the Borgias' kitchen!"

"But with the weapon Ibex has, it isn't necessary to poison the food or have direct physical access to the tribunal," said Eggart, not sure he was making his point. "They can wreak havoc simply by penetrating the complex. And with as many people as there are running around in there—"

"Eggart!" Brannigan responded, not unsympathetically. "I'm getting older, but I haven't yet slipped into senility. I'm aware of the problem. As I told you last time, I'm operating under definite constraints. I can't rush off to Nuremberg sounding the tocsin—you'll excuse the pun! If it will reassure you, things are not all as they seem. Ibex may or may not have agents within the Palace of Justice, but I assure you that *we* do. As a matter of fact, until you get us out of this mess, we've got a hell of a lot of them!"

Eggart felt put down. "With what we have now, we can move against Ibex at any time with reasonable certainty of arresting everybody but Grossbach," Eggart said. "The killing of Willach indicates that they're getting skittish. If they suspect we've got a hook into them, they might be inclined to act quickly. How much of a chance should we take?"

"If I was interested in bagging the Werwolf—even when I didn't know who he was—I sure as hell am interested in getting him now that I know who he is." Brannigan was emphatic. "But as far as taking chances is concerned— you take no chances at all! The moment they appear ready to move, we activate the operation. The timing of the strike—that's your decision!"

XXIX

From Frankfurt, Eggart drove directly to Kirchheim. Two weeks had passed since he had seen Barentz. He found a message Barentz had left in the drop at the church. Barentz wrote that he had been assigned to contact message centers in twenty-seven Württemberg towns, a task that would take him ten days, and that it was urgent he see Eggart as soon as possible.

For each day, Barentz had designated a place where he and Eggart could meet between 6:00 and 7:00 P.M. The next evening Eggart headed for Schorndorf, a forty-five-minute drive from Stuttgart. Following Barentz's directions, he turned left at the railroad station, crossed the bridge over the stream, and continued along the narrow, twisting road until he saw a large barn on the right. Going past the barn, he pulled off the road and switched off the car lights. Rain had been falling all day, and in the darkness the car was almost invisible against the barn. Eggart peered through the water-glazed windows, but did not see Barentz until he appeared like a phantom at the door.

Lashing the bicycle to the back of the car, Barentz got in and slammed the door. After he shook off the rain, he expelled a deep breath. "Willach has been killed," he said. "There is to be a meeting in Stuttgart of all Württemberg Ibex leaders."

"I am aware of Willach's death." Eggart saw no reason why he should pretend not to know. "Why was he killed? I thought Niehbar was pleased with him."

"It was done not on Niehbar's order, but on the fortune-teller's."

"For what reason?"

"She and the Werwolf concluded that Willach was an informer. She said there was no other explanation for what was going on."

"What was that?"

"Willach was wanted by the French Security Agency. Early in January, he was caught after a chase in the Allgäu, but an American general intervened, and he was let go. The fortune-teller has contacts with some Vichyite French officers who are afraid of a Communist uprising and would like to stage a simultaneous right-wing coup d'etat in France and Germany. They told her that Willach was an important person on the French target list and that, in order to escape being turned over for trial, he had to have high-level protection. A few days later, Willach went to Austria and tried to get information from Wirth on the Grafeneck toxin."

"How did the fortune-teller know what Willach talked to Wirth about?" asked Eggart.

"Wirth informed the Werwolf."

"How? Is the Werwolf in Austria?"

"I don't think so. But Wirth does have some communication with him. In any case, Willach's trip not only aggravated the Werwolf's suspicions, but made him extremely uneasy."

"Is that the reason for the meeting?"

Barentz nodded. "A mighty blow is to be struck against the occupation authorities. It is to be done immediately, so that nothing can go awry and the Americans do not have the opportunity to infiltrate another agent into the organization. The actitivies of everyone in Ibex are to be coordinated with the striking of the blow."

"The blow against Nuremberg?"

"I can only guess. But that's my impression."

"Are there to be meetings in cities other than Stuttgart?"

"I have heard about a simultaneous gathering in Munich, but I believe the Stuttgart meeting will be by far the largest."

"Why?"

"Württemberg has the best and the most extensive organization. The Werwolf has ordered that there is to be no activity of any kind in Nuremberg, so that no suspicions will be kindled."

"Where is the Stuttgart meeting to be held?"

"At the fortune-teller's."

"When?"

"A week from Monday, March 4, at ten o'clock in the evening. The people are to arrive in ones and twos from six o'clock on, so that it appears they are coming to have their fortunes told. They will stay until the lifting of the curfew on Tuesday morning."

"How many people are coming?"

"Perhaps fifty or sixty."

"Will Nichbar be there?"

"Definitely."

"Has he resolved his differences with the fortune-teller and the Werwolf?"

"Now that there will be action, I do not think there are any differences. My understanding is that Niehbar is being given an important role."

"Who will preside at the meeting? Do you think it is possible that the Werwolf himself will come?"

"That I cannot say."

Eggart handed Barentz a photograph of Theresa Hadler and asked, "Do you recognize her?"

Barentz looked at the picture for two or three minutes. "It is hard to tell. I have never seen the fortune-teller clearly, but there is a distinct resemblance."

Eggart took back the photograph. "Have you any idea how the blow is to be struck?"

Barentz shrugged. "None. That is a well-kept secret."

After arranging to meet Barentz again in a few days, Eggart dropped him off in Göppingen, then headed for Heidelberg. He reached his apartment at 11:00 P.M. It was clear that Brigadeführer Grossbach could not be permitted to proceed with his plans. Eggart was still mystified about how Grossbach intended to deliver his "*Gift*" to Nuremberg, but that made it all the more imperative for the CIC to strike. There was no assurance that Grossbach would be caught. But to Eggart that now seemed a secondary objective.

Eggart lay down on the bed for an hour, then spent the remainder of the night drafting plans for the operation. He set the strike hour for 11:00 P.M. on March 4, an hour after the Werwolf meeting in Stuttgart was scheduled to begin. Since the curfew hour was 10:30 P.M., the troops would be able to move through the streets without attracting attention. The main task force of eighty men would surround the house on Olga Strasse. Simultaneously, other teams would round up Ibex members who were not attending the meeting. Since it could not be known for sure whether a person was in attendance, the addresses of all known members would be raided between 11:00 P.M. and dawn. Also, to maintain security, only a few CIC agents would be informed of the mission and the targets before the night of March 4.

Early in the morning, Eggart put his draft of the plan on Colonel Campbell's desk. Four days later, on February 24, General Brannigan, informing Eggart that he was placing the security forces in Nuremberg on alert, gave Eggart authority to proceed.

There was an enormous amount of detail to attend to. Checklists had to be prepared. The CIC agents who were to participate had to be briefed, then briefed again. Decisions had to be made on the weapons with which the men were to be armed and what vehicles were to be used. To assure communications between various segments of the task force, the Signal Corps would have to set up a relay station atop the *Tagblatt* skyscraper, which had remained incongruously standing while all about it lesser buildings had been pulverized.

On Friday afternoon, March 1, Eggart interrupted his activities to drive to Calw, where he met Barentz beneath the towering railroad viaduct. After telling Barentz as much as he needed to know about the operation, Eggart gave him two stink bombs. Barentz was to pull the pins at 10:55 Monday evening, then hide the bombs in separate rooms of the fortune-teller's apartment. The bombs would activate in five minutes. Stench and smoke would fill the apartment, so that the occupants would be forced to throw open the windows and doors.

"Good luck!" said Eggart. Nearly a year had passed since he and Barentz had first met, and their lives had become interwoven. Though on the surface their relationship had remained professional, a bond had grown between them. It was almost with regret that Eggart thought that a few days more would see the culmination of all their work. "Be careful," he warned Barentz.

XXX

On Sunday, March 3, Eggart checked the Weimar Strasse jail to make sure a cellblock was cleared to receive the prisoners. At 6:00 P.M. Monday he drove to the Grosse Reiter Kaserne. Assembled in a special restricted area were the Fifteenth Cavalry Squadron and forty CIC agents. The main force—ten agents and seventy men—were to cordon off a three-block area between Olga Strasse and Urban Strasse, north of Charlotten Strasse. It was they who would stage the raid on the meeting at the apartment house. The remaining men would check the residences and gathering places of Ibex members and arrest any suspects found there.

A fine rain had been falling all day long, and as darkness descended fog shrouded the city. At 10:20 the task force left the Kaserne. With Reimer by his side, Eggart headed the Mercedes down the hill to the river, then led the main column into town along Neckar Strasse.

"If anything should happen, Bill—" Reimer said.

"Don't get melodramatic!" Eggart retorted.

"Just in case—you'll take care of Liselotte."

"I'd be delighted. But nothing's going to happen."

"How do you know?"

"I had Barentz ask the fortune-teller."

When they reached the Charlottenplatz, Eggart halted the convoy, and the men moved on foot the two blocks up the hill to the target area. At 10:50 they were in place. Eggart was to lead the dozen-man assault team on the apartment. Reimer had charge of the cordon. The combination of fog and the absence of street lighting produced a tar-black night. But the force was equipped with half a dozen powerful portable spotlights that were to be turned on when the assault began, and, thanks to the relay station atop the *Tagblatt* building, they had good communications.

Eggart watched the apartment house from the opposite corner on Olga Strasse. Heavy drapes covered the windows of the fortune-teller's rooms, but here and there chinks of light were visible. Eggart looked at his watch: it was 10:55. Barentz should be placing the stink bombs and pulling the pins. Eggart counted the seconds. Eleven o'clock. The bombs should be activating.

Eggart took out his gas mask, and the others followed suit. He did not yet put the mask on, for the fog would quickly cloud the eye pieces. Now it was 11:02. Eggart saw a rustle of the drapes. Twenty seconds more passed. The drapes suddenly were pulled aside and the windows thrust open. Two parallelograms of light fell onto the street. Coughing, gasping figures appeared in the windows.

Slipping on his mask, Eggart motioned to the men in the assault squad. They skirted the patterns of light and approached the building's door from the opposite side. At three and a half minutes past eleven, a locksmith set to work on the door, and in ninety seconds he had it open. Eggart passed through the short entryway into the main hall, where there was a stairway leading to the upper stories. He turned right. The door to the fortune-teller's apartment was open. Three people were standing in the hallway, and two were hunched over on the floor, coughing, gagging, and rubbing their eyes. Eggart charged past them—they would be taken care of by the tail end of the squad.

Brushing through the door, he found himself in the reception chamber Barentz had described. Several people were crowded together near the open window. Hydrogen sulfide gas veiled the room in dirty yellow. Two men were stumbling around. Eggart struck them a glancing blow with the barrel of his tommy gun, and they tumbled over each other to the floor.

He plunged through the half-open door into the room where Theresa had told Barentz's fortune. Several men were clustered about the window, but Eggart barely saw their forms through the haze. To the left, double doors opened onto a large room whose farther walls were hidden in the swirls of smoke. Eggart guessed that when the bombs had gone off, the meeting had been in progress in these two interconnected rooms. Tripping over a chair, he groped his way across the room. On the opposite side a door led into a dimly lighted hallway that was obscured by tendrils of smoke. Moving forward in a crouch, pivoting on the balls of his feet, Eggart searched for other entrances to the hall.

A shot ripped through the lower part of his mask's nosepiece. His head was jerked around, his eyes went out of focus, he felt as if someone had hit him on the jaw. Even as he fell to one knee, his finger reflexively tightened on the tommy gun's trigger. Through the blur of returning vision he saw a door opposite splinter as the heavy slugs tore into it. The metal thudding into the solid wood sounded like a series of small explosions.

Eggart ripped off the remains of his mask, and, firing, followed his shots through the door. His eyes glimpsed a stove, cabinets, dishes, pans, and to the right a coal bin with the top thrown open. A shadowy movement caught his eye; he fired again, a split second too late as a back disappeared into the bin.

Eggart paused in astonishment at the person's disappearance into the bin. Then he leaped forward. Inside the bin, steps led down into the blackness of the cellar. When Eggart squeezed the trigger, the gun kicked and reverberated in his grasp like a jackhammer; but the only response from the darkness was the whining, jumbled sound of ricochets.

Cursing, he inserted a new drum into the gun. Two men of the assault team who had followed the sound of the firing inched their way into the kitchen. Eggart directed one of them to take the powerful lantern-type flashlight he had on his belt and tie it to his carbine barrel.

Motioning to the GI to follow him, Eggart descended in utter darkness into the cellar. He dared not tell the soldier to switch on the light, for it would provide a clear target. With the tommy gun extended like a bar in front of his face, Eggart probed downward. After about twenty steps, his toes scuffed. He had reached the cellar.

He turned around, felt for the soldier, and pushed him down. Lowering himself to one knee, Eggart cocked the tommy gun and whispered, "Ready!" The soldier pressed the switch on the lantern and slowly moved the light back and forth above his head.

Illuminating an area thirty to forty feet ahead, the beam composed sharp lines of light and shadow into geometric designs. Eggart's eyes swept from one side to the other. The cellar was broad and sectioned off, with passages running this way and that. Along one part of the wall stood an array of laundry sinks, and beyond them were stalls whose black-coated sides indicated that they were coal bins. Pipes threaded along the walls and the ceiling. Debris, strewn along the floor, had accumulated here and there into small mounds.

The swinging of the lantern placed the scene in motion. From beyond the pale of light the red flick of a gun appeared like a flint struck in rapid succession. As bullets whipped overhead and ricocheted with small sparks from the pipes and the brick walls, Eggart pressed the trigger on the tommy gun. The gun became like a mallet pounding a gong into a crescendo of thunder.

Releasing his finger from the trigger, Eggart shouted, "Douse it!" to the soldier. Grasping the barrel of the soldier's carbine so that he would not lose his companion in the darkness, Eggart moved forward. He could see nothing, but depended on the image imprinted on his mind during the few seconds the light had been on. To reduce the crunch of his shoes, he walked on his toes, but remained in a half crouch. His ears strained for noises. After he had gone some thirty paces, a sudden rustle to his left caused him to swivel. He sprayed the darkness with the tommy gun.

In return, bullets whined and ricocheted around him like hailstones. As he dove to the floor, he released the trigger. Instantly the return fire stopped.

Eggart told the soldier to switch on the light. As the

beam projected into an empty coal stall, Eggart began suspecting that he had been ducking his own ricochets. Looking back, he could see a thick foundation wall with a jagged six-foot high hole through which he and the GI had passed. During the war the cellars of the houses had been interconnected, so that if a bomb blocked the entrance to one, people could move underground until they found an exit.

"Damn!" Eggart spat. He might as well be in the catacombs, with passages branching out in various directions. There was no telling where the people who had fled would emerge, and it was folly to grope after them. Taking the lantern and motioning for the soldier to follow, Eggart hurried back toward the stairs.

Some of the smoke and stench had cleared from the apartment. A dozen CIC agents and GI's had forty people lined up facing the wall in the outer chamber. One man, mortally wounded, lay in the street. He had been shot leaping from a window in an attempt to escape. When Eggart ordered the forty Ibex members to turn around, he recognized no one except Barentz.

Eggart loped out of the house and across the street, where a jeep had pulled up. Unhooking the jeep's radio microphone, he ordered the cordon expanded to nine square blocks. Any German appearing on the streets was to be arrested automatically. A house-to-house search was to be initiated. Eggart was wondering whether to request additional troops for the combing of the expanded area when a rattle of shots erupted from the direction of Urban Strasse.

Eggart sprinted toward the sound. A third of the distance down the flight of steps that formed a pedestrian way, a soldier lay doubled over, clutching his leg. Two Germans were hurtling down the hillside. The widening range was too great for accurate fire from the tommy gun, but as Eggart pulled the trigger one man's feet went out from under him. He tried to get up, but then collapsed and rolled forward.

"They came from there!" the soldier yelled, pointing. Eggart saw a wooden door to what looked like a tool shed built into the retaining wall of the garden. In actuality it must have been an entrance to the cellar.

Eggart grabbed the Very pistol carried by the soldier and fired a flare to attract attention. Then, spanning several steps at a time, he went after the second of the two men. Losing sight of him momentarily, Eggart picked him up again as he crossed into the Schlossgarten between the Staats Theater and the remains of the Neues Schloss.

As they skirted the burned-out palace, Eggart was closing the gap one step in every three or four. The man, wiry and hatless, zigzagged across Charlotten Strasse. Eggart could see that he was nearly bald, and as he plunged into the rubble of the Altes Schloss Eggart caught a brief glimpse of his profile. More by instinct than by recognition, Eggart realized that it was Siegfried Niehbar.

Flattening himself against the wall beneath the archway, Eggart pursued Niehbar into the courtyard. There, from amidst the rubble in the yard, rose a massive statue of a Swabian knight seated on his armored horse. Craggy-faced beneath his plumed helmet, his sword upraised to heaven, the knight seemed to ride incarnate out of the swirling mist. The castle was completely gutted. On the upper stories, jagged remnants of walls appeared and disappeared in the fog as if the structure were floating in the sky. Portions of the ornate pillars in the arcades surrounding the courtyard on the first three stories had crumbled, but sizable segments were intact.

There were scores of places Niehbar could have disappeared to. Eggart raised the Very pistol, and a flare snaked into the sky above the courtyard. Bursting and sizzling like a fiery sausage, it drifted down to ensnare the scene in infrared light.

The first shot ripped past Eggart's shoulder. The second missed by a wide margin as Eggart leaped sideways. The third ricocheted off the ground only six inches from his foot. Seeing the muzzle flashes in one of the large round windows that were arrayed like outsized portholes along the castle's third story, Eggart shot from the hip, and the bullets chiseled into the wall. But the statue of the knight was in the line of fire.

Like duelists, Eggart and Niehbar darted from position to position, fired, moved, then fired again. The reddish glare increased in intensity as the flare drifted down, but then, as it winked out, a shroud of darkness once more enveloped the castle.

Before Eggart had time to react, Niehbar jumped from the second-story gallery, rolled forward, came up in a crouch, and twisted toward a three-foot hole in the tower. Even as Eggart raised the tommy gun to fire, Niehbar slithered through the opening.

Eggart sprinted after him. A circular stairway led downward. At the bottom was a broad passageway formed by massive flying buttresses. Eggart fired a burst from the tommy gun, then aimed a flare along the passage.

The exploding flare sent white magnesium smoke whirling up in ghostlike forms. Bathed in orange-red, the underground way seemed like a tunnel through hell. Eggart dashed ahead, turned a right angle, and after a few seconds was again swallowed by the darkness. The hollow echo of Niehbar's steps drifted back toward him.

With only one cartridge left for the Very gun, Eggart groped forward. After three or four minutes, the passage narrowed into a cleft, so that Eggart had to turn sideways to edge through.

He was encompassed by the darkness of the blind; it gave him a feeling of terror. A faint sweet-sour odor, like that of burning flesh, drifted about him. Crooking the tommy gun under his left arm and gripping the Very pistol, Eggart used his right hand like an insect's antenna. He stumbled over something on the floor, righted himself, then continued on. A few seconds later his feet went out from under him. As he tried to catch himself, his arm brushed against an object. A drawn-out clatter, such as made by a collapsing shelf of books, followed. Then a bony hand pushed itself into his face.

Eggart, his heart jumping, flung out his forearm to knock the hand away. In the same motion, he fired the last flare. Ricocheting off a wall, it sprang to life on the rubble of the floor.

As Eggart's eyes adjusted to the light, he saw that he

had stumbled into a chamber of the dead. A dozen skeletal figures, some doubled over, some lying down, others sitting, stared somberly at him. A child, its blackened fingers clutching a pencil, bent over a table. Some of the people had been reduced to skeletons. Others still had fringes of burned flesh and clothing hanging from their bones. Evidently they had been trapped here during one of the great fire raids, and the air raid shelter had turned into their tomb.

Eggart could see no opening in the chamber except the crack through which he had entered. He had lost Niehbar. His enthusiasm for the pursuit was rapidly decreasing, and if he failed to make use of the flare's dying light he might not find his own way out. Picking himself up off the debris, he began his retreat.

XXXI

When Eggart reached the Weimer Strasse jail at 1:30 A.M., jeeploads of CIC agents and GI's were crisscrossing the city. Teams dispatched to other towns were returning with prisoners at fifteen-minute intervals, and Reimer was already interrogating the people who had been picked up in the fortune-teller's apartment. Eggart had Barentz pulled from the holding cell and brought to a separate room.

"I'm sorry," said Barentz. "I didn't know about the secret exit."

"How many people came to the meeting?" Eggart asked.

"Forty-five."

Forty-one were accounted for, so four had gotten away. "Was the forturne-teller there?" Eggart asked.

"Yes. Of course."

"The Werwolf?"

"No."

"Did you discover anything about the plan of attack?"

"No. But the fortune-teller had two black boxes, and was talking to Niehbar about them. I am sure they have some connection."

"What kind of black boxes?"

"They looked quite ordinary—about the size of shoe boxes. Each of them had three buttons."

"Have you any idea what their purpose is?"

"Only, I think, that they contain some sort of radio equipment. I overheard a few words, and Niehbar was talking about the communications at Nuremberg."

From Barentz's description, Eggart could not associate

the black boxes with any kind of radio equipment he had come across in the United States Army. Barentz, however, was unable to provide clarification.

"Damn it!" Eggart expelled a breath of frustration. "Are you aware that Niehbar and the fortune-teller escaped?" he asked.

"Yes."

"Where might they have gone?"

"I believe the fortune-teller planned to drive Willach's Opel. She probably headed toward the east: Nuremberg or Munich."

Eggart got on the telephone and arranged for three spotter planes to be put into the air. A fourth plane was to stand by and wait for him at the Stuttgart airport.

As he headed for the Mercedes, Peter Reimer intercepted him and handed him a crumpled slip of paper. "You might want to take a look at this," Reimer said.

Eggart smoothed out the paper. On it, smudged, was the pencil notation: "*Kammler—FZG 76.*"

Eggart stared at the writing.

"Mean anything to you?" Reimer asked.

"No." Eggart shook his head. "Where was it found?"

"That, with our usual thoroughness, we don't know. We cleaned out everyone's pockets and the stuff just got balled up in a pile."

"Do me a favor," said Eggart. "Call Brannigan's office and have them run the thing through."

Taking along the tommy gun, the Mauser rifle with the telescopic sight, and a carbine, Eggart headed for the airport. The rain was coming down hard and it was nearly 4:00 A.M. before visibility improved enough for the pilot, who introduced himself as Duane Moore, to take off.

In a few seconds they were airborne. In the universe of the overcast, they seemed suspended in a vast gray womb. At four thousand feet they broke into the clear. Below them was a sea of clouds, above a cupola of stars. Nuremberg and Munich were approximately equidistant from Stuttgart, one to the northeast, the other to the southeast, and the four planes attempting to pick up the radio signal from the

Opel's transmitter segmented the area. Moore, flying the most southerly leg, followed the autobahn from Stuttgart to Munich. Shortly after 4:30 A.M. the pilot of one of the other planes radioed that he had picked up the signals on the road leading from Donauwörth to Munich.

Evidently the driver of the car was steering a course midway between Munich and Nuremberg, and perhaps had dropped someone off on the road to Nuremberg. Moore swung the plane north. In a short while Eggart heard in his headphones the beeps from the car's transmitter.

Moore followed the Opel south as it skirted Munich and continued toward Bad Tölz. The roads were virtually deserted. The headlights of the car were probing through the darkness like the luminous eyes of a bug.

From Bad Tölz, the Opel took the narrow potholed road along the Isar River to Lenggries and the Alps. The eastern horizon became rimmed with blue and a thin streak of orange. At the onset of dawn, the auto arrived in the village of Fall. There the road ended. Beyond was an undulating quilt of rose-tinted snow and dark green stretches of forest.

When the Opel halted in front of a farmhouse, the radio transmission ceased. Moore flew the plane high and to the east, so that it was hidden in the rays of the sun. Eggart kept his field glasses focused on the Opel. After a few minutes, a line and a dot like a Morse code A appeared on the snow adjacent to the car. In the field glasses Eggart picked up a heavyset farm horse and what looked like the outline of a wagon—a few seconds later, as the angle of the plane shifted, he realized it was a sleigh. Then the Opel moved forward and disappeared into the barn from which the horse and sleigh had emerged.

From Fall, the sleigh crept forward toward the Alps of the German-Austrian border.. Eggart had the sensation of watching an ant crawl over an infinite sheet. The mountains stretched like an ocean of white and green-black waves, gentle here and cresting there, as far as Eggart could see.

The Stinson was running low on fuel, so Moore radioed for a relief plane to continue surveillance. As soon as it arrived, Moore headed for Munich. After the plane landed, Eggart called Brannigan. He reached the general immediately, briefed him on what had occurred, and asked if CIC Frankfurt had developed any information on "Kammler—FZG 76."

"We've come up with four Kammlers so far," Brannigan replied. "The most important is a Gruppenführer who was in charge of the V-bomb construction program. FZG 76 is a tough nut, but we'll keep at it. Do you draw any conclusions?"

"I don't know, sir," Eggart said.

Using Brannigan's authority, Eggart requested a detachment of ski troops dispatched to Fall. Then, before eating breakfast with Moore, he requisitioned a parachute and a pair of snowshoes.

"What the hell are you up to?" Moore inquired when the equipment arrived.

"I'm not sure. I might have to prove that the Eighty-second Airborne was wrong when they washed me out of jump school."

In midmorning, Moore and Eggart resumed their observation flight above the sleigh. It was traveling a cart road that was indistinguishable from the snowy landscape, except in places where it made a narrow cut through the forest or serpentined steeply up a slope. Moore throttled the engine back to reduce the sound and kept the plane high and to the south of the sleigh. Beneath was a wispy cloud formation. At twelve thousand feet the plane glided almost like a hawk watching its prey.

Eggart's eyes followed the road, which appeared like a segmented thread. About fifteen miles from Fall, the track divided. One leg continued winding over the Alps into Austria; the other led three miles to a frozen lake whose surface reflected the sun like a glazed mirror. Towering over one side of the lake was a sheer rock face, dark and devoid of snow. On the other side, the mountains formed a forest-rimmed bowl. At a point where the trees, the lake, and the gleaming chute of snow came together, a substantial chalet was cut into the mountainside. Hazy blue-gray smoke curled up from the chimney. Beyond the lake the track disappeared entirely, and it seemed improbable that any vehicle could penetrate farther.

The only man-made object Eggart could see was the chalet, but for the past half hour he had been thinking more and more about Kammler and FZG 76. A tingling sensation ran up and down his spine like a squirrel on a tree. Eggart had little doubt that the chalet was the hideaway of Brigadeführer Grossbach. As soon as the sleigh reached the chalet, Grossbach would learn of the events in Stuttgart.

The ski troops should be starting off from Fall at any moment, but Eggart had an overpowering, sixth-sense urge to get on the scene before their arrival. About two miles to the north of the lake was a small meadow, screened by the ridgeline. If the plane flew in low, it would be invisible to anyone in the area of the chalet.

Eggart strapped the snowshoes and the Mauser to his chest and packed the telescopic sight into his pocket. Moore tried to talk him out of jumping. The air was calm, but there was always the possibility of a sudden gust of wind carrying him into the trees.

Eggart, however, was not to be dissuaded. Moore swung the plane north in a wide arc, then descended steeply in his approach. When Eggart unlatched the door of the plane, an icy blast of air hit him, and he threw up his arm to protect his face. Moore reduced the plane's speed to about sixty miles per hour, but at a height of 700 or 800 feet above ground level the tops of the fir trees still flashed by with amazing rapidity.

Suddenly the trees disappeared like a shoreline, and there was only an expanse of snow beneath. Moore banked the plane slightly. Eggart, holding on, resisted the pressure momentarily, then pushed off, as if jumping from a diving board. He had a panoramic impression of sky and mountain, forest and horizon. After taking one deep breath, he pulled the rip cord. Following a throat-clutching second when nothing seemed to happen, he was jerked backward by an invisible hook as the parachute billowed over his head.

As he drifted forward at about twenty-five miles per

hour, the trees at the far side of the clearing rushed toward him. The meadow, which had looked level from the air, was actually on an incline of fifteen degrees. Eggart's feet hit the snow, but the chute did not collapse, and he found himself twisting like a puppet in the straps. A spray of snow flew into his face as he skidded downhill. Finally, almost with an audible sigh, the air went out of the chute. Leaving behind a crescent of plowed snow, Eggart tumbled some thirty feet farther before coming to a stop near the bottom of the meadow.

It was not the kind of jump he would want to make daily, but, except for a couple of bruises, he was all right. Moore circled back to check on him, then pointed the nose of the plane in the direction of the lake. Orienting himself with his compass, Eggart waved Moore off.

After strapping on the snowshoes, Eggart cut a strip from the parachute and tied it into a bundle to take with him. Following a gully, he started through the trees toward the top of the ridge.

By the time he reached the ridgeline an hour later he was sweating, though the temperature was not above 35 degrees. The second leg of the trek, however, was slightly downhill, and the going was easy. Here and there he could see the tracks of small animals in the snow. In places, the rays of the sun, refracted by the treetops, burst like incandescent diamonds. Only the sound of his breath and the whisper of the snowshoes disturbed the perfect stillness.

Not quite two hours after he had landed, he reached the tree line at the top of the bowl leading to the lake, which was about two-thirds of a mile below. When Eggart had looked at the lake and the chalet from the plane, he had seen no one moving about. Now, however, he observed several people busily engaged along the shoreline, as well as on the frozen surface of the lake itself. The arrival of the sleigh had evidently stimulated them into action.

Eggart was still too far from the lake to see clearly what was going on. Near the center of the bowl was an outcropping of rock that would offer an ideal observation point. Leading toward it was a slight depression. Eggart tied the white parachute silk around the upper part of his body, and, ducking low, headed toward the rocks. It took him about five minutes to traverse the distance. When he reached the rocks perspiration was dripping into his eyes from the tension and exertion.

Stretching himself flat against the back of a boulder, he took out the sniperscope and focused it on the lake, some four hundred yards away. He now had an unobstructed view of the whole area. As Eggart swept the cross hairs of the sight over the lake, he saw what had been hidden from him by the glare when he was in the plane: a ramp resembling a ski jump stretched over the ice. A dozen persons were pulled into view, half of them working on the ramp, and the others clustered about an object shapeless beneath a canopy of white cloth on the shore. Among them, the face of Theresa Hadler leaped toward him with startling clarity in the cross hairs—he had the illusion that he could smell the warm perfume of Benedictine on her breath.

Nearby, a man was busying himself over a black object that was set on a tree trunk. A cable, standing out starkly against the snow, led toward what appeared to be a small dark brown crate a short distance away. As the man straightened up, Eggart saw that the object on the stump had three buttons on its side; it was one of the mysterious boxes Barentz had described.

Men kept walking back and forth between the chalet and the object near the shoreline. After about ten minutes, several of them began pushing the object toward the edge of the ramp. Two of the men folded back the cover.

Eggart's breath escaped in an explosive puff.

There, magnified in the sniperscope, a shark-shaped device with stubby wings was visible on the ramp. Mounted on its rear was a jet engine. Its compact twenty-five-foot length was unmistakable, and Eggart had the odd thought that it was almost small enough to fit atop his Mercedes. During the last months of the war, Himmler had tunnelled into mountains all over southern Germany to protect factories and equipment from Allied bombings. Evidently, the SS had stored enough parts here to construct at least one V-bomb.

When the buzz bombs had attacked London, they had been equipped with rudimentary magnetic compass guidance systems of little accuracy. To launch a V-1 against the Palace of Justice, therefore, made no sense—*unless* the weapon had been modified and fitted with radio controls. That, apparently, was the purpose of the black box. Undoubtedly, it contained a guidance mechanism powered by a battery housed in the brown crate. Radio-controlled, the V-1 became a drone. It could reach Nuremberg in fifteen or twenty minutes. There, Siegfried Niehbar, in possession of a duplicate set of controls, could sit on a rooftop in sight of the Palace of Justice and with deadly accuracy guide the bomb into the wing housing the International Tribunal.

No great technological feat was involved in the modification. Yet the plot was one of such simultaneous horror and beauty that Eggart's eyes were riveted almost hypnotically on the V-1. He glanced at his watch. It was midafternoon, and the trial was in session. Even if the V-1 did not score a direct hit on the courtroom, the Grafeneck toxin that was undoubtedly part of the warhead would kill everyone in the building and its vicinity. The palace and all the records stored there would be contaminated. Dr. Eugen Grossbach would succeed in wiping out the discredited Nazi leadership and everyone connected with the trial. The continuing power and vitality of the SS would be dramatically demonstrated.

All the precautions General Brannigan had ordered taken within the Palace of Justice were useless, for neither he nor Eggart had anticipated that the attack would come not from within but without.

Taking his eye away from the scope, Eggart mounted the instrument on the Mauser. By delaying the launch for a couple of hours, he would give the ski troops the chance to reach the lake. Yet even as that thought passed through Eggart's mind, the men who had been working on the ramp and the V-1 scurried for the shelter of the trees. Eggart swung the sight and rifle toward the operator of the radio device, and saw his hand motioning toward the crew.

At the same instant, the vibrations of the jet engine,

magnified by the rock wall at the far side of the lake, trembled across the bowl. Yellow orange tongues flamed from the takeoff booster. As the buzz bomb shot forward, Eggart focused the sight's cross hairs on the chest of the radio operator, whose fingers rested on the buttons of the remote control box.

Eggart squeezed the trigger on the Mauser. A split second later, the radioman, struck by an invisible uppercut, reared halfway to his feet. His arms flew out, and he pitched backward to the snow.

Eggart desperately wanted to see what the buzz bomb was doing, but he dared not take his eye from the scope. Snapping a new cartridge into the rifle's chamber, he swung the cross hairs toward the black box. Once more he squeezed the trigger. A faint puff of snow just beyond the tree stump told him he had overshot the target. Inserting another cartridge, he aimed lower. As the bullet hit, the box somersaulted off the stump. Pieces of the apparatus sprayed into the snow.

Eggart looked up. The V-1, climbing steeply, was outlined against the mountain like a beautiful black flying shark. Momentarily, the destruction of the radio mechanism did not seem to affect it at all. Then it gave an almost human shudder. The left wing dipped. Like a high-wire artist with a balancing pole, the V-1 tried unsuccessfully to right intself. Flipping over, it screeched toward the lake in a wide arc, crashed through the ice, and fell startlingly silent. From the depths, a muffled explosion punched at the ice. A spider web of lines radiated across the lake like cracks in a window.

Eggart's ears were ringing. The rumbling vibration of the jet engine seemed to be continuing like an echo repeating and reinforcing itself. Eggart shook his head and pressed the palms of his hands to his ears, then released them rapidly to clear the pressure. But the sound only increased in intensity. Eggart had the impression that he was being dragged backward into the maw of a monstrous waterfall.

He swiveled his head. The whole mountain in back of him was in motion. A mist of snow, laced with iridescence by the sun's rays, swirled upward from the collapsing cornice. The intensified sound of the jet engine had vibrated the ridge of snow loose from the top of the bowl. The mass, second by second picking up weight and momentum, was crashing down the chute toward the lake.

Eggart dove to the downhill side of the outcropping and pushed himself against the face of the rock. As the first wave of the avalanche thundered across, snow poured down on either side of him and—projected from the top of the rocks as if shot from a cannon—blotted out the sun. He was trapped in an ice-white cave of roaring sound. The earth trembled. Periodically, huge masses of snow crashing against the outcropping exploded like thunder in his ears.

Then the sun broke through. Like fog lifting in the morning, the mist of snow disappeared. Eggart looked toward the lake. Only a few ripples remained on the surface of the snow. All but the roof of the chalet had disappeared, and one end of it was tilted, as if part of a wall had collapsed. All sign was gone of the people who had been working on the V-1.

Eggart was shaking. His lip was bloody where his teeth had bit into it. Snow had mounded up to his knees, but within two or three minutes he was able to dig himself out. Though he had lost the rifle, he still had his snowshoes. Striking out across the bowl, he headed for a rendezvous with the ski troops.

An hour later he met the thirty-man detachment as they came up the road. A snowcat (caterpillar tractor) was pulling a sled loaded with weapons, including a mortar and two machine guns.

Eggart briefed the captain in charge, who responded that he would attack immediately.

The detachment reached the edge of the clearing in less than a half hour. Through his binoculars, Eggart could see that two or three men had emerged from the chalet and were attempting to shovel a path through the snow.

The captain directed a dozen of his men to fan out along the side of the bowl, then set up the mortar at the edge of the woods. As the sun was blotted out by the trees and the bowl sank into shadow, the troops launched the attack. Rounds spit out by the mortar turned into fiery-centered plumes of snow bracketing the chalet. The snowcat, a machine gun mounted in its cab, lumbered forward. Troopers, almost invisible in their white camouflage suits, skimmed across the bowl.

Only the second-story windows on the chalet's downhill side remained above the snow line, and fewer than half a dozen shots were fired in resistance as the troopers crashed through the windows. By the time Eggart made his way into the interior, the chalet was secured. The seven remaining occupants stood lined up against a wall. There was no sign of Theresa Hadler. She had either been killed in the avalanche or had escaped into the mountains.

Although Eugen Grossbach was tight-lipped and refused at first even to acknowledge his identity, Eggart had no difficulty recognizing the Brigadeführer. He was an attractive man in his middle forties, trim though not athletic. Wearing a sweater, he looked like a pleasant, easygoing professor from an American college.

In a small tunnel, Eggart discovered a well-equipped workshop and enough parts and materials to construct another V-1. Questioning the SS men, he learned that FGZ 76 had been the original secret designation of the V-1.

One of the first-floor rooms of the chalet contained three steel cases that were filled with microfilm. The indexes indicated that they were the records of four of the seven departments of Himmler's *Reichsicherheitshauptamt*, the Reich Security Headquarters, and perhaps most importantly of German espionage operations in Russia.

Early the following morning, Eggart began transporting the prisoners down the mountain to Fall and Bad Tölz, and from there they were taken to Ludwigsburg. The cases of microfilm went directly to General Brannigan in Frankfurt.

Nearly two hundred members of the Ibex network were in custody. Siegfried Niehbar was arrested atop a bombed-out building within sight of the Palace of Justice. Friedrich Mussgay, the former Württemberg Gestapo chief, was picked up in Stuttgart. Efforts to track down Christian Wirth, however, failed.

XXXII

General Brannigan ordered Brigadeführer Grossbach to be segregated in a villa in Ludwigsburg. There Brannigan and other high-ranking officers came periodically to talk to him.

Under the special status accorded him, Grossbach rapidly became more communicative, and Eggart visited him almost daily. Grossbach combined an urbane charm with a razor-sharp intellect, and Eggart soon found that the SS general enjoyed intricate, chesslike conversations during which he was able to expound his philosophy. The restoration of Germany to world power was inevitable, he asserted, because ever since the eighteenth century Prussia had been the bulwark against Russian expansionism. The conflict between the Communist and capitalist worlds, which had been irrationally interrupted by the war, would be inexorably renewed.

Grossbach cited Winston Churchill's speech made at Fulton, Missouri, on March 5: "From Stettin in the Baltic to Trieste in the Adriatic, an iron curtain has descended across the continent. The safety of the world requires a new unity in Europe from which no nation should be permanently outcast."

The SS, Grossbach declared, had been created to combat communism, and it was in the interest of the Allies to preserve the organization. Since the Nuremberg trial abetted the Communists, it was, in fact, a disservice to the Western nations.

Grossbach nevertheless refused to answer any questions regarding the V-1 or his plan to strike at the Palace of Justice. He maintained that he knew nothing of the Grafeneck toxin, even though American scientists were taking samples from the contaminated water of the lake into which the buzz bomb had crashed.

Several of the other men who had been in the chalet were not so closemouthed, and Eggart learned a great deal from them. Grossbach had declared that by destroying the International Military Tribunal he would bring to an end the last vestige of cooperation between the victorious powers. When it became evident that the attack on the Palace of Justice had been launched from American territory, the Russians would accuse the Americans of perfidy. Russian-American relations would deteriorate rapidly to the point of war, and the Americans would lose interest in prosecuting Germans and instead recruit them for the fight against the Bolsheviks.

Grossbach was one of the most knowledgeable men on Russia outside the Soviet Union. Eggart learned that his doctoral dissertation at the University of Freiburg had dealt with German requirements for East European raw materials, and after Heydrich had recruited him he had become the Reich's economic intelligence coordinator for the eastern territories. He had been involved in the exploitation of the concentration camp population and in the transportation and allocation of slave workers.

When Eggart asked him if his conscience was not troubled by the misery and the deaths of millions of people, Grossbach shrugged.

"Self-survival, whether of an individual or a nation, is the paramount law of existence," he said. "Sometimes ten must die so that one may live. Slaughter is part of the human heritage. Yet mankind has not only survived, but multiplied to the point of discomfort."

"You gave no consideration to morality?"

"Morality and immorality are matters of fashion and convenience," Grossbach depreciated Eggart's question. "What is moral in one era or in one part of the world is immoral in another. Morality has no consistency. If each of us made his own judgments as to whether a directive is right or wrong, there would be anarchy. We obey orders as we obey laws—that is the only way to preserve order and civilization."

Eggart shuddered. There was an element of barbarism in a man's priding himself on his performance, no matter what the goal, yet it was precisely such mechanical execution by thousands of officials that had kept the Nazi machine functioning. Grossbach had emerged from German higher education as a brilliant analyst and thinker, yet he seemed more a machine than a human being.

As Eggart's questioning of Grossbach progressed, General Brannigan's interest focused more and more on the extensive network of agents Grossbach had built up in the Soviet Union. One day in early April, when Eggart went over to the villa, he was startled to discover that Grossbach was gone. Grossbach, Eggart was told, had been transferred to Frankfurt the previous evening by order of General Brannigan.

Eggart was perplexed. He started for Frankfurt immediately, but it was two o'clock the following afternoon before he was able to see Brannigan.

Brannigan greeted him warmly. But when Eggart explained that he needed to interrogate Grossbach further in order to complete the case against the Brigadeführer, Brannigan's expression became quizzical.

"I don't think I'm familiar with Brigadeführer Grossbach," he said.

"What?" Eggart blinked.

Brannigan remained silent, an enigmatic smile on his face.

"Grossbach!" said Eggart, tingling with an eerie sensation. "The Werwolf!"

"I have heard some mention of a Brigadeführer Grossbach who was in Berlin during the war," Brannigan said offhandedly, "but apparently he disappeared. Certainly neither I nor anyone else in American intelligence knows anything about him."

The truth was seeping in. Eggart stared at Brannigan. "Where is Grossbach?" he asked.

"He's no longer in Germany. Or, for that matter, in

Europe. I wish we could give you a medal, Eggart, though I'm not sure any medal would be adequate for the service you've rendered. The trouble is, we can't give overt decorations for covert missions."

"Am I to understand that Grossbach will not be brought to trial?" Eggart asked.

"Grossbach will not be brought to trial. There will be no mention of him in any proceedings."

"Why not, sir?"

"It should be obvious, Eggart." Brannigan swiveled his chair slightly. "You've provided us with an unparalleled intelligence expert on the Soviet Union. A man who will give us access to the network he established and put us in contact with countless agents whom we can take over. If the Russians found out that we have him, they'd immediately demand that we turn him over to them. The rest I leave to your imagination."

A grim smile pulled at the corner of Eggart's mouth. Everything Grossbach had done—including the aborted attack on Nuremberg—was being plowed under because of his importance to American intelligence. Eggart thought back to Theresa Hadler's words: every action takes place within a framework of circumstances, and the framework is more important than the action.

"You're amused, Eggart?" General Brannigan inquired.

"No, sir. I was just thinking what might have happened if the buzz bomb hadn't crashed."

"But it did, thanks to you. So we don't have to concern ourselves with that possibility."

"What I find funny is that I wound up saving Grossbach's ass. Here's a man who's as implicated in the deaths of hundreds of thousands of people as Kaltenbrünner or Frank, yet he's going to get off scot-free. He'll simply exchange a German desk for an American desk. What the hell's happened to justice?"

"Justice, Eggart? You aren't naïve enough to think that there's ever going to be justice when it comes to the murder of ten or fifteen million people?"

"Then why bother with the Nuremberg trial?"

"Symbolism. Symbolism, and the need for purging at least some of the hatred Hitler generated."

"Maybe that symbolism needs to be spread around a little," said Eggart.

"Where would you start? And where would you stop? Do you want to try Grossbach—and all the intermediaries and ancillaries? All the Germans guilty of complicity—and not only the Germans, but the Ukrainians, Lithuanians, Croats, and so on. How many would there be? One hundred thousand? Two hundred thousand? Five hundred thousand? How many would you hang? Where would you put the prisoners? Who would guard them? Who would pay the cost?"

"When I left the States two years ago, there wouldn't have been any question about that."

"Two years can be a long time, Eggart. You've been over here, totally involved in tracking down the SS. You've gotten yourself an education. But in America people think of the SS as Erich von Stroheim strutting around with a whip. They know he's bad, they know Göring and Hess are bad, so get rid of them. Hang them! But be done with it. They don't want to know the gory details. What they want to know is where can they get a new refrigerator, how much will they have to pay under the table for a new car, and what's the latest on Lana Turner's boobs and Betty Grable's ass!"

"Wouldn't it at least help if we did all we could to put the facts on record?"

"Historians write about the last war, Eggart. Intelligence prepares for the next."

"In that case," Eggart started to rise, "I've been wasting my time."

"If there's anything I can do for you, all you have to do is ask."

"Yes. There is." Eggart had kept Barentz with him in Ludwigsburg for safekeeping, but there were rumors among the SS in the internment camps that Barentz had been the *Spitzel*. "My agent, Johannes Barentz, volunteered to work for us because he wanted to make amends for some of the crimes. He has no future in Germany. I hope to get him to the U.S."

"I'm sure I can arrange it," said Brannigan.

"I'd appreciate that." Eggart rose, saluted, and started for the door. He had nearly reached it when Brannigan's voice halted him. Eggart turned around.

"I'll soon be returning to the United States, Eggart. There's talk of creating an intelligence agency that will give America the ability to compete on an equal footing with other powers. Experienced men will be needed. Why don't you drop in and see me in Washington?"

"Thank you, sir." Eggart's face was white. "But I don't think I'm cut out for it."

An hour later Eggart was driving back to Heidelberg. A one-armed veteran and a woman in her fifties wearing a shawl and a black skirt were hitchhiking. Eggart picked them up. He offered each of them a cigarette, and they gratefully accepted. Then he saw that they were faced with a dilemma. Should they smoke the cigarettes or save them because their value on the black market was so high?

"Smoke them!" Eggart ordered, and gave the man a box of matches.

"American tobacco. *Sehr gut!*" The woman inhaled, slowly blew out the smoke, then seemed to try to suck it back in again.

"Too bad nobody in Germany had the guts to kill your Lump of a Führer, or you could have been smoking American tobacco all along," Eggart spoke as antagonistically as he could.

"Ja," the woman nodded. "I never liked Hitler. They say he smelled bad and broke wind."

Madeleine had returned to France. On Sunday, April 14, Reimer was married by an army chaplain to Liselotte Feuerstein, who had reached her seventeenth birthday. Eggart served as best man. Liselotte carried a bouquet of daffodils, which glowed like yellow velvet against her blue-white dress. She and Peter were going on a honeymoon to Switzerland, then embarking for the United States.

Eggart wrote his final report, and wound up his affairs

in Ludwigsburg as rapidly as he could. General Brannigan's instructions were to forward all of the material to Frankfurt. For a long time Eggart contemplated the stack of papers on his desk. Then, carefully, he pulled out copies of his reports on the case he had compiled against Brigadeführer Grossbach. Wrapping them in oilskin, he tucked them under his arm.

It was three o'clock in the afternoon of a budding spring day when Eggart headed the Mercedes toward Stuttgart. If he drove all night, he could reach St. Etienne by five o'clock in the morning. Maybe, despite Madame Roche, he'd find a way to sneak into Madeleine's bed.

S.S. GLOSSARY

Rottenführer	corporal
Scharführer	sergeant
Untersturmführer	second lieutenant
Obersturmführer	first lieutenant
Hauptsturmführer	captain
Sturmbannführer	major
Obersturmbannführer	lieutenant colonel
Standartenführer	colonel
Oberführer	senior colonel
Brigadeführer	brigadier general
Gruppenführer	major general
Obergruppenführer	lieutenant general
Reichsführer SS	general (Heinrich Himmler)

Einsatzgruppen—special action groups formed to pacify the Eastern territories and exterminate so-called "enemies of the Reich," such as the Jews.

Gestapo—secret police.

Höhere SS und Polizeiführer—regional SS and police commander.

Kripo—criminal police.

Reichsicherheitshauptamt (RSHA)—National Security Headquarters.

SD—Nazi Party security and intelligence service.

Waffen SS—combat ss.